Published by New Generation Publishing [illegible]

First Edition

www.newgeneration-publishing.com

For my family, with all my love and thanks

SILVER LININGS

For Emma
with best wishes

Kimberley, South Africa

"G'night Steve. G'night Will," the security guard called out as the last vehicle left for home at the end of the day. Closing the gate behind them, he slipped the padlock through the thick link chain, tugged on it to make sure it was fully locked then headed into the wooden gatehouse to prepare for his first night-time patrol of the grounds for that week. His duties were easy; he had his supply of coffee and sandwiches, his newspaper, the latest best-selling crime novel and his radio. But he was not alone. In the corner of the hut, curled up in his basket, was a ferocious-looking but docile and affectionate Rottweiler, Nelson, and neither of them had reason to expect that this night would be any different to any other.

As he entered the hut, Nelson looked up at him expectantly. "Yes, it's patrol time, come on boy."

As they passed the gate Nelson seemed agitated, sniffed the air suspiciously and barked, his attention fixed on a spot beyond the fence.

"What is it?" the guard asked. "Some animal out there, is it?" He tugged on the lead but the reluctant dog baulked at being pulled away and resisted until a yank on the lead reminded him they had a job to do. "Idiot dog," the guard reprimanded as Nelson padded along beside him. "There's always animals out there in the brush, this is South Africa, remember?"

As soon as they were out of sight, a figure slipped out of the shadows, across the narrow dusty access road and sprinted across to the wire fence. Pulling out a set of wire-cutters from his jacket pocket, he snipped a hole large enough to crawl through and slithered along the ground on his belly to the nearby wooden office building. He checked his watch. He had thirty minutes before the guard and his dog came around again. It would be tight but it gave him enough time for what he needed to do.

At the office block, he used the key he had copied to let himself in then headed directly to the small room where the safe was kept. He checked again at the window. The yard was clear; no-one in sight. He pulled down the blind, turned on a small but powerful torch and knelt in front of the safe.

For three boring months, three tedious weeks, two days and nine hours he had worked for Jo Van Der Leiden, the mine company

manager, observing his routines, learning where everything was kept and waiting for the right opportunity. The work had been dull, Jo Van Der Leiden was a good man, but boring, and the days waiting for a result had been monotonous; each day the same as the one before. Waiting, waiting until the right stone was found. His customer in Britain had given him exact orders. No matter how long it took he **was** to work at the mine until a special diamond was found; nothing under three carats in weight!

The time had finally arrived. His flight to the UK was booked. In four hours he would be out of the country and on his way to more money than he had ever dreamt of.

Lifting a corner of the threadbare carpet, he lifted a loose block of wooden floor planking and found the key to the safe. Jo Van Der Leiden usually took any larger stones to the bank the day they were found but there had been a 'convenient' break in at his house that day which meant he had to rush home to wait for the Police.

Holding his breath, the man turned the key in the safe; he exhaled when it 'clunked' open.

Rifling through a number of papers and envelopes, he scattered them on the floor. There, at the back of the shelf…a small canvas bag. Was that what he was looking for? Yes! A large uncut yellow diamond fell into the palm of his hand. Three and a half carats in weight, worth a fortune and he would get a twenty-five percent share from his customer.

Voices! The gate chain rattled. At the window he saw the guard opening the gates and the Jeep he had seen leave earlier entered the compound. *Hell!* What had they come back for?

Hurriedly popping the diamond back into canvas bag he slipped it into his pocket, pushed the safe door shut without locking it again, turned off his torch and opened the blind; from the outside nothing should look out of place.

The guard was talking to the driver, while his passenger made a fuss of the dog. It had jumped up excitedly at him and was rewarded with a friendly ear rub.

Needing to make his escape while the men were busy talking, he left the papers strewn on the floor. There was no time to put them back in the safe and tidy up. He had to get out of the compound. At the door he hesitated, looked around the side of the building to make sure they

were not looking in his direction and fled, heading for the gap in the fence, the bushes and safety.

Nelson spotted the movement and growled savagely. He reared up, almost pulling his owner over. The intruder was speeding towards the still open gate.

"What the...? Will, quick! After him!" Will darted off in pursuit accompanied by the security guard and a now very fearsome looking Nelson, drooling strings of saliva, barking and snarling but still restrained by the lead.

But the thief was fast on his feet and darted through the gates and into the bushes to a motorbike he had concealed within shrubs during the previous weekend.

"Hurry...Steve! *He's going to get away. He's got a motorbike!*" Will bellowed as the motorbike engine roared into life and sped off along the road, throwing up billows of dust in his wake. Knowing they would never catch him on foot, Steve had already run back to the Jeep. The security guard bent down to release the dog.

"No point, Pete. Nelson won't catch him now, but we can. Come on, Will." Steve started the engine and pulled out as Will threw himself into the passenger seat. By now Nelson was in a frenzy, straining at the lead, desperate to join in the chase. His growls and barks were drowned out by the Jeep as it rumbled past them and out the gate and turned a bend in the road. They could just make out the motorbike in the distance; it showed no lights but moonlight glinted on the metal.

"There he is!" Will shouted. "Can we catch him?"

Steve put his foot down hard on the accelerator.

"You think it's the yellow?" Will asked. "But how did he know? Could it be someone we work with?"

"Probably," Steve replied, "or someone talked. Pity Jo had to rush off or it would have been in the bank by now."

Another turn in the road. "Hang on. Where is he? He's gone!"

"Oh, he's clever," Will replied. "I know what he's done. He's taken the dirt track. He knows we can't take the Jeep that way."

"Why not? What's wrong with it?"

"It's just that's all it is...a dirt track...narrow in places with a sheer drop down to the river on one side and a twelve-foot bank on the other...and no lights anywhere. The bike will make it but we

wouldn't."

Steve turned to look at Will. "Well, we're damn well going to try…"

"No. You can't, Steve. *We can't.* The track's rutted, rough…too…dangerous! Let the police handle it. I'm sure Pete will have called them by now."

"No. We're gonna have a go," Steve argued. "Look, once he gets to the town he'll disappear. We don't even know who he is. No description. Nothing to go on…!"

"…I know but surely if he's one of our guys, he won't show up for work on Monday and we'll know who it is…"

"…But he'll be long gone by then and so will the stone. He and it could be across the other side of the world by then. The police will never get him...it'll be too late. He's probably got a Cutter lined up already or a buyer who has."

"But, if we get stuck there's…there's…poisonous spiders, snakes and there's always hyenas and big cats around. If…"

Will never did finish his sentence. Steve found the turn-off and steered the Jeep onto the track.

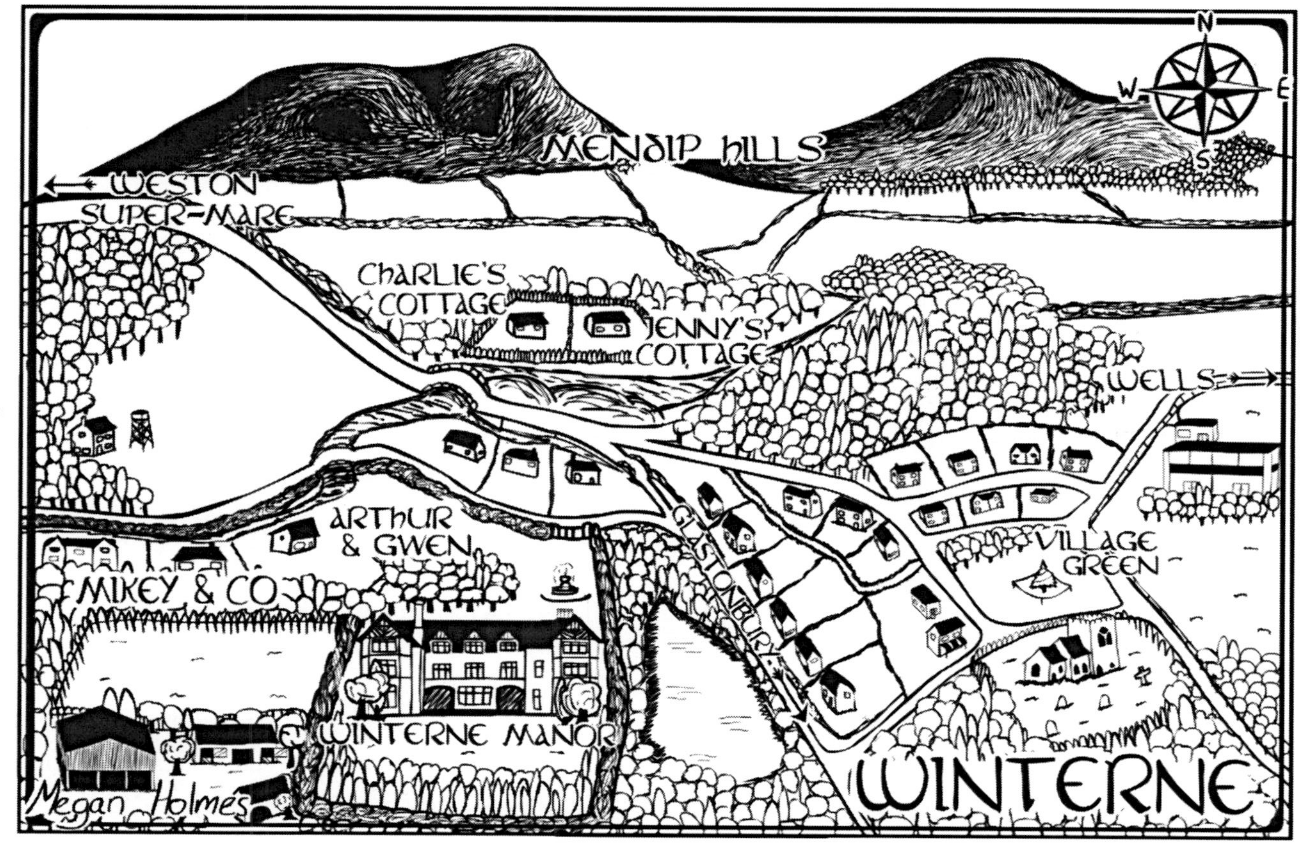

N
W
E
S
MENDIP HILLS
WESTON SUPER-MARE
CHARLIE'S COTTAGE
JENNY'S COTTAGE
WELLS
ARTHUR & GWEN
MIKEY & CO
VILLAGE GREEN
GLASTONBURY
WINTERNE MANOR
WINTERNE
Megan Holmes

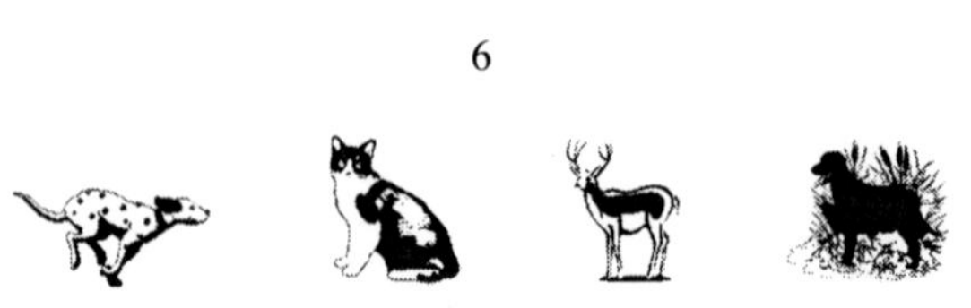

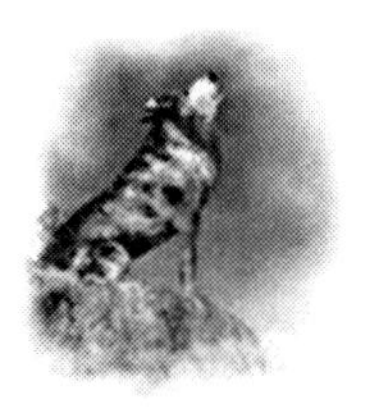

Chapter One

Jeremiah (Jerry to his friends) Atkins was feeling self-satisfied, smug. He had come a very long way from the back streets of the East End of London to become the wealthy Bristol businessman he was today. He had friends in high places, people of influence sought his company, asked for his advice; he was a very important person.

From his panoramic fifth floor office window he surveyed the fashionable office and apartment buildings in the new Wapping Wharf development, seven of them belonged to him; two office blocks, three apartment buildings, one very exclusive Italian Restaurant and a swish wine and coffee bar. The rents brought in an extremely good income. He had everything he ever wanted…well almost.

His gaze swept over the bustling city square below, where ant-sized people bustled between fountains and colourfully lit Christmas trees and hurried in and out of shops and cafés, many of them laden with designer labelled shopping bags.

Ahh, Christmas shopping. What a wonderful time to make money. A gratified smile spread across his broad, clean shaven face. At one time he had been considered to be quite a handsome man but at fifty years old recent years of good living had increased his waist, thickened his neck and now the only thin feature about him was his greying hair. But Jeremiah Atkins could send a shiver through your spine if you met his gaze; his eyes were dark, icy, pools, a smile never reached them and no-one ever dared to look into them for long. He always got what he wanted.

The youngest of four children to hardworking, church-going parents Jerry's life had been stable but boring. He wanted excitement, money,

travel. His two older brothers joined the Army and tried to encourage him to do the same but Jerry had no intention of seeing the world that way. His sister moved away after getting married and Jerry saw little of her after that. But that was no great loss to him.

Playing truant from school, he quickly slipped into the criminal world of the back streets of East London and his life outside of the Law began. He ran away from home, was involved in a number of robberies and never bothered with his family from that time on.

Having been left some money by his Great-Aunt Daphne, when the Police started taking him in for questioning on a regular basis, he left London and headed for Europe where soon he was making a well-paid, dishonest living selling houses he did not own to gullible people in Germany, Holland and Spain.

Several years later, with thousands of pounds in the bank and having upset a particularly hostile group of Eastern European criminals, Jerry returned to the UK but avoided London where he would be too easily located. Instead he made a new life for himself in Bristol after having invented a new background. It was there, though his new acquaintances, he met Harriet Jamieson, the daughter of a well-known surgeon and they married a year later. Through her family and friends Jerry rose within Bristol Society rapidly. He joined all the local business associations; he was wealthy, reputable, influential and popular with, as everyone believed, a legitimate business empire. Life was good.

But Jerry always wanted more. He knew how easily he could lose this comfortable way of life, how everything he had built up could crumble around him and he needed a back-up plan in case things went wrong, a stash of money or something easily saleable that only he knew about; a reserve to see him through hard times. Just in case. He had two survival plans in preparation. The first was out of his control at the moment. His man in South Africa was sorting that one out. The other was about to begin.

Turning away from the window he caught sight of a photograph of his family that hung on the wall. His thoughts turned to Harriet. He felt a short-lived pang of regret for everything that had gone wrong between them, but it was too late to put things right now.

At first, everything had gone well and soon they began looking for a large country home in which to raise a family. Having found Winterne

Manor near Glastonbury in Somerset, they knew it was the perfect place.

Two tall, wrought iron gates guarded the half-mile, pot-holed, drive that lead to the imposing but unloved twelve-bedroom residence. Either side of the driveway were untidy, neglected lawns overgrown by wildflowers and weeds. Jeremiah made a mental note to have the driveway and verges attended to before any other repairs. First impressions were important and the driveway could be seen from the road. No visitors would be invited until all renovations were complete.

For all its neglected condition, Harriet fell in love with the four-storey house at first sight. The agent, who showed them around, informed them that the house was reputed to have two resident ghosts. One, a prisoner who had been murdered in the cellar some centuries before and the other, a frequently seen apparition of a monk who was said to have been hidden in a priest-hole concealed deep within the walls, during a raid on the house in 1571. Unhappily, for the priest, the servant who hid him was knocked unconscious before he could tell anyone else what he had done. Some hours went by before he regained consciousness but not his memory, having forgotten entirely the events of the past few days. The trapdoor to the priest's hiding place could only be opened from the outside so the poor monk, with no way of escape and unable to be heard, perished. The family noticed a very unpleasant smell in that part of the house but the poor priest's body remained where it was until renovations were carried out in 1876. The priest was then given burial in the church graveyard but his ghost was still said to wander the corridors.

The property covered a little over one thousand acres of farmland, woods, a lake and had several cottages, some occupied, some empty. Although fairly dilapidated due to a previous owner going broke, Jeremiah and Harriet spent months and a considerable amount of money restoring it to a beautiful family home where their daughter, Meredith was born almost a year after they moved in. Harriet supervised most of the work as Jeremiah was occupied with his business empire and spent less and less time at home. When work on the Manor was finished, Harriet needed a new project and took charge of renovating the stables eventually creating a successful school riding business. With their wealth increasing from income from the businesses and the farm and stables, Jeremiah was content with life. He

had no worries that his unlawful activities would be discovered; he kept that side of his life well concealed and, if Harriet ever had any suspicion about what he was up to, she never mentioned it.

When Harriet's father told him there was gossip about them never spending time together, Jeremiah realised he needed to make more of an effort to be a family man even if it was only to keep his father-in-law happy. Harriet's family were very powerful locally and he knew he still needed her links to the people who mattered so, for a while, made an effort to be a family man. He was overjoyed when his son was born.

"I'll name him after me," he said aloud while Harriet dozed. "Jonah Jeremiah Atkins," he repeated the name to the cooing baby, cradling him in his arms as he walked to the window where soft sunlight shone through net curtains. The baby tried to suck his thumb and focus his bright blue eyes on the face above, "but you'll be called Jonah, not Jerry."

"Did you say something, dear?" Harriet asked sleepily from her bed.

"No, nothing important, I was just chatting with our son. Go back to sleep," he crooned. "Shhh…we must be quieter, my boy." He wrapped the soft white shawl closer around the baby. "OK, now, what do you think of your name, eh, Jonah?" The baby screwed up his face, hiccoughed, burped and was sick on Jeremiah's sleeve. "I'll take that as a yes then, shall I?"

As for Harriet, she never really trusted her husband. She knew how determined he was to be wealthy, influential, to have people look up to him. It was his biggest disappointment not to have been born into a prosperous and powerful family and she often wondered how far he would go to achieve his ambitions. Jeremiah wanted the children to join the local Hunt as he felt it would maintain their social status. Harriet though had other ideas. She was desperately against fox hunting and was equally determined to keep *her* children as far away from it as possible. Battle commenced and Jeremiah won.

Eventually, Harriet, worn-out by all the fighting, took to her room seeking peace and solitude, rarely seeing anyone. Jeremiah missed his wife occasionally but was too busy to think about her a great deal.

He checked his watch. His visitors would arrive any minute. Two of them, Mikey and Jake, were what Jeremiah called his 'security men'; it sounded better than 'henchmen'. They had been with him for years,

did anything he ordered and never asked questions. Another two, Henry and Chips worked for him on a casual basis, while the fifth was Mikey's young brother, Danny. Not having met him before, Jerry was unsure whether he could be trusted but Mikey had vouched for him and they needed someone at short notice. Henry and Chips would protest at someone new coming in but they would do as they were told. Back at his desk, he pressed a button on the intercom.

"Sandra."

"Yes, Mr Atkins," replied the tinny voice.

"I'm expecting a number of…gentlemen soon. Get coffee ready for six people then get off home. They can let themselves in."

"Yes, Mr Atkins." A few minutes later a dainty, blonde girl entered carrying a tray upon which were a jug of water and packet of fresh coffee. She opened a cupboard, slid out a shelf, plugged in the percolator and set out six cups taking care not to chip her newly painted pink nails.

"Is that all, Mr Atkins?" Sandra asked.

Jeremiah looked up.

"Yes, that's it. Thanks. Here take this. I'm sure you've got a lot of presents to buy for that enormous family of yours, all those brothers and sisters. Christmas must be expensive in your house." Sandra took the bundle of twenty pound notes he offered without stopping to count them. This was not the first time he had given her money to leave work early when he had visitors and, she, too, did not ask questions. Whatever was going on was none of her business.

"Thank you, Mr Atkins. See you Monday. 'Ave a good weeken'." She walked through the open door, closing it behind her without looking back.

A few minutes later the door opened again and three men entered. One of them was tall, dark haired and wore large dark glasses, another shorter, broader and going bald. Both wore smart suits. The third man was much younger, tall and with dark, gelled, spikey hair. He wore a pale blue shirt, dark suit jacket and jeans and appeared ill at ease, standing close to the man with dark glasses.

"Hi Boss," the tall one said.

"Hello, Mikey, where's the others?"

"Parking the car, Mr Atkins," the shorter man said, flattening his thinning hair across the dome of his head with his podgy right hand.

"Takes two to park a car, does it?" Jeremiah said scornfully.

"Before they get here, Mr Atkins," Mikey pushed the younger man forward, "this is my brother, Danny. Like I said, he can take over from Del, if that's alright with you?"

Danny paled under Jeremiah's scrutiny but avoided the intense stare by looking around the office, the enormous mahogany desk, the two enormous black leather armchairs by the window and the matching black leather sofas with the coffee table between them. There was a single large abstract picture on each of the three internal walls, each one with a different yellow, brown and black design. Aware of Jeremiah's penetrating gaze still on him, he sidled away to the window.

"'Ere, Mikey, it's like bein' at the top of the world." The early evening scene took Danny's breath away as the lights of the city mingled in the darkening sky with the Christmas illuminations.

"He'll do," Jeremiah turned away, to Danny's great relief, "but remember this, Mikey, you're responsible for him so make sure he does as he's told. Can he be trusted to keep quiet?" Jeremiah continued as though Danny was invisible but, before Mikey could answer, the door opened and two more men entered the room.

"You're late!" Jeremiah barked. "Get yourselves some coffee and let's get started. I'll do the talking and you do the listening." Helping themselves to coffee they settled down on the squeaky, squashy leather sofas. Henry noticed the stranger.

"Who's that?" he frowned.

"It's alright, it's me brother, Danny," Mikey answered quickly, "he's gonna take Del's place."

"Why, where's Del?" Henry eyed Danny and cracked his knuckles threateningly.

"Didn't you hear? Del's gone 'away' for a bit, so Danny's takin' 'is place, but don't worry it'll be fine," Mikey reassured.

Jeremiah who had moved to sit on the front edge of his desk studied the five men. Mikey, never without his 'shades' and always keen to impress but Jeremiah never quite trusted him.

Jake, was another matter. He was entirely trustworthy. Jake had worked for him for twenty years and they knew each other well. Considerably shorter and stockier than Mikey, his attempt to cover his bald head by covering it with strands of hair taken from the side looked absurd.

Henry, his remaining hair cut in a 'Number One', owed his flattened nose and scars to too many fights in and out of the boxing ring.

Lastly, Chips, a small weasely man, dark haired and dark eyed with thin, unkempt hair, and an insignificant moustache. Nobody trusted him. He had been called 'Chips' since Henry had said his hair was so greasy you could fry chips in it. Jeremiah didn't like Chips, nor did anyone else, but he was quick-thinking and an expert at opening safes.

He shifted his attention back to Mikey's young brother who realised he was being studied again and visibly shrunk into his seat, beads of nervous perspiration appeared on his forehead. Jeremiah wondered if Danny would be a weak link.

"Introductions over now? Then perhaps we can we get on." Jeremiah was impatient. He took out a map from the inside pocket of his jacket and left it, folded, on the coffee table. The men sat silently as he explained his scheme but they grew increasingly troubled as his plan unfolded. Mikey was so engrossed he failed to see his coffee cup leaning at a hazardous angle until he felt hot coffee running down his pin-striped trousers. The cup clattered to the floor as he stood up breaking into several pieces.

"I'm sorry, Mr Atkins," he said, reaching down to pick up the remains of the cup.

"Don't worry about that now, Mikey," Jeremiah snapped, handing Mikey a tissue to wipe his trousers.

"Thanks, Mr Atkins. Umm, Mr Atkins, did I hear you right? You want us to dig, under the earth like?"

"Yes, you heard me right. Is there anywhere else to dig?" he scowled. "I'd heard there was silver in the area and now I know where to find it. Until recently I was unable to pinpoint the right place," he went on, "...information was vague but a short time ago I heard a whisper about a possible seam near my home. I've checked it out, searched geological records and it looks good!"

"...but surely that's all they are, Mr Atkins, tales, stories," Jake cut in.

"No, not at all, Jake. I'll elaborate." Jeremiah paced the floor excitedly pouring out the details, waiting for their reaction.

"It's alright. He'll tell us this is all a joke in a minute," Mikey whispered to Jake.

"Was there something...Mikey?" Jeremiah smiled, dangerously.

"No, Mr Atkins," Mikey replied quickly, "I just asked Jake to pass me another tissue. "Trousers. Not quite dry."

Jake quickly reached out for the box of tissues, handing it to Mikey. Jeremiah ignored the interruption and unfolded the map on to the coffee table.

"We know silver was mined in Devon and that's only the next county on. There were silver mines all over the country at one time. This map shows another entrance to the caves near Wookey, not the one used by the public. Some of the caves are water filled but we can steer clear of them and no-one will see us."

"I like the 'us' bit!" Mikey whispered to Jake. If Jeremiah heard, he ignored it.

"We're lucky the land we have to cross has been neglected for some years. The farmer who owned it, can't remember his name, died a couple of years ago. There was no family and no-one's bought the land yet so we can move across it freely, but keep your heads down, I don't want to attract any attention." He paused to judge the reaction from his listeners.

Mikey leaned forward, peered closely at the map. "And the silver's really there then Mr Atkins?" he said pointing vaguely at the area.

"No doubt about it. Look at this." Jeremiah went to his desk drawer and took out a small cloth bag, opened it and tipped the contents out. Several small pieces of a dull greyish metal lay in the palm of his hand. "I took a look around a few days ago and found this. There's silver there alright," he gave each of them a look that left them in no doubt what would happen if they failed, "and you're going to get it for me." Jeremiah looked back at the small nuggets of silver ore in his hand. His eyes blazed.

"But, Mr Atkins, sir," Jake spoke up, "we're not miners, we don't know how to dig tunnels and…"

"You are what I pay you to be," Jeremiah snapped. "He looked at them each in turn. Does anyone have any objections? Anything they'd like to say?" He was daring them to speak.

"No, Mr Atkins," Jake sat back further in his seat. Mikey stood up. "No, none at all, sir. We can do it."

"Crawler," whispered Jake out of the side of his mouth. Mikey ignored him.

“That’s the spirit, Mikey,” Jeremiah smiled darkly at the group. “You’ll work at night. No one will be around Wookey Hole then so you won’t be heard. You’ll stay in one of the Manor cottages and, if anyone asks, you’re on holiday, members of an angling club, down for some private fishing. A little late in the year for fishing, I know, but as it’s private land you’ll get away with it. Any questions? No? Then it’s time you got on your way. Take enough clothes for a few weeks. I don’t know how long this will take and you’ll go down tomorrow. You all know where I live and it won’t take long to get there.”

“Are you going to be there as well then, Mr Atkins? “ Jake enquired cautiously.

Jeremiah folded the map. “Yes, some of the time. It would look suspicious if I was away from here for too long.”

As they left, Jeremiah knew none of them were happy about the job and he chuckled. Over at the cupboard he opened pull-down door, took out a large bowl-shaped glass and poured himself a brandy. “Here’s to success…again!”

Chapter Two

The caretaker threw himself back against the wall as hundreds of students swarmed through the corridor and out of the main doors of Redlands Academy, Nottingham. It was a dull and drizzly Friday afternoon, but that did nothing to dampen the spirits of the pupils at the sheer joy of school being over for another week and they created a racket of shouts and laughter that had to be heard to be believed. Rowdily pushing, shoving, shrieking out goodbyes to friends and insults to enemies, they streamed through the gates and out onto the pavement of the bustling main road. People on the pavement preferred to take their chances stepping into the road to avoid the crush of young people spilling out of the gates and onto the pavement.

Inside, once the stampede had gone, the caretaker retreated to his office for a restoring cup of tea leaving two Year Nine boys loitering in the now empty corridor while they waited patiently for their friend who had been given detention.

"Come on, Sam. How much longer?" Dave Russell looked at his watch. "How the Hell do you get detention on a Friday?"

"He didn't do it deliberately," Ranjeet Desai replied kindly, scanning the football team fixture list on the notice board.

"Well, I know that, don't I? But if he'd handed in his Geography homework for old Gibbins on Wednesday like he was supposed to, we wouldn't be hangin' around waiting for him. I've got better things to do than stick around here."

"He'll be out soon, it was only for half an hour and it's nearly up. There's Raj."

"What are you two up to?" said Raj, Ranjeet's older brother and school Prefect. "You should be off home by now."

"Sam's got detention. We said we'd wait for him," Ranjeet explained.

"Again?" Raj laughed. "Listen give Mum a message for me will you? Tell her I'm having dinner at Kim's and I'll be back later, probably about ten." He looked up and down the corridor. "I said I'd meet Kim here so I'll wait with you."

A few minutes later Sam ran down the corridor to join his friends.

"About time," Dave moaned.

"Got out as quick as I could. Tried to get out of detention but he's a…oh, hiya Raj…I…er…didn't see you there!"

"Weren't about to say something nasty about our beloved Geography teacher were you?"

Sam grinned. "Time to go home, I think."

A few minutes later, with their parka jackets zipped to keep out the cold wind and rain, Sam, Dave and Ranjeet were on the bus heading back to their homes in Daybrook.

"How's your Dad doing, Sam?" asked Ranjeet.

"Yeah, he's good. He'll be home soon 'cos his contract's nearly over and he'll be back for Christmas." Sam looked thoughtful. Dave and Ranjeet exchanged looks. "I hope he'll be able to stay," Sam finished quietly.

Changing the subject, Dave asked, "Hey, what was going on with you and Joanne earlier?" he winked at Ranjeet. "I saw you talking to her after lunch break. Ask her out?"

A pink bloom started at Sam's jaw and moved upwards, through his cheeks and ended at his hairline. "Don't be daft," he snapped, "I just talked to her, that's all."

"Don't get mardy. Just Adam heard you'd asked her to the Christmas Ball."

The pink bloom now became crimson. "Yeah, well…yeah I did. I asked her and she said yes…so what?"

"Ha! Thought you could keep it secret from us did you?" Dave nudged Ranjeet. "Told yer!"

"Well…she is very pretty," Ranjeet mumbled. "Going back to your Dad though," Ranjeet could see Sam was uncomfortable talking about Joanne, "when did you speak to him last?"

"A few days ago but he's phoning again tonight. He's trying to find out what's happening about his job so we might get to hear something tonight. It would be better if there was a job for him here in Nottingham."

"So what happens if they want to give him another contract in South Africa and there's no jobs for him here?" Dave was suddenly serious. The thought of losing his lifelong friend had never really crossed his mind before.

"I don't know," Sam frowned. "Mum and Dad rowed about that before he left. He wanted us to go with him but Mum said she wouldn't let him disrupt my schooling for just six months. She said if it was for a couple of years or more it would be worth it…"

"…But you don't want to go do you?" Dave interrupted.

Sam didn't reply. He just looked out of the rain-spattered window at the comfortable, familiar houses, shops and roads and hoped his father would find another job locally. There was still one working mine in the county and he had heard of people giving talks about the old colliery days. Perhaps something like that would come along.

This was really scary, much more nerve-racking than asking Joanne to the Ball.

"Please don't make us go to South Africa," he offered up a whispered prayer to whoever might be listening.

Chapter Three

Banishing Jonah to his room had probably not been a good idea. Alone he had time to gather his thoughts, build resentment and let unfair anger get the better of him. The accusation that it was his fault Peggy had fallen down the stairs festered and brewed his self-centred rage. He punched the wall in fury, skinning his knuckles. The pain increased his anger. "If she'd looked where she was going, she wouldn't have fallen!" he spat, completely overlooking the fact that Peggy had been carrying a rather large tray as she descended the stairs.

"She'd have seen the pens if she'd been paying attention. Idiot woman!"

His aching knuckles throbbed and he moved closer to the window to inspect the damage in the brighter light. The middle knuckles on his index middle finger were bleeding. "Idiot woman," he repeated.

A movement outside in the garden caught his eye. A pair of peacocks, the male trailing his beautiful 'eyed' tail behind him, picked their way across the lawn, scratching at the autumn-muddy grass in the hope of finding something interesting to eat before heading to their roost for the night. A thought crossed Jonah's mind. The peacocks were his mother's pride and joy. If he wanted to get back at her what better way...

At his desk, he rummaged around until he laid his hand on what he was looking for. His air rifle! "Yes!" He wrapped his fingers around it lovingly. Further searching found a small box containing lead pellets. He was ready and, yes, the peacocks were still in sight.

He was good with the rifle; his Dad had made sure he was involved with the local Shoot. He just needed to take a few deep breaths, be

calm, steady his hands that were still trembling with anger and take his time. The peacocks were perfect targets, they were in no hurry. He opened the window slowly.

Lining up the sight of the rifle with the peacock, Jonah hooked his forefinger around the trigger, closed one eye for a better aim and slowly breathed in. He took his time. He had all the time in the world. The peacock, unaware of the danger it was in, continued leisurely scratching at the lawn, moving slowly forward, searching for any edible morsel. Just a few feet behind, the peahen followed her mate, her movements mirroring his.

From the open window, the predatory Jonah got ready to fire. He hesitated. There would be Hell to pay for killing one of his mother's precious birds, but she would have to prove it was him.

Pleased with himself, he chuckled, leaned forward and rested his elbow against the window frame to steady his arm, wrapped his finger around the trigger, exhaled, breathed in slowly, gently squeezed the trigger and...swerved at the sound of a dog's bark! The peacocks fled just as the pellet flew. Then a scream!

Everything happened at once. Wilmot, his sister's Dalmatian darted out from nowhere and charged at the peacocks. They flew up into the lower branches of a nearby ash tree. At the same time, Arthur Sykes, the family's ancient gardener appeared from behind a maple tree just in front of where the peacocks had been.

Arthur's scream and the way his hand flew to his neck showed exactly where the pellet had landed.

"Oh Hell! That wasn't meant to happen." Jonah pulled aside the curtain, just enough to see what was happening as his sister Meredith, who had been following Wilmot, rushed to the aid of the stricken old man.

He dropped the curtain again in case Meredith saw him but convinced himself, she would have been too concerned with the old man to have thought of looking up. Why would she? Anyway, even if she had, she might guess it was him but there would be no proof.

The old man shook his right fist towards the unseen face at the window; his left hand still clutching his wounded neck. "LI'L 'OOLIGAN!"

As Meredith hurried towards the old man, a quick movement at the window of a second floor bedroom caught her eye. Her blood ran cold

as a terrible thought occurred to her. Jonah! Wilmot, having forgotten about wanting his dinner, barked happily as he bounded along beside her eager to join in the fun and, when they reached Arthur, she had to be very strict with the dog to make him calm down. Arthur leaned heavily against a tree, his hand at his neck. He was shaking from head to toe.

"Arthur, what happened? Are you alright?" she enquired anxiously.

"What you askin' that fer mith? You know know full well oo dun it. It were that brother of yourth, Mith Meredith. 'E 'it me with thummat, 'e did. 'It me neck."

Arthur's top set of false teeth had flown out of his mouth at the force of the impact. He covered his mouth with his right hand as he spoke and peered through watery eyes at the ground close to his feet. His denture lay in the grass at the bottom of the maple tree.

Unfortunately, Wilmot got to it first, sniffed at it, wagging his tail delightedly at his find. Without a second thought Arthur took a handkerchief out of his pocket, wiped the denture clean and to Meredith's disgust popped it back into his mouth. She pretended not to have seen and suppressed a shudder of revulsion, forcing herself not to gag. Then, teeth back in their rightful place, Arthur continued his tirade.

"I'm sorry Miss Meredith, but it were definitely Jonah. 'Im an' that blasted air rifle!" Arthur rubbed his sore neck. 'I'm sure on it. I'd not said anythin' afore now, but 'e's bin usin' squirrels an' birds for target practice. Oi've found their bodies; poor little creachers an' now 'es startin' on 'umans."

With a terrible sinking feeling in the pit of her stomach, Meredith knew it was Jonah at the window. He was more than capable of carrying out such horrible acts.

"Iss a good job I were wearin' me scarf, Miss. It could've bin a lot worse wi'out it."

A sore-looking red swelling was visible on the side of his neck just below the jaw. She did not want to think about how much worse it could have been; it was bad enough.

"Here, Arthur, let me help," she said, putting her hand under his elbow to support him and led him towards the house. "Come up to the kitchen. Mrs Renwick knows First Aid and that injury needs looking at. I can get Marjorie to make you a cup of tea. You could probably do

with a warm up too."

"No, no, don' you go to no bother, Miss, Oi'll get on 'ome to my Gwen," his whiskery face was ashen, "she'll tek care o' me though Oi'm much obliged fer yer concern, Oi'm sure."

"Then I'll get someone to drive you home. Yes, yes, I know it's not far, but you can at least let me do this." Arthur decided not to argue.

"We'll just walk round to the front of the house." Using her mobile phone, Meredith called the house and a few moments later a dark blue Jaguar purred into the front driveway just as Meredith, Arthur and Wilmot, still happily wagging his tail, appeared at the side of the house. The driver, a tall, dark haired young man, jumped out of the car and hurried toward them. Wilmot sprinted towards the newcomer, jumping excitedly around his legs.

"What's up?" Seeing Arthur's pallor he frowned.

"Arthur's been hurt, Stuart," Meredith said quietly. "Could you take him home please and ask Gwen to call Dr Brownlow to check him over and…could you stay with him until the doctor's been? I'd like to know he's alright?"

"No problem." Stuart took Arthur's arm and led him towards the car. "Come on Arthur, my old mate, let's get you home."

"Oi don' wan' no fuss. You 'ear me?" Arthur protested as Stuart helped him along.

"An' you'll get none from me," Stuart grinned as he eased Athur into the car. Once he was settled comfortably Meredith explained to Stuart what had happened. "I'm sure Jonah's behind this."

"Don't worry. Arthur's a tough old bird. He'll be fine." Stuart climbed into the driver's seat, started up the engine and waved as the Jaguar sped off down the drive. Meredith sighed. *Now for Jonah!*

At the back door, she braced herself before going in. On a normal day, she would kick off her boots in the small lobby before entering the kitchen but this was not a normal day.

Chapter Four

The Atkins' home, Winterne Manor, was an impressive blend of stone and black and white Tudor timbering. Originally built in the twelfth century, the manor had started life as a baronial hall. Over its legendary history, it had gained a reputation for a series of unfortunate events. At one time a hundred year curse had been placed on the manor which had caused all kinds of terrible things to happen to its residents.

Fires, accidents, early deaths, all sorts of unexplainable things had haunted the manor until around twenty years before the Atkins' family had moved in, but Meredith often wondered if the curse was still active, toying with her family. In all honesty though, she knew the only thing wrong with the house and indeed her life, was her family.

Her father was never at home, her mother led an almost reclusive life and her brother, Jonah, was a nightmare in every way.

On an almost daily basis he caused havoc in the village and at home. She had sincerely hoped that this day would be a peaceful one. She was too tired to cope with trouble. Unfortunately, her hopes were dashed at the sound of Arthur's scream.

After making sure Arthur was being taken care of by Stuart Seymour, son of their cook, Marjorie; Meredith gathered her strength for the battle to come with Jonah. Shaking with rage, she stormed through the back door into the wide, vault-ceilinged kitchen only to find both Dorothy and Marjorie waiting for her.

Mrs Seymour, a plump, grey haired woman in her sixties, floury hands on her hips was clearly very angry. A mixing bowl, half full of cake mixture, stood unattended on the marble-topped table beside her. Dorothy Renwick, the Housekeeper, was sitting in the huge green armchair by the fire, fidgeted crossly with a large ring of keys on her chain belt. The brightly blazing open fire was the only cheerful thing in the room. Meredith knew the signs.

"What's he done now?" she dreaded the answer.

Dorothy scowled. "Where would you like me to start?" She would not meet Meredith's eyes. "I fell for it. Again! He said he'd got a bad headache, he said he felt sick," she looked away, "and I fell for it," she repeated. "I said he could have the day off school. I'm such a fool!" She finally looked up at Meredith. "Of course he was faking…again. Then he got bored…and we all know what he's like when he gets bored, don't we? She paused for a moment and when she spoke again it was in a quieter but cold, harsh tone. "Dr Brownlow's been here earlier to see young Peggy."

Meredith felt her stomach flip. Marjorie said nothing.

"This time he's gone too far! He'll kill someone one day," Dorothy shook her head.

"What happened?" Meredith wanted to be somewhere else, anywhere else.

"Your precious brother," Dorothy stopped in mid-sentence, "oh, I'm sorry dear, he's not your responsibility." She sat back in the armchair wearily, as if just talking about what happened had drained every bit of strength from her.

"Pens! He left pens on the stairs deliberately to see Peggy fall. She was coming down the stairs with your mother's lunch tray and didn't see them. The poor girl fell from the top of the stairs to the landing. She could've broken her neck… and he thought it was funny!"

Meredith's knuckles whitened as she gripped the back of a chair. "Is she alright?" Marjorie wiped the flour off her hands with a tea-towel, and laid a reassuring arm across Meredith's shoulders while Dorothy continued more calmly. "Yes. Dr Brownlow said she was lucky and it's just a slight sprain. She's shocked of course but a couple of weeks rest will help. I've been on to the agency for another maid until she's better...I just hope she wants to come back. I couldn't blame her if she resigned."

"Neither would I," Meredith said weakly. She was about to leave the kitchen to confront her brother, when Marjorie cleared her throat. "Umm, before you go dear…there's something else. Look at this," she opened a cupboard door, "he's been in the larder and helped himself. The cakes I made earlier have gone, all of them. And, just look at the mess! Egg bowl, smashed on the floor, along with two dozen eggs, flour everywhere and biscuits all trampled into the floor," Marjorie

sniffed tearfully.

Meredith pulled a wooden chair out from under the large, rectangular wooden table and flopped into to it.

"Oh my, but you look all done in," Marjorie said tenderly, "you just sit there and catch your breath while I make you some tea, dear."

Meredith nodded her thanks. She looked around the large, warm, cosy and usually welcoming room. It was a haven she always looked forward to at the end of a busy day but not on this day. Today it was no sanctuary. There was no comfort to be had until she had dealt with Jonah.

"I'm not sure how much more of this I can take," she sighed. The two older women exchanged worried looks. They knew tears were threatening to fall. "He's definitely excelled himself today," Meredith continued, her eyes fixed on the fire, "and to think all I expected to have a go at him about was what he'd done to Arthur." Dorothy and Marjorie exchanged questioning looks. "He just used Arthur Sykes as target practice with that damned air rifle of his."

"He never did!" Marjorie gasped. "And I was worried about eggs!"

"But...Arthur must be eighty if he's a day!" Dorothy exclaimed. "That's awful! How is he?"

"I don't think it's serious. His scarf stopped it from being any worse."

"When I lost my job ten years ago and your Mum took me in, I couldn't have been happier. You were a lovely little girl and Jonah was such...a...sweetheart, in those days," Dorothy said quietly, staring into the fire. "Your Mum was always my favourite cousin and I'd do anything for her...but, the way things are now I'm just about at my limit with Jonah." She turned to face Meredith. "I've even thought about resigning, you know. I have a little money put aside now and I'm not so old I couldn't get another house-keeping job..."

"...but you can't!" Meredith cried, "I'd never cope...not without you."

Dorothy smiled, "You didn't let me finish. I'm not there quite yet. Not quite at the point where I'm ready to give in...yet. This house's been home to me for ten years and I'm part of this family...they say you can't choose your relatives." She gave a chuckle. "Jonah I mean. No, no, I'm not going anywhere just yet." She gripped Meredith's hand reassuringly. Meredith smiled with relief.

It was easy to see that Harriet and Dorothy were related with their red hair, green eyes and similarly strong jaw lines. Dorothy, at fifty-two was the older of the two, her hair slightly fading now with age, but still a striking woman.

"Stuart's driving Arthur home," Meredith said. "I've asked him to wait until Dr Brownlow's been, then he'll let us know how he is." She sat wearily back in her chair as Marjorie handed her a mug of tea. "I'm at my wit's end with Jonah. He's vicious! He's a truant…never takes any notice of anything I say. Why can't he be like other kids of his age?" She took a sip of her tea. "I wish Dad was here more often. Things might be different then."

"Bless you m'dear," Marjorie soothed, "but I wouldn't want the responsibility of him. I never had any trouble at all with my Stuart, except for…" she paused a moment, recovered herself and went on, "well, that'll do another time." She frowned at a memory she was not prepared to share. Meredith and Dorothy said nothing, made no sign they had noticed.

"I need to talk to Dad," Meredith looked at Dorothy hopefully, "have you heard if he's coming home soon?"

Dorothy shook her head. "No, I haven't heard from him recently, so probably not."

Meredith stared down into her mug as if looking for inspiration. For a few moments, no-one spoke; the only sound was the crackling of the fire. Loyalty prevented Dorothy from criticising Harriet but she dearly wished her cousin would spend more time with her children then perhaps these problems would never have started. It was grossly unfair that, at eighteen, Meredith had so much on her plate. With maternal concern she watched as Meredith finished her tea, took a very deep breath and summoned her strength for battle.

"OK, let's get this over with," Meredith sighed as she rose from her chair. Wilmot stood up, ready to go with her as he always did. "Not this time boy. Lie down, stay!" Wilmot sniffed huffily but flopped down again, obedient to her command. He stared after her as she headed out of the swing door that led to the hallway before dejectedly laying his head on his crossed front paws. The two older women watched her go, sending their silent support but anticipating the fallout to come. Marjorie picked up the empty mugs and put them on the sink unit.

"Poor wee thing," she said softly. "I wouldn't want to be in her shoes right now." Dorothy nodded. "Changing the subject, Dorothy," she said with a sly, sideways grin at her friend, "Ernie popping in later is he?"

"Now don't you go making more of it than it is, Marjorie Seymour, you...wicked old match-maker." Dorothy's face grew warm under Marjorie's steady blue-eyed gaze, "Ernie's just calling in for a cuppa during his rounds, like he usually does."

'Aye, o'course he is." Marjorie picked up the empty mugs still grinning and enjoying the obvious embarrassment. "You mark my words, Miss Renwick, our policeman's got a soft spot for you."

"Nonsense!" Dorothy rummaged in her pocket for a handkerchief, trying to hide the rosy tint spreading across her cheeks by turning away to avoid her tormentor's knowing smile.

Meredith ascended the three steps that took her to the dark hallway. She flipped the light-switch and two enormous crystal chandeliers suspended from the carved ceiling glowed into life illuminating the oak-tiled floor and panelling lining the walls. To one side of the hallway stood two long floor-standing glass cabinets, locked for security, containing small swords and daggers. Above them, more glass cabinets displaying lethal-looking swords including claymores, scimitars and sabres together with a number of axes exhibited in pairs, formed part of a collection that any museum of warfare would have been proud to own.

Secured to the wall that formed the side of the staircase, pikes and helmets from the English Civil War were arrayed together with shields showing the Coats of Arms of previous owners of the manor. The entire collection was completed by two gleaming suits of armour standing guard duty at the bottom of the wide staircase. The entire collection was treated with loving care by a local armoury expert, hired by Meredith's father, to keep it in prime condition and Jeremiah Atkins, immensely proud of this martial aspect of the manor, thoroughly enjoyed showing it off to visitors whenever he was at home.

Meredith glanced at the cases containing the daggers, ran her fingers over the glass and suppressed a murderous impulse to break in and steal one of the weapons, if only to threaten Jonah a little but, she realised with relief, if she was unable to get to them, so was he. Heaven only knew what damage he would do if he got hold of a sword!

Pushing that horrible thought out of her head, she sprinted up the portrait-hung staircase to Jonah's rooms, stormed along the red-carpeted corridor, her anger building, to find Jonah waiting defiantly at his door for her.

"So you're here to sort me out, I suppose," his smile revealed a metal brace across his teeth.

"No!" she snapped, pushing past him into the room, "I'm here to give you a medal." Slamming the door behind them, she exploded into anger. "Hurting people's just a game to you, isn't it?"

Jonah brushed by her, an expression of boredom on his face. "I don't know what the fuss is about? It was only a bit of target practice," he laughed. "How was I to know you and that stupid dog of yours would show up like that? Anyway Arthur was a great target." He would not admit it was an accident and that he was trying to hit the peacock. Why let her think he couldn't hit what he aimed at? "I give myself points for every moving target I hit," he said remorselessly. "You have to admit it was funny when old Sykes jumped." Meredith opened her mouth to say something but he cut her short. "Oh, I'm sorry, didn't you find it amusing?" he gave her a sarcastic grin.

Meredith couldn't believe her ears. "You really have no idea what you've done, do you?" Jonah looked away. Meredith thought she fleetingly saw shame in his eyes but it flickered out far too quickly for her to be sure. "You nearly killed two people today!" His dumb insolence inflamed her rage; tears of frustration filled her eyes. "What did either of them ever do to you?" She took a deep breath. Could she reason with him? "Look, Arthur's a dear old man and Peggy didn't deserve what you did to her, can't you see that?"

"Oh I knew you'd get to hear about that. Big mouth Dorothy been talking has she?" Jonah smirked. "Don't worry about Peggy, she's stupid…and Sykes, a dear old man! That's the point, he's old! You know…old, decrepit…and anyway, he's only a gardener. It's time he retired…I'm sick of seeing him around the place. And, as for that Peggy…we can always get another servant. Why so bothered about people who don't matter?"

Meredith was dumbstruck. Moving quickly to his bed, she picked up the offending air rifle and the plastic tub containing of the tin pellets. "These are going. Right now!"

He made no move to stop her. "I'm pretty good with that, you

know." He moved closer to her smiling wickedly. "Did you remember the Edwards' cat?"

Meredith recalled their nearest neighbour's ginger cat having had its eye removed by the Vet after a mysterious injury a few weeks previously. The Edwards had never discovered what happened, but he knew and now Meredith did too.

"What happened to you? You're sick, twisted...you're...not...the same person...not..." she struggled to find the words, "not my brother any more," she said despairingly. The conversation had become so much stranger than she had anticipated. "We need to get you some help...before you actually do kill someone. I'd better phone Doctor Brownlow...see if he can recommend someone."

As she spoke, she glimpsed a flicker of misgiving in his eyes and a moment of pity caught her off guard. Perhaps something of the old Jonah was still in there? For a split second she wondered if all this spitefulness was a cry for attention and watched as he turned away, without speaking, towards the window. His right hand went to his hair and he twiddled a lock around his finger, a gesture he would make as a small boy when he was scared or worried. She felt an impulse to go to him but he spun around, his face and hers almost nose to nose.

She had the sudden realisation that, at fourteen years old he was as tall as she was and wondered when that had happened. *Why she had not noticed it before?* Time had gone by so quickly and it had been so long since they had spent any real time together.

He sensed a softening in her manner and sniggered again, snapping her back into reality. *Perhaps her little brother, the Jonah she knew had gone after all.*

"What you have become...I...don't know you anymore," she said coldly, staring directly into his eyes, "I'm actually ashamed to be related to you."

He shrugged his shoulders and turned back to the window.

"It's time I called Dad. It's time he knew what you've been up to," she said, heading away towards the door.

He turned around to face her, not appearing the least bit concerned.

"It's not just about Arthur and Peggy," she continued, "I've heard quite a bit about your...recent activities." She waited for him to respond, but he just glared at her.

"Dr Brownlow's tyres were slashed last week. I know it was you.

You were seen running off and don't bother to ask, I'm not going to tell you who saw you. You've been playing truant from school and they've had complaints about you bullying the younger pupils. Well, no more! Do you hear me? I'm sick of this and I'm sick of you! You're lucky not to be suspended."

There was still no response from the sullen boy so she continued talking, struggling to maintain an even tone. "You know it's only because Dad's who he is that you were brought home in the police car the other day when they caught you hanging around the pub and in school time too. Anyone else would have been taken back to school, or worse, the police station! Don't you have anything to say for yourself?" His arrogant silence infuriated her. "OK, that's it! I'm done with you," she snapped.

For a brief moment he seemed uneasy, then smugness slid back into his eyes and a cynical sneer spread across his face. "Find someone who cares. Get our loving Daddy to come home? You'll be lucky," he shouted, moving away from the window and advancing towards her, angrily. "Where are you going to find him, eh? Are you going to leave a message with his secretary so she can make you an appointment with him? It's for sure you won't get hold of him and he never comes home except when he wants to schmooze business people, make an impression," he stopped ranting and lowered his voice. "He doesn't care about us," he said, more calmly than she expected. "Don't kid yourself. We come way down his list of priorities."

Meredith thought his outburst was over but then he looked her up and down, screwed up his face and pinched his nose between his finger and thumb. "God, you stink!" She had forgotten she was still wearing her waxed jacket, jodhpurs and riding boots.

"You still stink of those rotten stables! Go back there and do some mucking out, why don't you? Get back there and leave me alone!"

There seemed no hope of finding any common ground no matter what she said or did.

When their parents separated, Meredith and Jonah had become very close until the accident at the stables when Jonah had shown how irresponsible he was. There had been times after that when Meredith wished they could forget the past but the gulf between them was now far too wide. She tried one last appeal to his better nature, if he still had one.

"Why can't you stop behaving like this? Arthur and Peggy deserve better. Peggy's really good with Mum." But Jonah just stared back in dumb insolence triggering her anger again. "I'm wasting my time aren't I?"

Jonah rolled his eyes upward. "Oh, go on tell Daddy, he sneered, "if you can find him that is!"

They were so angry the air between them crackled with hostility, her hazel eyes glared fiercely into his brown eyes. But he was right. Their father only used them and the manor when he wanted to influence some business deal. He had no real interest in the family. Sometimes he brought reputable businessmen, but they were unsure about others; some seemed very shady. Her father's offhand attitude toward his family and social climbing had created the rift between their parents. Neglect by both parents had hurt the children but Meredith, being older, seemed able to deal with it better. It was Jonah she was unable to cope with alone.

He no longer spoke of friends and Meredith guessed his behaviour scared them away. He probably had no friends. One minute she was trying to understand him, the next she was furious with him. Exasperated, her hand itched to slap him very hard, but what would that achieve?

"Is there anything else I can do for you," Jonah enquired with a nastily sweet smile, "or are you going back to the stables where you belong, sister dear?"

"Oooooh! Don't push it you little…little…," for a moment she was too infuriated to think of a suitable word, then it came to her, "…pig!" She prodded her forefinger hard into his chest, forcing him backwards. "Just remember, what goes around comes around. You must have heard that saying, brother dear?"

"Get out! GET OUT!" Jonah screamed at her as she stormed off, her head held high. His mocking laughter followed her as she walked along the corridor but she refused to give him the satisfaction of turning round and missed seeing his scornful mask slip.

As he watched her walk away he felt an unexpected surge of misery and recalled the pain in Arthur Sykes' face and the sheer terror on Peggy's as she tried desperately to keep her footing on the stairs. He had watched from behind the banisters as she fell, her scream echoed again in his mind just as it had several times that afternoon. It seemed

to be on replay in his head.

Guilt welled up from somewhere deep inside. He felt nauseated and almost called Meredith back, but pride or perhaps, stubbornness stopped him.

Another memory he thought he had buried long ago, crept back. "NO!" he shouted to the walls. "No, not now!" He took a long deep breath and rubbed his eyes as though it would help erase what he did not want to see again in his mind's eye. Forcing the memory from his mind, he closed his eyes and told himself to forget but tears threatened.

He heard Meredith's footfalls on the stairs and slammed the door, defiantly shutting everyone out again. Once again he was alone.

"Good. She's gone. I don't need her…I don't need anyone. They can go to Hell!" But his voice went unheard beyond the now empty room. He booted up his PS4 and chose a game from the case he kept inside the drawer, a game for one player.

Chapter Five

"I'm home, Mum," Sam called, flinging his wet jacket on the banisters.

"Hi Sam, have a good day?" his mother replied from the kitchen.

"Not bad, Gibbins had a go at me for not handing in my homework though and I got detention."

"I thought they had to give you notice of detention." Jane came through to the hallway to meet him. "Surely you shouldn't have had to stay today?"

"It was my choice. I wanted to get it over and done with." Sam checked his appearance in the hall mirror. Good, still no spots, he thought, and walked with his mother into the kitchen where he tugged off his school tie, opened the neck of his shirt, dumped his school bag on the table, helped himself to a carton of orange juice from the fridge before reaching up to the shelf of a wall cupboard for the biscuit tin.

Sam was a good looking boy with even white teeth, blond hair and wide blue-grey eyes and, even though he was not really aware of it, he was very popular with the girls at school but he was usually awkward and tongue-tied around them. He did not mention to his mother that he had asked Joanne to the Christmas Ball at school. She would only ask questions.

"Dad's phoning tonight isn't he?"

"Yes, after work and don't you get stuck into those my boy, dinner won't be long."

He shook his head, his mouth too full of chocolate digestive to speak.

"Kids!" she said, grinning at him.

"I wone aff emme mo," he mumbled, trying hard not spit out crumbs.

"It's chicken casserole tonight, is that OK with you?"

"Yeff…fime."

Up in his room he spent the next hour getting his German and Maths homework out of the way. He usually phoned Ranjeet for help but thankfully it was geometry and not too difficult. Later over dinner, he and his mother talked about how their respective days had gone and Sam told her about the episode with Mr Gibbins, briefly mentioned the concert and the ball, but still left out telling her about Joanne.

After dinner, and under protest, he helped with the washing up and then fed their very large, very lazy black and white cat, Portia. She woke up when she heard Sam getting her food ready and purred around his legs while he filled one bowl with food and the other with water.

"I've got my homework out of the way and I'm going on the XBox till Dad phones," he called from the bottom of the stairs into the front-room where his mother was glued to Emmerdale on the television as she did the ironing.

"OK. I'll give you a call when he phones."

Sam ran up the stairs two at a time, sat at his computer desk and got out his FIFA 14 game. He played for an hour or so then got bored so he looked up some friends on Facebook, posted comments on updates and sent some messages but he was so impatient for his father to call that nothing seemed to interest him for very long and it was difficult to concentrate. He missed having his Dad around. They were not a proper family apart but the separation was unlikely to last much longer. His father would be home for good soon or they would go to South Africa…but that was another problem.

He stretched out on his bed and, having no interest in any of the programmes his mother would be watching on television, watched a recording of the previous night's 'Top Gear' on his bedroom television, then read for a while until he realised it was ten o'clock. His father had still not called.

"Mum, I thought Dad was going to phone tonight," he shouted down the stairs.

"He was, but you never know, maybe he's worked late," she called back. "He does sometimes. Perhaps he couldn't get a connection, but don't worry, he'll probably call in the morning. Anyway, it's getting

late and time you settled down. If he does call have got any message for him?"

"Yeah, tell him next time phone earlier. I really wanted to talk to him tonight. G'night Mum."

"G'night Sam."

Climbing into bed, Sam pulled his 'Stig' duvet over him, turned out his bedside lamp and snuggled down to sleep. It seemed he had only been asleep for a few moments when a persistent telephone ringing broke into his dream. It took a while before he understood. The phone in their hall was ringing.

He heard his mother's bedroom door open, the landing light click on and strip of light showed underneath his door. He heard her run down the stairs and the click of the hall standard lamp. Sam groaned when he saw the time. It was twelve forty-five in the morning. It can't be Dad. Not at this time of night. He pulled the duvet back over his head. It better not be a crank caller or a wrong number! Throwing back the duvet, he put on his dressing gown and tiptoed to the door. He opened it quietly hoping to eavesdrop.

"Yes, yes, this is Mrs Johnson. Oh, Mr Van der Leiden. What's happened? Is Steve alright?" Sam heard her ask. "Oh God! How badly hurt is he? How did it happen?

Chapter Six

Hurtling down the stairs at break-neck speed, Sam missed his footing, slid heavily down the last six steps and almost ended up in a heap on the hall floor but he somehow managed to stop himself by grabbing the banister. With a jarring jolt, he pulled up hard wrenching a muscle in his right forearm that sent a searing pain shooting through the inside of his elbow.

Not realising he was hurt, his mother rolled her eyes in exasperation. There was so much static on the line she found it difficult enough to hear without any of Sam's nonsense going on.

Sam had been too pre-occupied with his painful arm to pay attention to his mother but soon realised she was trembling and her face was ashen. Although he had never actually seen anyone faint, he guessed that if he had they would look just as his mother did at that instant and ran into the kitchen to get a chair for her, startling poor Portia who scuttled under his feet bolting for cover. Sam had to use some very skilful foot-work to avoid tripping over her before she disappeared under the hall sideboard and hissed furiously at him, her coat standing on end and her tail fluffed out like a bottle brush.

Ignoring the pain in his arm, Sam struggled through the door and back into the hall, by holding it open with his left foot and shoving the chair along the laminate floor. He set it down beside his mother and gently guided her into it, while moving his head closer to the telephone as he tried to hear the other side of the conversation. He still had no idea of what had actually happened but obviously something was dreadfully wrong.

"Yes, Uh-uh, yes. Mr Van der Leiden. Er…Jo. What? But how bad is it? Is he conscious?" Her voice shook and her eyes brimmed with worried tears. "Sorry…I missed that…did you say Steve was

conscious? Oh, thank goodness…yes. Oh, yes…but how long ago did you find him?" She put her free arm around Sam's shoulder.

"So he was out there for…for how long?" Sam mouthed questions at her but she shook her at head him and put her hand over the mouthpiece.

"I'll tell you everything in a minute, just let me hear it all first." Sam frowned but nodded; waiting was hard when you were so anxious.

"What did the consultant say? Yes, yes, I understand. Good…um… that's a good sign isn't it?" She moved her hand, gripped Sam's right arm and he turned his face away so she could not see him wince.

Portia, unused to all the activity so late at night when she should have been cosily nestled down to sleep on Sam's bed, cautiously peeped out from her refuge underneath the sideboard to see if was safe to come out. Reassured no-one was about to step on her, she ventured out into the hall, sat down and proceeded to lick her tail while taking occasional peeks at the humans, in case she needed to dash off again.

Sam, frustrated at not being able to hear any of the distant conversation, hovered agitatedly in front of his mother, who was making signs at him to calm down.

"They what? Why not? No I don't understand the company's position…Oh I know, I'm sorry…but yes, Mr Van der Leiden, I mean Jo, yes of course, I'll come out. Thank you for getting in touch with me so quickly. Yes, I'm sure I can get a flight today. I don't know which airline yet, but I…I WILL get a flight today. I'll call you as soon as I've sorted everything out."

By now Sam, desperate to know what was going on, paced the floor anxiously. Portia looked up at him, her small pink tongue poking out. Sam stuck his tongue out back at her. She stopped grooming herself, stood up and with a dignified swish of her tail flounced away to the living room.

"Well? What's happened?" he whispered urgently to his mother. Again, she shushed him to be quiet. "Wait!" she snapped in a loud whisper.

"Sorry…um Jo, yes, I'm still here and I quite agree, the sooner I get started, the sooner I can let you know the arrangements. Please give Steve our love and tell him I'll be there soon. Yes…I do have your number and I'll call you later. Thank you for everything Mr Van der

Leiden…sorry, Jo. We're very grateful." She put the telephone down, inhaled deeply and, to Sam's annoyance, did not move from the chair.

"What Mum? Mum…come on, tell me." He hovered around her, following her into the kitchen Mum. What?"

"Sorry, Sam. Just give me a minute. I need tea and time to take it all in, make sure I've remembered it right…but...it's alright, your Dad's OK." Well that was something, he supposed.

Without a word, she picked up the kettle, filled it and switched it on. Sam thought he was going to burst. *Why wouldn't she talk to him?* He chewed his thumbnail impatiently, watching as she seemed to take forever, tying the belt on her rose coloured dressing gown, brushing her hair away from her face with her hand and, he was sure, avoiding looking at him. After what felt like hours, she finally sat down at the kitchen table and pulled out another chair, indicating he should sit beside her. Sam had been trying to convince himself that nothing too awful had happened. Then he noticed how she was pressing the heels of her hands together to stop them trembling, they were white from the pressure. More quietly he asked, "OK, Mum, just tell me!"

Turning to face him she took a deep breath, "Your Dad…" she reached out for his hand, "it…it was a car accident." Gathering tears threatened to spill. "It was somewhere off the main road, down a dirt track…that made it difficult to find them. Her voice quivered every bit as much as her hands. "That was his boss, Mr Van der Leiden."

"Yeah, yeah, I know that but what's happened to Dad."

"It…it seems that he and…and Will, I think his name is, were chasing a thief on a bad back road and it was dark…and…," she looked up, "well, to be honest I'm not sure of all the circumstances but the important things is that his injuries aren't life threatening…but they are bad. He's broken a couple of ribs…both his legs are broken," tears welled up in her eyes, "the right femur, that's the thigh bone, has been broken in two places and his jaw's dislocated but," she stopped and took a deep breath, "there's also possible spinal damage and that's worrying the doctors most. They're carrying out tests, doing X-rays and MRI's and so on to see what the damage is." She stopped for a moment to let Sam take it all in.

"We've got to get out there...be there with him."

"Wait a minute, Sam, let me finish." She looked grave and Sam had a nasty feeling he was not going to like what she was going to say next.

"He's got to stay in hospital there for a week or two. His medical bills and sick pay are covered, so at least that's something and Mr Van der Leiden…Jo, told me the consultant's confirmed his injuries aren't life-threatening but they'll take time to heal. They'll know more after the results."

Sam's mind was racing; all the things he would need to pack, how long they might be away for and was only barely listening to his mother.

"Sam? Are you listening to me?"

"Sorry, I was just wondering how long we'd be away for and how much to pack."

"Ah, yes. Now that's where we have a problem," she turned away unable to look him in the eye, "and I'm going to need your cooperation. I need you to be very mature and understanding…can you do that for me…for your Dad?"

"Yeah, of course. What do you want me to do?"

"Stay here."

"Stay here? No! Oh no." He jumped so quickly his chair fell backwards and clattered on the floor. He walked over to the sink unit and stared out of the window to the dark, starlit sky. He could not believe she wanted to go without him. Putting her arm around his shoulders, she tried to comfort him. "Sam, please. I understand how you feel but you can't come for a number of reasons and I want…, no, I need you to understand."

Sam's heart slipped to somewhere below his knees; his face a picture of misery as he faced her.

"Why?" he pleaded. "Why can't I come with you? I can't stay here while you're there. I won't know how Dad is…" he paced the kitchen floor, "…I won't be able to…to concentrate at school or anything and, anyway…I always wanted to see South Africa," he ended lamely.

"I know, I do know, believe me." She cupped his face with her hands, looking into his blue-grey eyes, "but there's no way I can take you. If we'd won the lottery or we earned more, if your Dad had a permanent job, it would be different, but..." Sam's face was a picture of frustration and confusion. "Sit down again and I'll explain. I don't want to go without you either and if there was any way," she trailed off. How could she make him understand? She wanted so much to make him feel better but what could she say?

She moved over to the work-top, took two cups down from the hooks and put teabags in them. "OK, Sam, firstly, although we're not broke we're not very well-off either and, there's just not enough money right now for an extra ticket there and back plus hotel rooms. We'd have to pay the adult fare for you now, and we just can't afford it. On top of that…"

"But Mum?"

Ignoring him, she poured boiling water into the cups. "No Sam, no 'buts', and this is the second reason. I've no idea how long I'm going to be away and I'll be at the hospital all day. There'll be nothing for you to do, no school, no friends, you'll be utterly bored doing nothing all day, hanging around the hospital. Oh, don't look at me like that. Don't make feel worse than I already do, please. I would take you if I could but, as well as only paying for my flight, I'm being given a single room at the hospital. They will only help your Dad's next of kin…me. He needs me and I don't have a choice." She gave him a weak smile trying to offer some comfort. It didn't work.

Sam fought back tears. He was too old to cry and deep down he knew she was right. No matter how he tried he could not find any way around the situation and realised he would just have to resign himself to staying at home. "It's OK. I'll be fine and I'm sorry to make things tough for you. I didn't mean to be mardy."

She squeezed his hand and he forced himself not to wince. "That's more like it," she smiled oblivious to his pain.

"So what happens now?"

"I'm going to call Aunt Cathy to see if she can come here to look after you while I'm away."

"Aunt Cathy! We haven't seen her for years, not since before she married…what's his name"

"Charlie. Remember? Cathy sent us an invitation to the wedding but you had Mumps and we couldn't go."

"But that was ages ago. I don't know them…well I don't know him and I can't remember her very well, so it's the same thing, isn't it?"

"I'm sorry, love, there's no-one else. We're a small family and Cathy is my only other relative." She put her arms around his shoulder and kissed the top of his head. "Sometimes things happen we have no control over and have to be dealt with as best we can. Right now we have to put your Dad first. If you think you've had a shock just think

how he must be feeling. He's thousands of miles away from us and badly hurt," she reminded him. "You know I wouldn't leave you behind if I had any choice and it should only be for a couple of weeks," she said, crossing her fingers behind her back.

"Yeah but that's not the point is it? I...I...wanna go too."

"I know but it's impossible. If it was my choice, you'd be on that plane with me but it's not." She spoke more firmly than she intended and felt awful. "I feel bad enough about leaving you," she said sympathetically but she had to stay strong, be firm. "Now, I have to get things organised so why don't you go back to bed and let me get on? It's very late and you need your sleep. We have a busy day ahead."

"You don't honestly think I'm gonna sleep again tonight, do you?" Sam forced a smile. She ruffled his blond hair and smiled encouragingly at him but he had never seen her so worried.

"OK, OK, I'll get out of your hair, but I promise you I won't sleep. Night Mum."

After he had gone Jane threw away the forgotten tea, took another cup from the hooks and started making coffee, she was going to have a long night packing, making arrangements and making telephone calls. Pre-occupied by her thoughts, she didn't hear Sam come back into the kitchen and jumped at the sound of his voice.

"Are you sure you don't need my help?" he grinned. "Didn't mean to scare you, sorry."

"No son, thanks. I'm going to make some coffee, then I'll phone Cathy, book my flight, then phone Jo Van Der Leiden but you go back to bed and try to get some sleep," she shooed him out of the door before turning back to the boiling kettle.

Try and sleep, Sam thought, as he climbed the stairs. He tried to put himself in his mother's place. She was in a difficult position. Was there any other decision she could have made? Probably not. Sliding under his duvet, he knew he wouldn't be able to sleep, his mind was buzzing with everything that had happened. His old teddy bear was sitting on the bedside chair, he picked it up and placed it on his pillow straightening its legs and arms so that it sat properly. He was much too old for cuddly toys but his Dad had bought 'Scruffs' when Sam was just two days old and although it was a bit tattered, he would not part with it, especially now.

He remembered when his father had told him he had got a job in South Africa after being made redundant when the coal mine closed down. He had looked for other work for a long time before finally accepting the offer of the job thousands of miles away and now his Mum would be there as well. It just wasn't right! He tried to recall what his aunt looked like and a hazy picture appeared in his mind. He could just about remember the last time he saw her, but not where. He knew she lived in a village somewhere in Devon…Dorset? Somewhere like that, and she had a big thatched cottage with a huge garden but couldn't remember anything else about it. She and his mother regularly spoke on the phone and they seemed very friendly but how close could they be when they hadn't seen each other in years? He got out of bed and shouted down the stairs.

"Mum, are Aunt Cathy and that man still down in Devon??"

"It's Somerset and…oh hang on a minute…I'll come up," she called back.

A minute or so later his door opened. "No point in shouting up the stairs. Yes, they're still there. It's near Cheddar Gorge or Wookey Hole, one of those two cave places. And, for goodness sake, his name's Charlie, not 'that man'. It's a shame we've all been too busy to meet up and I've no idea what he's like but Cathy seems happy, so he's probably very nice. Now, will you get some sleep, we've got a busy day tomorrow," she paused, "make that, today." She blew him a kiss as she went out.

Sam snuggled back under the duvet and wondered if his Dad would be in a lot of pain but guessed his doctors would be making sure he was comfortable. His door had been left slightly open and he could hear his mother on the telephone, probably talking to his aunt. It might not be so bad he thought. If he'd gone to South Africa he wouldn't have been able to take Joanne to the Christmas Ball at school and it had taken him ages to pluck up the courage to ask her. He smiled. Perhaps staying wouldn't be so bad after all. She was right though, hanging around a hospital all day would have been boring.

He strained to hear the conversation going on downstairs but his eyelids grew heavy, like lead weights. His mother's voice sounded further and further away. He was vaguely aware she was making another call and guessed it was to book her flight. He was fast asleep

by the time she called Mr Van der Leiden giving him the time of her arrival.

Sam didn't know that she finally broke down, crying over her fourth cup of coffee. Jane Johnson felt terrible about leaving Sam behind and, after talking to her sister, she dreaded telling him about the arrangements she had just agreed to.

Chapter Seven

In the village of Winterne, Cathy and Charlie Nowell had been asleep, Charlie snoring loudly as usual, when the telephone rang. It was ten to two in the morning! Cathy rushed downstairs to answer it while Charlie got out of bed, threw on his dressing gown and followed after her. No-one ever called so late at night without it being an emergency.

"Jane, darling, whatever's wrong?" Cathy plonked herself down to sit on the small sofa in the hall beside the telephone table. "Oh, that's awful! How badly hurt is he?" Charlie leaned a little closer.

"Yes, of course you must go and yes, we'll look after Sam but, I'm afraid he'll have to come down here; we can't be away for long this near to Christmas because of Charlie's work." Cathy watched Charlie's reaction.

A large black dog disturbed by the activity, stood up, stretched and nuzzled Charlie's hand, demanding his attention. A second dog raised its head, curiosity aroused, but not enough to be worth getting up for, he settled back down to sleep.

"Of course he'll be fine with us. We can sort out something about temporary schooling, if need be, and we've lots of young people in the village. I know he's a 'Townie' but I'm sure he'll like it here…once he gets used to it. Now don't worry about anything. We'll get ready and drive straight up. At this time of night there'll be very little traffic so if we leave soon we should be with you in about four hours or so. I'll explain everything to Charlie as we get ready. No it's no bother. What are family for but to help out when needed. Try not to worry too much, I'm sure everything will be alright and we'll be there as soon as we can, so you just get on with whatever you need to do. We'll find a way to

explain everything to Sam, or at least Charlie will. He's terrific with children. Oh yes. I'd forgotten he's fourteen now, not a child anymore." Charlie nodded his approval of her arrangements. Cathy smiled at him gratefully.

"Yes, I know, Jane, dear, you must be feeling dreadful. It's a nasty situation, but you'll be with Steve soon and Sam will be fine with us. Now off you go and get yourself ready. We'll be there soon."

Cathy looked thoughtful as they went through to the kitchen. We'll have a cuppa before we go, Charlie." She filled the kettle from a filter jug on the worktop, then lifted two cups off hooks underneath a wall cupboard as she explained to Charlie what had happened. "I'll leave a note for Sarah and she'll keep an eye on everything while we're away. She'll take the dogs next door for a while and they'll be no problem for the rest of the night. Umm…now then, if we feed the cats and shut them in the kitchen, they can let themselves in and out through the cat-flap. What do you think Charlie?"

He had been quiet all the time she was talking and she suddenly realised he had not said anything. He was staring out of the window, into the night apparently deep in thought. She went to him and laid a hand on his arm.

"You're very quiet. Are you alright?"

The big man turned to her, put his hands gently on her shoulders, and smiled warmly, his eyes crinkling at the corners. In a rich, deep voice he replied.

"There's nothing else to be done, Cathy m'dear. Yer sister needs our 'elp an' she'll get it. Now you get yerself dressed, I'll make the tea then take the dogs for a quick walk an' we'll be off."

Relieved, Cathy gave him a hug. Charlie was tall, just over two metres and fairly wide around the middle, and when she hugged him, she couldn't quite get her hands to meet behind him. He was a big bear of a man with the heart of an angel, and she loved him dearly.

"You're a good man, Charlie Nowell." She stretched up on to her tiptoes to kiss his cheek then quickly headed up to get dressed. He smiled as he watched her go, made a pot of tea, put milk in both cups then listened for a moment at the kitchen door while the tea brewed.

Satisfied Cathy was busy upstairs he noiselessly opened the back door, took down a lamp from the shelf, struck a match, lit the wick and carefully, so as not to make any noise, opened the back door.

On the doorstep, he held the lamp aloft and waved it high above his head seven times, all the while listening for Cathy coming back downstairs. He blew out the lamp, put it back on the shelf, slipped back into the kitchen and poured the tea, putting the biscuit tin on the table.

"Tea's ready," he called. Two cats, which had been asleep in baskets either side of the wood burning stove awoke. Their indignant expressions at being disturbed were comical but, as the humans were up there might be food around too. Arching their backs, they stretched elegantly then, one following the other, they padded over to Charlie hoping for some milk and pieces of dropped biscuit.

Cathy, now dressed, came back into the kitchen as Charlie poured the tea and the cats purred around their legs. One, tortoiseshell and white with a long fluffy coat, jumped up onto Cathy's lap demanding to be made a fuss of. She stroked it absent-mindedly, while they discussed Jane's situation and finished their tea.

The dogs, having seen the cats begging, joined the company and sat between the couple, turning their heads from Cathy to Charlie, as if following the conversation closely, waiting for any goodies that might just drop their way.

"I think we should jest get on the road up there," Charlie suggested, "instead of sittin' 'ere blatherin' we can talk on the way." Charlie picked up the teacups and headed for the sink. He seemed eager to get on the road, so Cathy gently lifted the protesting cat off her lap, setting her down on the floor.

"I can be ready in five minutes," Cathy said running the cups under hot water. "I just have to write a note for Sarah then I'm about done."

"An' oi'll get the dogs out fer a quick walk then we'll be off. We'll be no more'n foive minutes." He opened the door and the dogs bounded through excited to be going out again.

The minutes went by, five, then ten, then fifteen. By the time Charlie and the dogs returned Cathy was quite anxious.

"Is everything alright? I was getting worried."

"Daft dog!" He nodded towards Benny. "'E' trailed off after somethin' in the field an' it took me a while to get him back...daft thing probably jest a bit excited, that's all."

"Well as long as everything's alright, dear, let's get going. It'll probably be about six when we get there."

With the cats settled back in the kitchen, and the dogs in their beds in the hall, Cathy and Charlie, wrapped up in warm coats, went outside and climbed into their Land Rover. A clear, cloudless night sky displayed thousands of twinkling stars and a silver crescent moon shone down onto the glistening frosty ground. Cathy shivered and tucked her scarf closer around her neck.

"Once we get going the heater will warm us up," Charlie smiled.

The only sounds were the hooting of an owl and a dog barking somewhere in the otherwise hushed village until Charlie started up the Land-Rover and the peace was broken by its harsh, rattling sound engine

"Hope we didn't wake anyone," Cathy giggled.

Chapter Eight

It was the busiest time of the year for the Winterne Elves so they worked in a shift pattern;

One group would eat and rest while the other worked. Those who were resting in the home cavern on this particular night were waiting for friends to arrive before the evening meal could be served and it was getting very late. Some were getting tetchy.

Piggybait was bored and kept talking about television programmes to his friend Claptrap, who wanted nothing more than to read his newspaper in peace.

"What under Earth are you going on about Piggy?" Claptrap said exasperatedly as he poked his silver-blond head up over his Elfland Chronicle. "You've been watching that electric box thing again, haven't you? You waste far too much time in front of it."

"Don't!" protested Piggybait huffily, "I like Coronation Street and Emmerdale, you learn a lot about humans watching those programmes and I like practising different accents, they're fascinating." he sulked. "Anyway, what's your problem?" Piggybait picked up a slice of hazelnut bread, spreading it with honey freshly stolen from the Manor Farm beehives earlier that morning. It had bits of honeycomb in it. It was much nicer with honeycomb, made it crunchy.

"So come on then, Claptrap, what's your problem?" Piggybait was not going to let the matter drop. "Can't I have a bit of fun on my evening off? I'm not hurting anyone." Taking off his cap, he threw it playfully at his friend, Claptrap, who caught it in his left hand, without looking up. Piggybait's light brown, curly hair, now released from the confines of his cap, fell forward across his face.

"Nice catch." he laughed, "You can still do it then. Glad to see you're not as engrossed in the paper as you said you were, so you can

kindly explain to me why I shouldn't watch the 'box' so much. The Chief gave it to us so I'm only showing the appropriate gratitude."

Claptrap threw the cap back and Piggybait tipped his head, skilfully managing to catch it on his head.

"My dear Piggy," Claptrap began disdainfully, "I am perfectly well aware where the…*thing* came from, but you practising foolish accents is very distracting from my more serious occupation reading the newspaper." Claptrap removed his monocle and looked down his nose at his friend. "You really should read the paper, you might learn something."

Piggybait raised an eyebrow. "Yes, dear friend, even *you* might learn something," Claptrap ended.

Claptrap grinned over his paper then disappeared behind it again but continued talking. "There's always something fascinating going on in the human world, especially at this time of the year and you might actually find it informative. You never know what might pose a threat to our way of life and the Chief trusts us to make sure everything gets looked after safely. So Piggy, do stop the nonsense please, you sound utterly ridiculous!" He smoothed a crease in his burgundy velvet jacket and fingered the top of his ears reassuring himself they were standing up at the correct angle.

Piggybait poked out his tongue. "Well, you look utterly ridiculous!" he muttered under his breath.

It was almost time for dinner and the elves were gathering in the main chamber. The other elves present were used to the banter between Piggybait and Claptrap, their good natured bickering was always good entertainment for the clan.

Claptrap considered himself to be quite sophisticated and dressed in a manner he felt befitted his refined style. The other elves treated his rather pompous airs with friendly humour, affectionately nicknaming him Claptrap because he talked so much rubbish, and to keep his little elf feet firmly on the ground. His motto was '*An elf should always look his best. One never knew who one was going to meet,*' and he endeavoured always to live up to it.

Piggybait, was a complete contrast. He had no airs or graces and continually dressed scruffily, mostly to upset Claptrap.

Claptrap was the older of the two, being two hundred and fourteen years old with Piggybait being three years younger. In elf-years they

were in their early middle-age. No-one could remember how either of them had acquired their nicknames and most of the younger elves had no idea they even had birth names.

This particular evening, when Claptrap went back to reading his paper, Piggybait looked around the cavernous split-level chamber that had been their home for centuries. Warm and dry, the accommodation was perfect during winter months and provided a cool respite from the heat in summer making the perfect haven for this clan of Elven folk. Several small cosy sitting rooms, with squashy sofas and chairs, led off the main chamber. Surprisingly, one of these side rooms had an old-fashioned television and radio sitting side by side on an equally ancient wooden sideboard. Strangely though, there were no wires attached to either of these devices but around the television were a circle of eager elves all enthralled by a particularly gripping episode of Dr Who.

The entire sandy floor was covered by a matting of reeds mixed with herbs that released a light fragrance of rosemary, lemon verbena and thyme when anyone walked across it and mingled with the smoky essence of roasting pine cones that crackled and sputtered on the open fire from which trails of wispy smoke filtered away through a series of natural chimneys and pot-holes, eventually dispersing far away in the woods.

The lower walls were hung with tapestries depicting scenes from elf-lore and garlands of fallen red, gold and brown leaves were strung high above. Higher on the walls were limestone layers resembling cream coloured cake icing that had oozed over the sides before setting hard. Situated around the chamber, one hundred small fir trees, bedecked with fire-fly lamps stood in tubs, making the cave shimmer and glow.

At the far end of the cave, a stairway built into the cave wall led to the upper level, where the clan had excavated to provide sleeping alcoves and bathrooms under the roots of a massive oak tree that grew above on the side of the hill. Obscured from human view on the outside, several small round windows lay hidden among the roots of the tree which allowed in some natural light. A number of the roots were raised up out of the ground concealing a convenient, and very much used, second entrance or exit to their home.

Piggybait loved his clan. Unobserved, he smiled as he watched some of the younger elves play darts with starched ears of wheat while

Primola, matriarch of the Winterne clan and mother to the twins Rondo and Rondina, bustled about efficiently arranging the table ready for the evening meal.

Piggybait looked for her twins and found Rondo leaning against an open doorway casting long and mournful glances towards Ellien who appeared not to notice. There was no hope for Rondo. Ellien had already given her heart to another.

Rondina, he found sitting in an alcove sewing dock leaves together for curtaining windows in the upper levels, her eyes screwed up in concentration trying to keep her stitches tiny and neat, just the way her mother liked them.

His gaze fell on Ellien, the daughter of Jimander, their clan leader. She had a gentle, kindly temperament and was adored by all, especially the younger male elves. With silver-blonde hair that fell in soft waves to below her knees and emerald-coloured eyes, Ellien glowed with a luminous beauty. She and her two female companions harmonised in an ancient Elvish song, their voices clear and soft as birdsong, while they wove fibres from the plant, Old Man's Beard, to make warm winter jerkins.

In a corner by the open fire, four elderly males listened to the music while they sat around a small cut tree-trunk table, playing dominoes with discarded lady-bird wings. Everything as it should be, thought Piggybait contentedly.

The central focus of the room was a magnificent oak table that, on this night could barely be seen due to being so heavily laden with bowls, plates, cups, huge earthenware tureens, candlesticks and wooden cutlery ready for the evening meal. Laid out in the middle of the table were four large baskets containing crusty loaves of warm, delicious hazelnut bread. Fat cheeses, slices of pumpkin pie and a variety of oddly shaped pots containing honey and jams were placed around the table amongst large bowls of dried mushrooms, raspberries, hazelnuts and almond tarts. There was so little room left on the crowded table that when a second set of twins, Halmia and Halmar, brought out more food they found it difficult to find space and kept moving crockery and utensils to make room. Seating was in the form of two long benches accommodating fifteen elves each and two ornately carved chairs with wide arms were placed at either end. Piggybait pulled up a stool near the blazing fire where copper kettles hung on hooks heating water for

the herb teas favoured by the elves. Elderberry wine and dandelion beer were also popular and a tray stacked with tankards and wooden cups stood ready on a shelf in the kitchen. Although the evening meal was prepared, not everyone was there. The clan were waiting for four more of their companions to arrive and could not begin their feast until everyone was present.

Claptrap rested his feet on a lump of rock that bulged out from the wall while he continued to concentrate on his newspaper, completely unaware of the late hour and the overdue dinner, until a chill breeze blew through the cavern. He shivered and the corner of the page he was reading flipped over with the gust that heralded the entrance of four caped and hooded elves.

Ellien smiled warmly as she put down her work and stood to greet the arrivals, one of them her father. Her silky hair enveloping her in a radiant cloak that almost covered her long, gold-thread embroidered moss-green gown. With a loving smile to her father, she almost glided on tiny bare feet into his affectionate embrace before helping him remove his cape and brushing the dampness off his hood as she laid it on a stool near the fire to dry.

"Ah! At last! You're here," said Primola, putting down her sewing and pursing her mouth. "Good, now perhaps we can eat. Come on everyone, up to the table."

"Greetings, my friends," said Jimander, who moved forward as the other members of his party stood back, allowing him to go first in deference to his rank. He gave a wry smile at Primola's scolding; she never made any complaints when they brought her something useful.

The elves never killed animals for food or clothing, but were not against using leather or sheepskin when they came across it and were expert at recycling clothes and footwear. Many pairs of outgrown children's boots and shoes had made their way to the cavern and their food stores were continually kept topped up by superstitious locals who always baked an extra cake or pie and left it on the window sill for the 'fairy folk'. And many a local farmer scratched his head at the disappearance of eggs, milk, jams or cheeses that the enterprising elves just happened to find unattended.

Jimander, at almost four hundred and seventy five, was the oldest and wisest elf of his community and the leader by right of seniority. Generally the life-span of an elf is around four hundred and fifty years

old but, even though Jimander was way beyond that, he had barely aged other than a few streaks of grey in his dark, shoulder length hair.

"So, you're finally back." Claptrap's paper slipped to the floor but he picked it up and laid it neatly folded on the arm of his chair under a withering and disapproving glance from Primola. "We were about to send out a search party for you, weren't we Piggs?" he grinned. "So now you're here, we can eat."

Jimander chuckled good-naturedly at Claptrap's teasing as Ellien kissed her father on the cheek, put her arm through his and led him towards his usual chair at the head of the table. He patted her hand and allowed her to shepherd him along, but Claptrap was impatient and would not allow Jimander to get away as easily as that.

You know," Claptrap continued as he walked by Jimander's side, "I had the most peculiar feeling something was wrong earlier. My ears were almost shuddering."

"No, everything's fine," Jimander replied, "but we spent so long talking we still haven't got round to the feeding and exercising yet and I'll need some volunteers. Don't worry everything's all set for the big night but right now I'm starving, so let me at that bread and honey. We can talk later."

Jimander took his place at the head of the table in one of the armchairs with Ellien on a bench on his right with Piggybait beside her and Claptrap on the bench opposite.

"Oh yes, I'm ready for this," Jimander said, eagerly. "Aah, this bread's still warm. He inhaled the delicious aroma deeply and gave a satisfied smile. "Wonderful baking again, Prim." He saluted the motherly female elf who blushed with pleasure at his praise. "I hadn't realised how hungry I was. It's the cold weather that does it. Piggy, do me a favour, pour me a tankard of the dandelion beer. It's very welcome on a night like this and...I'll have some of that pumpkin pie, pass it over there's a good elf." Jimander handed a platter of bread and cheese to Ellien, just as she turned to speak to Piggybait. Her lovely profile reminded him again, as it always did, of another face he had loved many years ago and the recollection triggered a bittersweet memory. He sighed deeply. Elves lived very long lives and were rarely unwell but they could be injured, sometimes fatally, and that dreadful memory came flooding agonizingly back. A few weeks before Christmas, when Ellien was just a tiny elfling, Jimander's wife,

Malliena, decided to collect mistletoe to decorate the cavern. She knew of a large, healthy plant growing on an oak tree a short distance away from the cavern. As an expert climber and a child of Nature the woods held no fears for her and none of the clan foresaw any danger in her making this short trip alone just as she had done countless times before.

In no time Malliena was way up amongst the upper branches and close to where the mistletoe grew thickly. Nimbly, she stepped along the bough and was about to reach for the plant when she surprised a young pine marten concealed amongst the leaves. He had been about to pounce on a young blackbird and was so intent on seizing his prey that he was entirely oblivious to her presence (and she of his), until she almost stepped on his tail. In fright and frantic to escape, the pine marten darted between her feet, forcing her to one side, she missed her footing, grasped at a nearby branch to prevent her fall, but it was too weak and it snapped under her almost imperceptible weight, hurtling her to the ground below and into the jagged teeth of a poacher's trap. The spring snapped shut. Malliena was mortally wounded.

When she had not returned by twilight, an anxious Jimander organised a search party. It was already dark by the time they found her, unconscious but still alive. Prising open the teeth of the trap, tenderly and skilfully they released her from the jaws of the trap and, refusing all offers of help, Jimander gently carried her broken body home where he laid her on a goose-down mattress in their small chamber, keeping vigil over her. Over the next few days he searched deeply into his knowledge of elf-lore, desperately seeking a way to heal his wife's terrible injuries. The clan cared for baby Ellien, while the tragedy involving her parents was played out in another room.

Malliena drifted in and out of consciousness. At times, although she seemed to be aware of everything going on around her, she was too weak to talk. At others her mind drifted to times and places he could only vaguely remember. It was during one of these feverish episodes of delirium that Jimander discovered how the accident occurred, as she whispered of pine martens and blackbirds. During her lucid moments, her eyes watched Jimander whenever he left her side. He tried, for her sake, to be positive, talking to her of the future, but they both knew the truth and when she slept, he raged, cried and mouthed bitter curses at the poacher whose trap had destroyed their happiness. On the fourth day as evening fell, Malliena was fully awake and clear

eyed. Jimander held her hand while he talked to her about anything, Ellien and how she was growing, what they would do when Malliena recovered, the elves plans for Christmas, anything that came to mind. He talked simply for the sake of talking, while his hand lovingly brushed her damp hair away from her forehead and he tried not to meet her eyes in case she saw the truth there.

Turning her ashen face towards him she smiled weakly and mouthed something he was unable to hear. Jimander kissed her cold hand and leaned closer. This time he was just able to make out her words.

"I will wait for you," Malliena whispered, her eyes dimmed and she spoke no more.

Silent tears trailed down his face as he helplessly watched the life-light fade from her eyes, just as it did from his heart. At the door, grief-stricken Claptrap, Piggybait and the Chief stood in quiet respect, saying their goodbyes to a precious friend, while the other elves waited within the great hall unable to believe the blow that Fate had dealt them.

Inconsolable, Jimander vanished from the cave that night leaving the clan to care for Ellien who was too young to understand her mother had gone. The elves were anxious about Jimander but the Chief believed he would come to no harm and would return when he was ready.

The unfortunate poacher, whose trap had killed Malliena was found dead a few days later having met with an accident while laying another trap. Somehow he had become entangled in its wires making it impossible to escape and had starved to death. He had no family to miss him, but when his neighbours realised he had not been seen for a while, they searched the woods and found his body near to an old mistletoe covered oak tree. His death was accepted as an unlucky accident and those who had their suspicions that Nature had fought back, simply kept quiet.

Jimander returned two days after the poacher was found. No-one ever spoke of the poacher in his hearing. Over the next few months horrific accidents befell poachers in the Winterne Woods, some fatal. Soon, word spread. There was talk of ghosts and ghouls sucking the blood of anyone foolish enough to enter the wood but one local man, determined to continue catching pheasants, refused to be scared by what he considered as sheer fantasy and was boldly determined to put an end to the wild tittle-tattle. Soon after entering the woods he ran

screaming into his cottage where he was found cowering in a corner of his bedroom. It was said his screams could be heard for several miles. From then on, no poaching took place in Winterne Woods and the elves never spoke of the incidents.

Jimander never fully recovered from the loss of his wife. He missed her dreadfully, and focused all his energy on the clan, his young daughter and his work. Spending time with Ellien, who grew more like her mother with every passing year, gave him consolation. As she grew, he often talked to her of Malliena and found comfort in the belief that she remained with him in spirit and they would meet again on the far shores of Alfheim when his time was done. His reverie was interrupted by a voice nearby.

"I'm glad you're back, Jimander," said Halmar, slipping onto the bench beside Piggybait, "we've were getting worried."

Jimander, turned away for a moment to blink away the threatened tears, but looked back in time to see the adoring look that passed between Halmar and Ellien and noted the pink bloom that crept up her cheeks how she quickly dropped her glance when she saw her father watching them.

The son of Jerrill, a clan Elder, Halmar was a handsome young elf with shoulder length, dark blond hair and deep navy blue eyes. He had always been courteous, responsible, intelligent and likeable. Jimander could not complain at Ellien's choice and was prepared to give the union his blessing, when Halmar got around to asking; he would make a fine husband for her.

"Like all the good things life has to offer, my dear young elf. I'm worth waiting for."

Chapter Nine

When the meal ended, Primola chivvied the younger elves, some of them reluctant, into helping clear away the dishes and Claptrap and Piggybait volunteered to help Jimander with the duties he still had to complete that evening. Ellien stood very close to Halmar, both deep in conversation as Jimander blew her a kiss goodbye. She returned the kiss and waved as he put on his cloak, then turned back to the handsome young elf as Jimander went to join the others.

At the entrance, he stopped for a moment to watch them, unobserved, and saw the tender looks passing between them. It brought him comfort to know she would not be alone when his time came to join her mother. Halmar was a good young elf, a credit to his father and the clan. Ellien could do no better than to than choose him for her husband. He turned away to join his waiting companions who had already collected and lit two crystal lanterns and together they entered a long rocky tunnel.

"So what happened tonight? The Chief doesn't usually call you so late?" Claptrap enquired, his silver-blond eyebrows knitted together in a deep frown.

"Nothing major really. There's a little problem he has to sort out and just wanted to let us know he may be away for a day or so."

Piggybait, who had been examining the walls for any interesting colouring in the rocks, now paid attention and listened. "He's going away?"

"Don't worry. It's only for a day or so. He used the dogs as an excuse to get out so late…just a minute, we're here." Jimander stopped, put his right foot on a projecting rock and pushed hard. With a

rumbling sound a small section of the cave wall slid downwards revealing a number of hidden woven reed bags. A blast of cold air from the opening blew into their faces as Jimander reached in and pulled out one of the bags. Placing his foot on the rock again, the door slid back to hide the cavity and contents again.

"I know *he* needs feeding, but do we have to keep his food this cold?" Piggybait shivered.

"Well…yes," Jimander grinned and passed the chilly bundle to him.

"But it's freezing," Piggybait groaned hoisting the bag over his shoulder, "and why is it always me that carries it? It's not fair!"

"Don't moan, Piggy, you know *he'll* take it better from you. He likes you more than me and this is the price you pay for popularity," Jimander winked at Claptrap as they walked on with Piggybait muttering under his breath, "that shouldn't mean I have to carry it though."

"Now where was I?" Jimander ignored Piggybait's complaints. "Oh yes, I was talking about the dogs! We'd have been able to talk more if they hadn't been there, but under the circumstances they had to be."

"But he usually only walks them earlier in the evening," Claptrap remarked, "and this was much later, wasn't it?"

Jimander shrugged, "It's not the first time but it's rarely that late. He was in a hurry so all he had time to tell me was that things might be a bit difficult for a while but didn't say what the problem was. He thinks he should be back tomorrow but it may be the day after and, in the meantime, we just carry on as normal. He'll let us know when he's back."

"If it's only for that short time it should be fine," said Claptrap, who began chuckling at Piggybait's continuing struggle with his burden.

"Yes, he's been doing…huff…this too long and he's too…puff…careful to let anything affect the routine," Piggybait panted as he swung his burden onto the other shoulder. Thankfully the bag was warming up a little but, on the down side, his back was getting damp as it thawed.

"You're not very fit are you?" Claptrap smirked. "Have you thought about taking some exercise? You've definitely let yourself go a bit, old friend."

Piggybait tried to give him a withering look but it just looked like a scowl which made Claptrap chuckle all the more.

The route took them higher as they skilfully negotiated their way over deep-dug tree roots that spread in close but irregular intervals across the uneven rocky floor and, apart from Piggybait's grumbling, they walked in silence until a grey rabbit, in a state of panic, darted from a concealed burrow on their left, careered straight into them and fell under Claptrap's feet, tripping him up. Claptrap fell heavily, his lantern flew into the air and his monocle slipped to the ground. Jimander twisted and caught the lantern in mid-air in time to stop it smashing on the hard tunnel floor and, to make matters worse, Piggybait, trudging close behind Claptrap, fell over him, catching him a glancing blow with the bag and almost stepped on the monocle. The rabbit, horrified at having caused such a mishap, was most apologetic.

"I'm most dreadfully sorry," he cast a nervous glance over his shoulder, "um…there are ferrets about tonight…you know...in the tunnels. Do be careful."

"*Be careful*!" roared Claptrap, rubbing his knees and head alternately, "it's you who needs to be careful! Look what you've done!"

Piggybait, in a heap on the floor, the bag having landed on his legs, moaned miserably as he inspected a tear in the elbow of his jerkin. Jimander, on the other hand, found the whole incident extremely amusing and was doubled up with laughter, adding to the indignation of both his companions. The offending rabbit, sitting up on his back legs, whiskers twitching nervously, decided it was a good time to leave and scampered away down the tunnel, his white tail bobbing out of sight.

"Well! By Alfheim!" Claptrap exclaimed, picking himself up and brushing off his clothes. "I never realised a rabbit could do so much damage." Jimander, still chortling away to the annoyance of the other two, picked up the monocle and passed it back to Claptrap, who wiped it clean on his leggings and returned it to its rightful place in front of his right eye.

Piggybait stood up, brushed off his elbows and checked for any further damage before picking up the bag again and moaned bitterly about not only having to carry the bulky bundle, but now he had sore arms too.

"Ferrets indeed!" Claptrap moaned. "That blasted rabbit's caused more trouble than a whole pack of ferrets. Anyway, if a ferret shows

his face I'll soon see him off. I don't much care for ferrets and after tonight I've gone off rabbits."

Piggybait, now saw the funny side and joined Jimander in laughing at Claptrap's rant which just annoyed him all the more and now it was Claptrap's turn to grumble as they headed along the downward slope.

A short while later the tunnel widened out and they were able to walk side by side. They walked down five roughly hewn steps and turned a sharp corner where a light in the distance grew brighter as they approached until it was soon as bright as daylight and the lanterns became redundant. A muddled sound of engines and voices came from beyond the tunnel exit that increased in volume with every step. They emerged from the tunnel onto a wide ledge about half way up an immense cavern looking up at a vast domed ceiling that towered some fifteen metres above. Reflected light from flaming torches highlighted seams of minerals in shades of pink, cream, gold and yellow that blazed in their flickering glow.

Piggybait leaned against the safety barrier built to prevent anyone falling the ten metres or so onto the cave floor. Below was a bustling hive of activity, filled with elves scurrying about, loading and unloading boxes from two long conveyor belts while others darted along the cave floor on quad-bikes. Two elves stopped to hitch up trailers to their quad-bikes and load them with boxes and parcels from the belts, while those already full just hurried straight through. Each trailer was labelled with the name of a destination country.

"Busy tonight," Claptrap commented. "Do you think they need any help?"

"Nah," Piggybait replied, picking up the soggy sack, "there are plenty of them down there and they'll let us know if they need help. We'll be back here soon enough. Come on, let's go. I want to get rid of this bag." He nudged Claptrap who was gazing dreamily at the quad-bikes. "I'd love a go on one of those. Maybe next year."

The ledge circuited the sides of the cavern ending at two tunnel mouths side by side immediately opposite the one they had come out of. As the three elves continued around the ledge, they took occasional peeks over the barrier to watch the bustle below and someone spotted them.

"Piggs, hey, Piggy!" A voice was heard over the din. Piggybait waved to an elf below who was wearing a soft woollen hat pulled low over his brow.

"How goes it, Corp?" he called. "It looks a bit hectic tonight...where's this lot going?"

"Over to Europe...," the other replied, "through the Chunnel."

It is not generally known by humans, but while the Channel tunnel was being excavated, the elves were digging their own right alongside it as they felt it was the perfect opportunity to take advantage of the situation. While the human digging and construction was underway, the elves worked in parallel helped by a number of friendly dwarves, expert in tunnel-digging who sometimes *borrowed* materials or tools they needed when the workmen were careless and left them lying around. However, they always put back any tools they used before they were missed, and were meticulous about ensuring they were returned in the same condition in which they were found. It was due to the resourcefulness displayed by the enterprising dwarves, they were able to finish their task considerably earlier than the humans.

"Good to see you Corp but we've got to go...we're on night patrol," Piggybait called down, "I'll see you later. Maybe a glass or two of acorn wine?"

"Nice elf, Corporal," he said as they set off again, "pity about his ears."

"But it doesn't show when he's got his cap on," Claptrap replied sympathetically.

Passing by the first exit, they took the second tunnel where Claptrap opened the small glass doors on the crystal lanterns and blew inside each one gently. Instantly flames flickered into life, steadily increasing until the steps rising upwards through the dark tunnel could be clearly seen. Soon the rocky floor levelled out and they reached a very large boulder that blocked their way. Jimander pushed it aside easily allowing in a rush of fresh air through the gap. To human eyes the boulder appeared to be a solid mass of rock, far too large to be moved without the use of a crane. However, it was made of an elven substance they called Challim, which they could make into any shape or form they wished and they used it whenever and wherever they needed to

hide their secrets from human eyes.

Piggybait and Claptrap followed Jimander out into the night where clouds had developed into a patchy mist and the foggy clumps allowed them to slip from the cave into the surrounding woods unseen other than by eyes belonging to the nocturnal wildlife of the woods. Shapes loomed and strange noises filled the night, but nothing made the three elves feel uneasy. They knew every inch of the woods and what or who was in it. It was what lay beyond the woods that gave them concern.

"Even in this fog, I'd be a lot happier if we didn't have to cross the field. It's a pity the trees weren't just a little bit closer," Piggybait fretted. "Why?" asked Claptrap, "the wall stops us being seen and so does the fog." He pointed to the two cottages. "The family next door to the Chief are asleep and there's nothing but foxes, owls and bats or maybe the odd cat silly enough to be out in the cold that might see us tonight. All the same though, I'll be glad to get back in front of the fire this evening; never keen on night patrol at this time of the year."

Approaching the field they stayed very close to the garden wall. Reaching the safety of the next group of trees, they were almost invisible within the woody undergrowth. Owls called and bats flew in zigzags above their heads, and somewhere far off a fox gave its high pitched yipping bark. The fog was thinner amongst the trees and their excellent vision, aided by the lanterns, ensured they could clearly see the path. From somewhere nearby a blood-curdling canine howl stopped them in their tracks.

"Why does he do that?" Piggybait asked, not really expecting an answer.

Veering off to the right they arrived at the bottom of a small hill surrounded by bushes. Jimander pushed aside the curtain of overhanging ivy to reveal an old wooden door covered in mysterious covered symbols. He turned the handle with ease and they entered a small round cave which was the lobby to a much larger area beyond. Bales of straw were stacked to the right of the cave, and on the left, sacks of oats were piled high, with buckets placed on top. Near the bales a spring of clear, ice cold water gurgled from a gap in the wall. It babbled and gushed down the wall before disappearing into a crevice in the floor. Rustling noises and a long snuffling sound came from the large area beyond and a low growl made Piggybait spin around to look into the grinning, open jaws of a wolf.

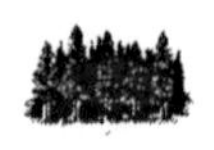     

"We wondered where you were tonight," the wolf said, drooling and sniffing the air. "It's kind of you to remember us, *finally.*"

"No need for that," Jimander scolded, "we got here as soon as we could. I had something to deal with earlier but we're here now."

The wolf hung his head apologetically and sidled off to stand beside Piggybait who pulled a sizable chunk of raw meat out of the bag. The wolf pounced, greedily disposing of it in no time at all, bones and all. Piggybait shuddered. "You'd think I'd be used to seeing you eating meat by now but it still revolts me." He grimaced. "I don't know how you can eat it."

"Easy. I just open my mouth, bite off a chunk, chew a bit and swallow." The wolf gave a wide grin revealing tattered bits of raw meat stuck between his teeth. "It was a little too cold for my liking though, warm it up a bit next time will you?"

"Yeuk!" Piggybait exclaimed with an expression of disgust which greatly amused the now satisfied wolf.

In the chamber beyond, Jimander and Claptrap filled nine buckets of oats and carried them through to the back of the cave, where nine large brown animals occupied a separate byre each, above which was a gleaming brass plate displaying their name. Obviously as hungry as the wolf, they rushed forward, making snuffling sounds, each of them eager to get at their own bucket of oats, which they slowly chewed in dignified silence. The elves swept up and bagged the dirty, loosely strewn hay and replaced it with a fresh supply while the animals watched while chomping through their evening meal. Eventually, with the cave now smelling of sweet new hay, the buckets washed and filled with spring water, all nine animals allowed the elves to slip rope halters over their necks and one by one they were led out of the cave.

The only one making a noise was the wolf who growled and jumped around as he usually did whenever Piggybait tried to get a leash on him. They played a rough, noisy game of tug-o-war until Jimander lost patience, scolding them both soundly.

"What under Earth are you two playing at? In the name of Alfheim, why *do* we have to put up with this every night?"

Piggybait apologised, so did Wolf, who hung his head promising to behave and walk properly if they, in turn, did not harness him. Jimander agreed but only on condition Wolf kept his promise. The elves took three ropes each, leading the reindeer outside into the woods

with Wolf padding noiselessly alongside Piggybait, unleashed, but on guard. They strolled along the dark pathways between the trees following a regularly used trail, listening for any strange noises.

Jimander found Wolf as a cub in northern Canada after a trapper killed his mother and took away his two brothers and sister. He somehow missed the tiny fourth cub huddled close to his mother's body for warmth, terrified and starving until Jimander, travelling in the area, came upon the tiny orphan. Moved to tears for another unnecessary death, he checked to see if there was anything he could do for the mother and found the near dead cub hidden beneath his mother's cold neck. At the sight of the elf, he tried to wriggle further under her body.

More concerned for the cub's survival than finding and punishing the trapper, Jimander picked up the whimpering cub, tucked him inside his cloak for warmth and hurried to the nearest elf tunnel speeding back to his clan where, with round the clock attention, they saved the life of the frail cub.

Although he owed his life to Jimander and showed him great respect, the wolf was still a little afraid of him. On the other hand, he had formed a strong bond with Piggybait, who returned the affection and they walked alongside each other in companionable silence.

After an hour of exercise it was time to return the reindeer to their cavern home for their evening grooming. Within another hour all nine reindeer had clean hooves, antlers and teeth and smooth, gleaming coats. Wolf lay down in the corner, watching and contentedly licking his paws while Piggybait moved on to inspecting and polishing reins and sleigh-bells. When the grooming and equipment inspection were over, Piggybait shuffled toward the wolf with a brush.

"Oh no you don't," Wolf snarled, "I might like you but don't push your luck. I'm perfectly happy as I am thank you." His lips turned back in a malevolent grin revealing gleaming white fangs and he growled threateningly as he darted into the farthest corner of the cave, daring Piggybait to get him out.

"OK…if that's the way you want it, fine! But you smell awful. One day I'll get you," Piggybait grinned, "just you wait and see."

"Not if I can help it," Wolf muttered circling in his corner. Piggybait laughed out loud as he joined Jimander, Piggybait, who were preparing to leave. "OK, you win this time, Wolfie. We're leaving now but if I don't get to clean you up sometime soon…I can tell you the

Chief will. In the meantime, I'll leave you to your duties guarding the…ladies." The wolf shuddered and glared at Piggybait who chuckled loudly as he went out the door.

Chapter Ten

Sam slept fitfully and awoke at the sound of voices downstairs. He checked the time on his alarm clock. It was only seven-fifteen! He groaned. If Aunt Cathy had already arrived he thought he had better get up. He tried sitting up but flopped back down on his pillow; after the night he had just had, he was still dog tired.

Scruffs had fallen off the pillow and onto the floor during the night. Sam picked the teddy bear up and laid him gently back on the bed, then he got a whiff of bacon.

The smell of grilling bacon and coffee wafted up the stairs making him feel hungry. He jumped out of bed, put on his dressing gown which was at least four inches too short and went out onto the landing. Leaning over the banister he strained to hear what was being said, but the voices were still muffled. Tidying himself up quickly in the bathroom, he crept downstairs, carefully avoiding the creaky floorboard: he didn't want anyone to hear him until he was good and ready, and tiptoed along the hall, trying to ignore Portia who appeared from nowhere and prepared to launch herself onto his shoulder.

"No, not now, not now, Portia," he whispered. But she had no intention of going away and purred loudly, rubbing her head against his legs until he picked her up. She cuddled into his neck and rubbed her nose against his jaw. "Yes, yes," he whispered impatiently, "I'll feed you soon, just please be quiet."

The kitchen door stood slightly ajar but it was still difficult for him to hear what was being said. Portia jumped down and padded in through the door, pushing it further open giving him a narrow field of vision into the room. There were two other people in the kitchen with his mother and he craned his neck to try to get a better view of them but he could still only see part of the man, but he heard him well enough;

heard his deep, booming broad west-country accent and felt a bit nervous about meeting him.

He could see his mother and was shocked at her red eyes and the dark circles of exhaustion underneath them and he realised she had been up all night while he slept which made him feel very guilty. The three adults were deep in conversation and what Sam heard her say next rooted him to the spot. "Well, if you don't mind Sam staying with you, it would probably be the best solution all round although he's expecting to stay here."

Sam's world collapsed. No that's not how it's going to be, he thought angrily. *No! I'm staying here*! It had never occurred to him he might have to go away. He wondered why he had never considered that possibility. He moved closer to eavesdrop. "I'd hoped I wouldn't be away too long and you might be able to look after him here..." she broke off as Sam burst into the room, his face a picture of fury.

"So the plans have changed have they?" he shouted, his heart pounding, mouth dry, "without telling me. No-one thought to include me in this plan of yours." Sam glared at his mother furiously.

"Now Sam, don't be angry," she tried to placate him, forcing herself to stay very calm, "you're being very rude. We're trying to do the best for everyone. Cathy and Charlie have very kindly agreed to help us out, at very short notice, I might add..."

"*I don't care*!" he screamed at her. "They can just turn around and go right back where they came from. I'm staying here!" He almost shrieked with fury, shaking from head to toe with emotion. Cathy looked horrified but his new uncle stared at the floor, a wry grin on his face.

"You'll apologise for your rudeness, Sam Johnson, right now!" Jane shouted, clearly embarrassed by Sam's outburst.

"*I will not!*

Jane turned to her sister. "Sorry Cathy, but to be fair this has been sprung on Sam and it's all been a shock for him." She turned to face Sam and took a deep breath.

"I repeat Sam, your aunt and uncle made a special trip in the middle of the night to help us out. I won't have you being hateful to people who are putting themselves out for us." Sam's eyes stared back at her in dumb insolence. "It has to be this way, Sam. Charlie can't be away from work for long and we don't know how long I'll be away with your

Dad. It's selfish to expect Cathy to leave her home and commitments for too long to stay here alone."

"No, but it's not selfish of them to expect me to go there just to fit in with *them!* Sam cut in.

Jane ignored his interruption and went on. "I know you've had a shock and we didn't mean to upset you. I had hoped to have time to break it to you gently, but you burst in here before I could explain things," she looked as miserable as he felt. "What else can I do?" She turned her back on him. He felt a little ashamed that she was so upset with him, but he was adamant, he was staying.

"Well, I'm sorry for upsetting you but I'm not going anywhere." He already had an alternative in mind. "I can stay with Dave." He turned to the older couple who had patiently watched the angry scene being played out in front of them. "So thank you Aunt and Uncle," he bowed to them, rather sarcastically, "but your services won't be required," he said coldly. Cathy took a deep breath and walked past Sam, without looking at him, and out of the kitchen into the hall where she collected her coat and went for a walk in the garden. Charlie did not follow her but instead he continued to observe the hostility between Sam and Jane without interfering.

Jane finally snapped. "You will NOT stay with Dave!" she almost screamed at Sam who was taken by surprise at the strength of her anger; he had never seen her so furious. She forced herself to continue in a calmer tone. "His mother's got enough on her plate as it is and you want to add more, well frankly, I'm astonished by your lack of consideration, your selfishness." He glared defiantly back at her. "Just to get your own way you'd dump yourself on the Russells. I can't believe you'd be so unfair. Bill's just lost his job, he's desperately looking for work, Megan's got the measles and there's the new baby coming." By now her strength was beginning to wane and tears were threatening. "Don't you think Pat's got enough to worry about as it is?" She braced herself for another round of battle. "No, absolutely not! So you'd better get your head around it because one way or another you're going to stay with Cathy and Charlie! Now get upstairs and pack, and don't give me anymore grief." The threatened tears now streamed uncontrollably down her face.

Sam ran out of the room, slamming the door behind him as Portia scuttled away under the sideboard again frightened by all the noise.

Cathy, walked back into the hallway just in time to see Sam dash past her and thunder, to steps at a time, up to his room. The house shook as he banged shut his bedroom door.

"I'm so sorry," Jane apologised for her son, "only all this has happened so fast and it's all been such a shock for him and..and to know how badly his Dad's been hurt, they're so close you see. He's not normally like this."

"I understand that," Cathy replied patiently, "but you've had a shock too, but I don't see you slamming doors and showing off," Cathy put her arm around Jane's shoulder sympathetically.

"If it's alroight wi' you, Jane, I'll 'ave a word wi' young Sam. Let's see if we can sort this out, man to man."

"You can try, but I don't think he'll listen," Jane smiled gratefully.

"He might when I take him a bacon roll," Charlie put a couple of now cooling rashers on a crusty roll, set them on a plate and headed out of the kitchen door banging his head on the top of the door frame on the way. "Ow! You know, Jane m'dear, you're gonna have to get bigger doors if we're gonna keep comin' up 'ere."

Cathy was convinced he had done it on purpose to lighten the atmosphere and was glad to see Jane giggle through her tears.

Charlie knocked on Sam's bedroom door but did not wait to be invited in. Sam was hunched up at the top of his bed, his chin resting on his knees, and hugging his legs with his left arm and cradling his right arm in his lap. He was staring out of the window but not really seeing anything. Books were strewn across the floor and Scruffs lay face down in front of the wardrobe. Charlie picked up the discarded bear, laying it at the bottom of the bed.

"What do you want?" Sam spat.

"Jest thought I'd come up and 'ave a chat, man to man loike, an' Oi thought you'd be hungry, fancy a bacon roll do you?" He handed the plate to Sam who rudely snatched it away and set it down on the bedside cabinet and continued staring blankly through the window and out at the grey, damp morning.

Charlie tried again. "It's nearly Christmas, you gotta 'elp out an' be good or Santa won't come."

He received a scornful look for that remark. "Don't be stupid! I'm not a kid," Sam snapped. "This 'as all been a bit 'ard on you, ain't it?" Charlie said quietly. "But you know it's harder still on yer Mum 'cos

she's torn between trying to get to yer Dad, not wanting to leave you behind and not wanting ter upset you either. Difficult situation all round really."

Sam understood Charlie was trying to help and he looked around at the big man who he had expected to start arguing with him. Instead he found himself looking into a sympathetic face with a pair of the brightest, bluest, crinkliest, laughing eyes he'd ever seen and felt his resentment draining away.

"I know things are tough for Mum and Dad, and I really don't want to make things more difficult, but you don't understand. There's all the Christmas stuff at school and there's…there's Jo…" Charlie appeared not to have noticed the hesitation. "I'm old enough to look after myself if I can't go to the Russell's," he was almost pleading. "I know how to iron, use the microwave, make sure the door's locked when I go out, and I can look after Portia. I really don't see the problem. It's not as if it's going to be for that long anyway." Charlie weighed his words carefully not wanting to drag things out any longer than necessary.

"I can understan' how you feel m'boy, but apart from anythin' else, leaving you 'ere ain't legal. Yer under age to be left on yer own an' yer parents could get arrested. 'Ow d'you feel if that 'appened on top of everythin' else? No old son, better resign yersel' to comin' wi' us, we ain't that bad yer know," he grinned. "Now then, why don't you get yerself downstairs to yer Mum an' tell 'er yer sorry and we'll say no more about it an' givin' 'er a hug wouldn't go amiss either. Then get yersel' back up 'ere and get packed. Yer Mum'll 'ave to leave soon, so we'll need to get a shake on."

Sam's had no idea how but his anger had simply dissolved. All he knew was that he was going to do exactly as they wanted, and it had been painless.

Jane looked up from the table as he entered the kitchen. The strain she was under was plain to see, and he knew his surrender would make things easier for her.

"Sorry Mum. Sorry Aunt Cathy," he mumbled, ashamedly, with eyes downcast. Portia, sensing that calm had returned to the house crept out from her hiding place and began pestering Sam for food. Brushing against Sam's legs again hopefully, but was again ignored as Jane held out her arms and Sam walked into them, consoled by the knowledge he was doing the right thing.

Cathy heaved a sigh of relief. “We’re not so bad Sam. You may even get to like us,” she said giving him a warm smile.

Uneasy about his earlier outburst, Sam had avoided looking at her before but now he smiled back. “Sorry.”

“Ow!” Charlie bumped his head again as he entered the kitchen and laughter relieved the remaining tension. “Dunno how many bruises an’ bumps Oi’m gonna ‘ave by the toime Oi leave ‘ere today,” he boomed. “Everythin’ alroight now is it?

Cathy was five years older than her sister, about the same height but slightly plumper, her mousy-grey hair was cut in a collar length bob which she wore with a heavy fringe and Sam noticed indentations either side of her nose indicating that she wore glasses often enough to leave marks but she wasn’t wearing them now, and she was dressed for comfort in a pair of old khaki coloured camouflage style combat trousers with a dark blue tee-shirt, under an open dark blue denim shirt, and navy trainers. Sam thought she looked pretty cool for her age. But it was her hands that Sam took note of. She had very long, slim tapering fingers, and it was then he remembered she was an artist. She painted and sculpted and he vaguely recalled seeing some of her paintings a long time ago at an exhibition somewhere. He also remembered the pottery cups his mother kept on a shelf in their conservatory. It was all coming back to him now. A surge of long forgotten affection for his Aunt flooded back with the memories and he knew everything was going to be alright.

Charlie, on the other hand was large, so huge in fact that Sam felt a little scared of him, even though he was obviously a very kind person.

His hair and beard were a silvery white and a Christmas card image of Santa Claus flitted through Sam’s mind. He dismissed it as just too silly for words. Besides Charlie was much too ‘country style’ to ever have worked in a city department store. Funnily enough Charlie and Cathy were dressed in a similar style, as he wore an old black army-style jumper with tabs on the shoulder, patched blue jeans that had seen much better days and an equally old pair of battered black boots. But it was Charlie’s eyes Sam noticed most; warmth and kindness shone out of them and they were so bright they actually sparkled. Charlie grinned at Sam, aware he was being studied and his eyes crinkled into laughter lines. “Oi think we’re going ter be great friends, aren’t we Sam? So don’ you worry yer ‘ead none, Jane, m’dear, Sam and I understan’ each

other," he said, cheerfully winking at her. Sam nodded as Charlie held out his hand for Sam to shake.

Jane's relief was obvious. All she needed to worry about now was time and getting to the airport. "Sam, I went to the cash machine earlier and took you out two hundred pounds. Cathy will look after it for you. It's for pocket money and to cover any expenses you may have while I'm away. It should last a while as long as you don't spend too much on Christmas presents. I don't know how long I'm going to be away, it's important your education doesn't suffer so Cathy's going to talk to the local secondary school and arrange for you to go there temporarily."

Sam groaned.

"You'd only get bored being home with me," Cathy broke in.

"So I've given Cathy a letter making her your guardian and, on Monday, she'll contact Redlands to explain what's happened and arrange for your regular work to be sent down to you, so this shouldn't affect your exams," Jane explained. "Right, so you'd better hurry up and pack. I've got to get a move on if I'm to catch that plane."

Sam looked around at his Aunt and Uncle. He really hoped he was going to get on with them. Jane disappeared upstairs, only to re-enter the kitchen a few minutes later with a small flight case in hand.

"I think that's it for now," Jane said, "but there's still a little time if we think of anything else. Why don't you pop up now," she told Sam, "and get your stuff ready, we haven't got very long now."

Sam meekly did as he was told. He filled two large holdalls with clothes and books, and was just looking around to see if he had left anything when he remembered Portia had still not been fed. Dashing down the stairs, he found the very disgruntled cat in the empty kitchen, mewing angrily.

"OK girl, I'm sorry. We forgot about you." Then it hit him. Portia! Who would look after her? She gratefully pounced on the bowl of dried food he set down on the floor before anyone could take it away from her.

"Hey Mum, what's happening to Portia?" Sam called to Jane who was now in the sitting room having coffee with Cathy and Charlie.

"She's going next door to Ken and Emma. All sorted," she shouted back. Sam stroked the cat who purred loudly as she ate. "I'm going to miss you, girl, but we'll be back soon, and you'll be well looked after

hile we're away. You probably spend as much time next door as you do here anyway," he told her.

Sam still could not explain why he had changed his mind so easily. All Charlie had done was talk to him and all Sam's objections had suddenly seemed very unimportant. The concert, the ball, even Joanne, none of it mattered. There'd be other concerts and balls and Joanne would still be there when he got back. What mattered was his mother catching her flight and his Dad getting better.

While Portia finished her breakfast, he wondered what it would be like in the countryside. At home he had cinemas, bowling alleys, football, the Ice Stadium and he could meet his friends at the Broadmarsh or Victoria Centre shopping malls. There was always something to do. What do you do in a village for fun? He wondered if his Aunt and Uncle even had a computer. They looked too 'arty' or 'hippie' to even have television and computer games? He doubted whether either of them had even heard of a PS4 or Xbox and decided there was little point in taking his.

Running back up to his room, he grabbed his holdalls and carried them downstairs to wait for the taxi with his mother.

"Now have you got everything? It'll be too late to get back in once I've gone and you're on your way." She brushed a few of Portia's hairs off his jumper, obviously making a real effort not to become emotional; they had never spent time away from each other and were both finding the parting difficult.

"Don't worry," she said softly. "Cathy and Charlie will look after you well, and you'll make friends at your new school. No, now please don't look at me like that, honestly you will, and you'd only get fed up doing nothing all day. Most of the young people your age in the village go there and Cathy will arrange everything so your school work here won't be too interrupted. They're on a different curriculum at St Merriott's, but she's sure they'll let you keep up with your own work. She's going to talk to the head teacher, he's a friend of Charlie's, to get things sorted out and don't worry about your Dad. He'll be fine and I'll be in touch as often as I can."

"Sam?" Charlie poked his head around the door, "Have you got yer computer games and DVDs and such? You'll want them if the weather's bad and you can't get out much." Sam dashed back upstairs. They did have TV and they knew about

cool stuff after all. Snatching cases off the shelf, it took him two minutes to grab his favourite games, DVDs, and his consoles before dashing back down the stairs and out of the front door where Charlie was waiting for him.

"Thanks Uncle Charlie," Sam's smile reached his eyes for the first time that morning. Perhaps things wouldn't be so bad after all, he thought. Charlie took the bag and Sam winced as a pain shot through from the wrist up to the elbow.

"That pulled muscle will be pretty sore I wouldn't wonder, Sam. I'll give it a bit of a massage for you later," Charlie promised.

"Is that everything?" Jane asked him. Sam tried to speak as a lump filled his throat. "Portia's already gone next door. Right then, give me a hug and I'll have to go or I'll miss the check-in time at Birmingham," she told him. "I really mustn't miss this flight. Mr Van der Leiden will be meeting me at the airport and your Dad knows I'm on my way. Be good, Sam and keep your chin up," she smiled, "we'll be back before you know it. Make sure you help Cathy and Charlie, and remember a change doesn't have to be scary, see it as a new adventure and enjoy your stay." Sam nodded as he fought back his tears, giving his mother a final hug.

"Bye Mum, have a good flight. Give my love to Dad and don't worry, I'll be fine. Just make sure you call me when you get there," he said, putting on a brave face. His mother's eyes were glistening and her chin started to quiver. He knew exactly how she was feeling. As he let her go, he saw the Land Rover, it was old and mud-spattered and suited Charlie perfectly. Jane said her goodbyes as she got in to the taxi, but she wound the window down to blow a kiss. "Love you Sam. I'll be back with your Dad before you know it," she called as the taxi started up. "I'll be in touch." Then she was gone.

Sam climbed into the Land Rover feeling miserable as he watched his mother's taxi turn into the main road and out of sight. As he settled into the back seat and reached for his seat belt, a sharp pain shot through his lower arm and Charlie, who was just getting to the driver's seat, saw him flinch.

"You'd better let me 'ave a look at that," Charlie leaned over from the front seat, reaching out for Sam's arm. Cathy turned to watch. As Charlie took his arm, Sam felt a tingle run all the way up to his

shoulder but, as he pressed gently on Sam's wrist, for a second or two it increased to a blinding pain making Sam's gasp, then it was gone.

"That'll feel much better in a few minutes Sam, you'll see," Charlie reassured him, "sorry, if I hurt you." He gently turned Sam's wrist back and forth a few times.

"There that should do it. Better?" he asked, still holding Sam's wrist. Sam had to admit it was and nodded his reply. "Good, we'll get on then," Charlie said, turning back to face the steering wheel and fastening his seat belt.

Cathy frowned, "Sorry about the dog hairs on the back seat. We do try to keep it clean but we left in such a hurry, we didn't have time, and push those old papers over the back if they're in the way. If you want to sleep, there's an old blanket somewhere about you can use as a pillow, I think it's over the back, but it's probably a bit doggie too."

"Thanks Aunt Cathy but I don't want to sleep," Sam said glumly. Cathy tried to cheer him up. "No formalities, you can drop the Aunt and Uncle. It's Cathy and Charlie from now on, eh Charlie?" Charlie nodded.

"Roight then, orf we go," Charlie boomed. As Sam watched his neighbourhood slide away out of sight he realised, in all the rush, he had not told Dave what was going on. He took out his mobile phone, tapped out the number and waited for the connection. Mrs Russell answered. She said Dave had already left for football training which Sam had completely forgotten about. He explained what was happening to Mrs Russell telling her he would call Dave later.

It was a grey, misty morning, typical of late November and Sam thought it reflected his feelings exactly. As if she had read his thoughts, Cathy turned around again, struggling to manoeuvre against the seat belt. "How's the arm now, Sam?" she enquired.

"It's absolutely fine." Sam still had no idea what Charlie had done but he was grateful that the pain had gone and he could move his arm normally.

"Charlie's a bit of a healer, you know." She glanced affectionately at her husband then turned back to Sam. "I know things look a bit bleak to you right now, but you might find you like the country life. Every cloud has a silver lining, so they say."

Sam tried to force a smile. He could think of very little to make him feel optimistic about this enforced holiday except the hope it would be

a short one. As the three occupants of the Land Rover knew very little about each other, making conversation was difficult and, after an awkward silence, Sam asked Charlie what he did for a living.

"Oi'm the local part-time postman for the Askam's, they run the village sub Post Office an', o' course this toime o' year we're gettin' pretty busy with the pre-Christmas post."

Cathy interrupted, "He's got another job too."

"Oi was jest gettin' to that, my dear," Charlie said patiently. "There's a manor house just outside Winterne with a farm business that's got a few acres set aside for opine trees, an' when they're grown enough, they sell 'em for Christmas trees. I work there part-time too, getting the trees in good condition ready for cuttin'."

Cathy interrupted again. "But his main field of expertise is as a tree surgeon on the wood surrounding the Manor. There's nothing he doesn't know about trees isn't that right, Charlie?"

"Well, Oi've learnt a bit over the years, Oi s'pose."

"You're just being modest, dear," she patted his cheek. "If Charlie goes missing anytime, it's a safe bet he's probably in the woods somewhere."

Chapter Eleven

The following morning Meredith knocked at the door of the Sykes' cottage and waited in the shelter of the porch, there was a chill in the air and although she was dressed warmly, the breeze made her eyes water. Wilmot, on the other hand was completely unaffected by the cold and was far too busy sniffing at the large basket she was carrying; something inside was very interesting.

Hearing footsteps approaching the door, Meredith commanded him to sit and unusually he did as he was told first time, but just before the door opened he jumped up and wagged his tail expectantly. Gwen Sykes appeared in the open doorway and smiled a warm welcome as she wiped her wet hands on her apron.

"Whatever brings you here m'dear?" Gwen said eyeing the basket.

"I thought I'd check how Arthur is," Meredith said, "after…yesterday…well you know," she ended awkwardly.

"Well it's roight nice o' you to call but the least said abou' what happened the better, Oi say. But don't stand aroun' in the cold, yer letting all the warm air out the 'ouse, come on in and bring tha' daft dog o' yourn too." She stroked Wilmot's head as he bounded past her into the narrow hallway. "We got no problem wi' dogs in this 'ouse although Oi can't say the same for some 'umans I know."

Meredith followed Gwen through to a bright, spotlessly clean sitting room where Arthur sat in a rocking chair by the window reading the paper, smoking his pipe and surrounded by a tobacco haze. Gwen tutted loudly as she went through to the small kitchen.

The first Arthur knew of his visitors was when a cold, wet nose nuzzled his hand. "'Allo Wilmot, old feller. If you're 'ere then that

Mith Meredith mutht be too," he chuckled as he stroked the dog affectionately. Ith good to see you Mith. You vithitin' my Gwenny?" Meredith didn't need to look to know he didn't have his teeth in this morning.

"No Arthur, I've come to see how you are. Stuart told me Dr Brownlow said your injury wasn't serious, but it was a horrible thing Jonah did and I'm terribly sorry."

"Iss not you as should be sorry, m'dear." Meredith turned to see a scowling Gwen who was now standing in the doorway.

"I understand how angry you must be Gwen. I got rid of the air rifle." She gave a small laugh, "Jonah called me a few unpleasant names, but I don't care. I can't apologise enough for his terrible behaviour and, to be honest, I'm sick of doing it."

"Hmmph!" Gwen grunted. "You shouldn' 'ave ter 'pologise fer 'him. Iss time tha' boy learnt 'is lesson…"

"No, it ain't your fault Mith," Arthur agreed, rocking his chair back and forth. "No long term 'arm done eh?"

"No 'arm done, huh?" Gwen snapped indignantly. "No, damn 'arm done?"

"Oh hush woman!" Arthur muttered impatiently. "That'th not ter thay it don't hurt still, 'coth it do, but the Arnica cream'th 'elped but' 'e do need t' be stopped," he told Meredith. "Tith a good job that air roifle'th gone and not before toime, I moight add, but it'th yer father should be thortin' thith out, not you. 'E needth ter gi' 'im a good 'iding 'e do!"

"Silly old beggar didn't wanna see Dr Brownlow. Kicked up no end o' fuss, but Oi med sure 'e did," Gwen interrupted. "Oi didn' loike the look o' that welt. Stoopid old man!" she added crossly.

"Oh hush woman," Arthur broke in, "yer futhin' about nothin'."

Meredith was caught in the crossfire between the two arguing old people and she didn't like it much. She felt awful that the incident had been the cause of so much trouble between them.

"But Arthur, Gwen was right to make sure you saw the doctor. It was me who asked Stuart to call him and I hope you told him how it happened. If Jonah thought the authorities know just how much trouble he's causing and that he's actually inuring people like you and Peggy it might make him think again, might make a difference but I somehow

doubt it," Meredith shrugged sadly. She then explained what had happened to Peggy.

"Definitely toime that boy was locked up," Gwen sniffed indignantly. "Yer'll 'ave a cuppa tea wi' us?" she asked.

"Thanks Gwen, but I'm just on my way to the stables. It's Angelo's exercise time." She got up to leave. "I promise I'll try to keep a better watch on Jonah from now on and again, I'm really sorry for all the trouble." She held out the basket she was holding. "Gwen, I've brought you some eggs and cheese from Home Farm and there's a cake Marjorie made for you. I hope you can use them," she handed the basket to Gwen.

"Very good 'o you Meredith, I'm sure, but you shouldn't 'ave bothered," Gwen said putting the basket on the table. "Oi'll see you out, then."

Meredith stopped at the door. "I really am very sorry about all this Gwen but, I just don't know what to do anymore. I had hoped Jonah learned his lesson a while back, but it doesn't look like it."

"Oi know you're sorry m'dear but so's everyone else on the estate *and* the village, sorry he ever came 'ere…but it shouldn't be all on your young shoulders, bless you. Try givin' yer Dad a call." She gave a sad smile and went to close the door as Meredith and Wilmot turned to leave. "Oh Meredith, Oi forgot. Say thanks to Marj for me will you? It were good of 'er to make that cake for us."

Meredith nodded and called Wilmot to her side before waving Gwen goodbye. She pulled the collar of her waxed coat higher up around her neck and began walking briskly down the lane towards the stables; Wilmot running in and out of the hedges following any interesting scent and inspecting rabbit holes along the way.

As they turned a bend in the lane she was surprised to see two white vans parked outside an estate cottage that had been empty since September. One van belonged to an industrial cleaning firm she had never heard of but the other she recognised immediately as it belonged to a local plumber and gas appliance fitter, Donald Evans. Meredith knew him quite well as she had been at school with both his sons and it was his company her father had chosen when they were renovating the manor. Just as she approached, he came out of the cottage, opened the back door of his van and began rummaging around inside; Meredith's curiosity at seeing the vans and particularly Don was stirred; she

wondered what was going on and called Wilmot to her side and he reluctantly gave up investigating a scent he had been following.

"Good morning Don," she called. Having been concentrating on finding whatever he was looking for, Don Evans had not been aware she was approaching and jumped on hearing his name, thumping the back of his head on the doorframe as he stood up. "Ow!" He turned to see who had called him. "Oh it's you, Meredith. You made me jump sneaking up on me like that." He rubbed his head. "You checking up on me for your father?" he asked a little grumpily.

"Sorry about your head and no, of course not," she replied, "I'm just on my way to the stables when I saw you." So, her father was obviously up to something and Don assumed she knew about it. She played along. "So how's it going?" she asked, nodding toward the cottage.

"Not bad," he replied, "the boiler and radiators are working fine and the cooker's been fixed, so all I need to do now is change a couple of tap washers and I'm finished. He wiped his hands on an old rag he pulled out of his boiler suit pocket. "The cleaners are almost done too so my guess is that we'll be out of here in an hour or so." He took a few steps towards the cottage. "Tell your Dad I'll leave the radiators on to warm the house up for your guests." Meredith's heart sank. So her father had invited people without telling her and she guessed Dorothy had not been told. It looked as though he was trying to hide something. Surely he would realise they would notice strangers being around the grounds.

"That's great. Thank you, Don. I'll let Dad know." Meredith worried all the way to the stables, her mind raced with jumbled notions of what he father could be up to. Wilmot padded along a few metres ahead, completely unaware of her concerns, lost in his own world of curious scents that needed to be explored.

At the stables, she found a woman waiting for her wanting to discuss stabling her daughter's pony and her worries were put to one side while they talked. After her visitor left, Meredith steeled herself to call her father; talking to him was never a pleasant experience, and had just dialled the number when the vet arrived to see a horse with tendon problems. She put the phone down before the connection was made.

By the time the vet left about thirty minutes later, all thoughts of making that call had slipped her mind and Angelo still needed exercise.

He was a magnificent 16-hand Cleveland Bay with a dark, gleaming coat and mane and a very good nature. He whinnied a greeting as she opened his stable door and began saddling him up. A few minutes later they were trotting along the tree-lined lane with Wilmot running alongside. As usual, when riding Angelo all her problems disappeared. The cottage and its mysterious guests were forgotten in the joy of freedom.

Chapter Twelve

Cathy and Charlie chatted happily as they drove home apparently unaware of Sam's worry of how little he knew about them. They seemed nice enough but, even though he had felt a connection with them earlier, it felt different now they were away from his home. After all, they were practically strangers and he was not at all sure he was going to enjoy his stay.

A swirling mist and with the autumn late afternoon dusk visibility was reduced as they entered the village to just a couple of metres on either side. Sam shivered in the cold and damp evening air. Was it colder in the countryside than in the city?

Some homes had already switched on their Christmas lights and it saddened him to realise just how close Christmas was. Perhaps his parents would make it back in time so he could spend the holiday with them but deep down he thought it was probably unlikely. He thought of Joanne and wondered who would take her to the school Christmas Ball if he was not there. He suddenly felt very lonely, his eyes felt warm. He sniffed, choking back the tightening in his throat and coughed.

"What was that dear?" Cathy had been dozing but she jerked her head up at the sound.

"Sorry Cathy, just coughed."

"Are you alright?" she asked, concerned.

"Mmm," Sam forced himself to smile but in his heart he just wanted to turn tail and head back to Nottingham.

"Time you woke anyway m'dear," Charlie said, "we're nearly home."

Sam felt as though his world had been turned upside-down overnight: what would Christmas be like without being at home without his parents. No parents at Christmas probably meant no presents as it

was her habit to leave everything to the last minute; she loved the atmosphere in the shops close to Christmas. The more he thought about it, the more depressed he became so the more he tried to think of something else, but whatever he thought of always brought him back to the same point. No parents, no home and no presents. Then he remembered his father's situation. Dad's in hospital with broken bones and stuff and here's me thinking about presents. Selfish or what? Anyway they'll make it up to me when they get back. I'm doing it again. Stop it! His head whirled with worry, guilt and disappointment, his thoughts all muddled up.

Cathy's voice broke through his thoughts. "Of course although they'll have cast the parts for the school Christmas play, I'm sure Mrs Wilkinson, she's a friend of mine, will find something for you if you like Drama. Jane said you're quite talented and although the rehearsals have started, I don't think it will be too late to for you take part." She peered out of the window through the mist. "We'll be home in about five minutes and I hope you're ready to meet the dogs. They'll love you."

"What type are they? I mean what breed?"

Cathy laughed, "They're not too big, they're only Mastiff crossbreeds"

Charlie chuckled. "Don' you go tellin' the boy lies now, Cathy. Don' you listen to 'er, Sam. They're a fair old size our boys. Being Mastiff crossbreeds, they're pretty big. They're crossed with Labradors and they're not small either. They're both young and strong and they tek a bit o' handlin' but they're well-behaved, loyal, fairly intelligent but most of all they're boisterous. There's no temper in either of them.

"What do you call them?" Sam asked.

"Benny and Bjorn," she answered. "We both like Abba."

Great! Abba fans! Sam thought, catching himself before he rolled his eyes I bet they've never heard of the Kaiser Chiefs.

"It sounds like they're huge." Sam had never had a dog but he's always wanted one.

"We have two female cats as well," Cathy told him, "but they tend to keep to themselves, until they want something, like feeding. They might take a little while to get used to you though." It didn't matter to how long they took, they weren't Portia and he was missing her already.

"They're not named after the women in Abba, are they?" Sam joked.

Cathy laughed. "Uh-huh. You've got it. We tried to think of other names but it just seemed the logically thing to do."

Sam groaned.

"I'll introduce you to Jenny and Simon who live next door tomorrow," Cathy went on, craning her neck around the head-rest. "Jenny's your age but her brother, Simon, will be sixteen in February, I think. Is that right Charlie?"

"S'roight, leastways I think so, don't hold much wi' birthdays. I loike Christmas meself, it's the same day for everyone an' a big family time and, 'o course, it's possible you could be wi' us this year." Sam's heart slid down into his stomach.

"Don't be too upset," Charlie said, reading his thoughts. "We'll make sure you enjoy yerself an' they do Christmas really well here in the village," Charlie continued. "Oi'm sure you'd rather be at home but we'll do the best we can for you if you're still 'ere."

That was no real comfort to Sam but for their sake he tried to be positive. Charlie had voiced what he'd been thinking all along and the possibility that he would be without his family at Christmas, for the first time ever, was not something he would look forward to; he really hoped they would make it back in time. There were still a few weeks to go so, perhaps…

They pulled into a narrow lane bordered by tall hedges. "Almost there," Cathy said. "Just two more minutes and we'll be home." Sam was relieved, the journey had seemed never-ending and now they had arrived he was unable to see anything clearly through the mist and darkness, just a few hazy Christmas lights. The Land Rover pulled up outside a semi-detached, white-walled thatched cottage and from what Sam could see both cottages mirrored each other. The lights were on in their cottage and from inside he could hear dogs barking loudly. Charlie took the bags out of the Land Rover, slammed the doors shut and the barking inside the cottage became frenzied; Sam suddenly felt uneasy about meeting the dogs, they sounded terrifying.

"S'OK boys, yer Daddy's back an' he's brought a new frien' for yer," Charlie called out cheerfully.

Cathy opened the door and stood to one side as two massive black shapes flew at Charlie, jumping up at him, their tails wagging furiously

almost bowling him over, before running back to Cathy who braced herself against the wall before impact.

"They're a bit excited Sam, sorry," she shouted over the din.

When they had calmed down a little they noticed the stranger and padded over to Sam slowly and with, perhaps, a little suspicion. Sam stood nervously still as the huge dogs walked around him, sniffing warily. He slowly extended his arm and turned his hand over bunched up in a fist. The larger one of the two sniffed it suspiciously, the slightly smaller one held back a little at first then he too came forward.

"That's roight, Sam, let them sniff your 'and first. Once they get yer scent, they'll know you're alroight," Charlie advised.

Benny, the larger of the two, and Bjőrn stalked around him, sniffing and lazily wagging their long tails until they were satisfied he was a friend. He knew he was accepted when Benny sat down and lifted a paw for him to shake immediately followed by Björn gave his hand a sloppy lick.

"That's Benny. He's jest cleaning yer 'and before he takes a bite!" Charlie said with a straight face. Sam grinned. The dogs being so friendly put him more at ease than he had been all day. Once the canine greetings were completed, they led the way back into the cottage in front of their human companions. Having been accepted so easily by the dogs, for the first time Sam felt that he might actually enjoy his visit.

From inside a warm, delicious smell of cooked chicken and pine reached Sam's nose making him realise how hungry he was and he entered what looked like another Christmas card picture.

The white-painted hallway had black painted wooden beams crossing the ceiling and to the right, was a large red-carpeted room with two wide, slightly-bowed black beams on the ceiling. The room was half-screened from the hall by three, black painted, wooden poles reaching from the floor to the ceiling, each one was hung with bunches of dried flowers and little figures made of ears of wheat with ribbons and dried flowers attached. Tapestries depicting country scenes adorned the walls and Sam felt as though he had walked into the past.

Then he saw the fireplace. It took up the entire middle third of the wall. Sam had never seen anything like it before. Above the hearth was a huge black wooden beam with an old coin nailed into the middle

of it. On the mantle stood a large carriage clock and beside it were several photographs of Charlie, Cathy and the dogs.

But what astonished him was that there were two small photographs of himself and a larger one with him and his parents and it was then that he finally understood Cathy and Charlie really were his family and relaxed.

In the open hearth, a roaring log fire blazed a welcome.

"Pine, Sam. Burns well and smells good, but you gotta wait a few years for the wood to season properly, let it dry roight out like." Sam jumped not having realised Charlie was there.

"Loike what you see so far?"

Sam nodded. "Yeah. Yes, Charlie, I do. I've never seen a fireplace so big." Either side of the hearth stone seats had been built in where at least two people could sit comfortably side by side. Gleaming copper kettles hung from hooks around the side of the fireplace and two large copper scuttles, one full of coal, the other with logs were placed in front of one of the seats.

Two three-seater settees faced each other in front of the fireplace with a low, dark wood coffee table in between and two very large matching armchairs were positioned either side of the bay window. The settees, chairs and curtains were all in a warm shade of deep rose. From outside Sam would never have thought the cottage was so big inside, it was a big like Dr Who's TARDIS.

Leaving the sitting room, Sam wandered down the hall, looking at all the pictures and knick-knacks on shelves in the hall, and into the kitchen where Cathy was about to serve up dinner. How she had managed to set a fire in the sitting room and organise dinner so quickly was beyond him. They had only been in the house about ten minutes!

"Bless, Sarah Richards." Cathy said on seeing him. "She lives next door. Jenny and Simon's Mum…you know, I mentioned them earlier." Sam nodded. "We do favours for each other," Cathy continued, "and she popped in a while back, got the fire going and put a casserole on timed to be ready when we got here." Sam was convinced she and Charlie could read minds.

"Could you give me a hand setting the table, Sam? You'll find mats, plates and cups in the cupboard over there, and knives and forks in the drawer on the right side of the sink."

Sam took a good look around the kitchen. Again, the room was painted white with black trimming and high up, all around the room was a black, wooden picture rail with plates of all descriptions standing upon it. Some were animal portraits, some floral scenes and some were royal occasion souvenirs and, hanging from the same rail all around the room, were jugs, small, plain jugs, Toby jugs, floral jugs, patterned or plain jugs.

Oh, this is just too old-style. Sam tried not to laugh.

"There are jacket potatoes in the oven and peas and carrots in the other pot. There's fresh bread in the bread bin over there, Sam, so let's get sorted. Charlie's already taken your bag up to your room. I'll bet you're starving aren't you?" She set out three plates on the worktop. "Could you give Charlie a call and let him know dinner's ready. He's just outside with the dogs."

Sam looked down as something brushed against his leg. A large tortoiseshell and white cat with huge round amber coloured eyes looked up at him.

"That's Agnetha," Cathy said. "She's not normally that friendly but she seems to have taken a shine to you." Agnetha purred as he bent down to stroke her while she moved in and out around his legs. Cathy and Charlie are nice, the dogs are fun and now the cat likes me. Maybe it won't be so bad staying her after all.

"Where's the other cat...Frida is it?

"She's probably out mousing – she's quite a hunter is our Frida but she likes to bring her trophies home for us as gifts," Cathy pulled a face. "We've had baby rabbits, squirrels, mice, birds, all sorts. Mostly they're still alive when she brings them in so Charlie takes them outside to the barn and, it's funny, you know but they all seem to survive once he gets them away from her.

Agnetha left Sam's legs and, tail high, padded over to the armchair near the stove, jumped up, circled a couple of times, licked a paw, then wiped it around the top of her head and her ears, purring loudly. She stopped grooming herself and stared at Sam, slowly closing her eyes and opening them with a contented smile on her face then circled a couple of times again, lay down, tucked her tail over her eyes and went to sleep. As Charlie entered the room she flicked her tail crossly looked up and frowned at the disturbance, then resumed her nap.

It was after eight thirty by the time they had cleared up and Sam was feeling tired. His previous night's sleep had been disturbed and it had been a long day. He hoped his mother was alright and that her flight had gone well and wondered whether she had landed in South Africa. He checked his watch and guessed she would have been there for a while by that time, might even be at the hospital with his father. He wondered if she was already at the hospital and how long before she called him.

"You're looking tired, Sam," Charlie said, "you ready fer yer bed?"

"I think so, if it that's OK but can I call my mate, Dave, first please? I told his Mum I would and I haven't yet."

"Yeah, o'course. The phone's in the hall, 'elp yerself."

Back in the hallway, Sam noticed a door he had not seen earlier. He turned the round wooden handle, but the door was locked.

Charlie was watching him. "We don't use that room Sam. It's kept locked fer safety," Charlie moved nearer. "The people who built this cottage about three hundred years ago built it around a well and it's still there, roight in the middle of the cottage. We think it fills up from the river underground and it's pretty deep. To be 'onest we're not sure how safe the shaft is either so I don't let no-one in there. Can't 'ave no-one fallin' in so the room's kept locked." Sam thought Charlie seemed a little less friendly than before but dismissed it as his imagination and headed for the telephone.

Dave answered quickly. "Dave, it's me. Did your Mum tell you what's happened?"

"Yeah. So how long you gonna be down there, wherever you are?"

"Dunno. Dad's pretty bad and Mum's shot off over there to look after him, so I'm down here."

"What are they like…you know, the people you're staying with?"

Sam looked around to check Charlie wasn't still about.

"They seem OK, I think. Don't know them very well and it's weird here…everything's so quiet but they've got a couple of dogs and they're OK. I hope I'm gonna be back for Christmas but I'm not sure. I can't stop long. Just wanted to let you know what was happening. Do me a favour, try and keep Jamie Sullivan away from Joanne, if you can."

"No problem, mate. You should've seen what a numpty he made of himself at football practice today. Showing off doing 'headers' and

headed the ball right into the cricket clubroom window. Smashed to bits! Me 'n' Raj were in bits laughing. Shame you missed it."

Sam wished he had been there. He would have liked to see Sullivan squirm. After arranging to talk again later in the week, Sam felt better. He told Charlie he was ready to go up and called out goodnight to Cathy who was still in the kitchen.

On the stairs, Sam was astonished to discover they turned to the right twice and was mystified. From downstairs they appeared straight! This place is weird! I expect it's more left-over weirdness from those original builders Charlie was talking about. As they climbed the stairs, Sam took in all the wooden-framed paintings lining the staircase walls. There were landscapes, portraits of people, a number of them with animals. Sam thought he recognised one of the two dogs and another of Agnetha, but wasn't sure which of the other cats might be Frida. A little further along a painting of a young girl, probably in her early teens caught his eye and he stopped to study it more closely.

"Yep. That's yer Mum. Cathy tells me she'd 'ave been about your age when it was done. Cathy did all of these. Good ain't she?" Charlie had stopped at the top of the stairs and waited for Sam to catch up. "She's damn good, even if I do say it meself. She's 'ad any number of offers to sell her paintin's but she don't like sellin' 'em. Says God gave her a gift an' it ain't roight to make money out of it, she'd rather give it away. I dunno, to my mind it's a shame. She could do really well for 'erself, perhaps even become famous one day, who knows? But Cathy, she don' wan' that. Says she don' do it for commercialism. She's probably roight not to."

Once Sam had joined him at the top of the stairs, Charlie pointed out the different rooms leading off the hallway. "To the left, down there's the spare bedroom, the bathroom and the airing cupboard and this way," he turned right, "are the bedrooms. This one's ours and this one," he opened the stood back to let Sam pass through, "is your room. It overlooks the back garden an' woods. I think you'll be comfy."

Sam looked around. The room was large, warm and well decorated. The walls and ceiling were cream and there were, of course, more paintings on the wall. It was cosy and warm. The brass-framed bed was covered by a patchwork quilt with cream, blue and green squares and had warm, cream brushed cotton sheets. Sam was ready to just slide into its comfort. Opposite the bed there was an unused fireplace

with brass accessories on the hearth and two large leather straps hanging on either side, each with four horse brasses in a vertical line. The window frame was painted black and hung with heavy cream velvety curtains, which would keep out the draught when closed, and beneath it was a large double radiator that threw out plenty of warmth against the cold night. Charlie had already unpacked Sam's holdalls, his clothes were now stowed away in a large dark wood wardrobe and chest of drawers standing side by side against the wall.

"I've put everythin' away for you Sam but I don't think you'll 'ave any trouble findin' anythin'."

"Thanks Charlie. It's nice," Sam smiled as Charlie turned to go. "And thanks again for everything. You've both been great and…and I'm sorry I was such a pain before."

"Not a problem, all forgotten. Oi'm jest glad we could 'elp. Roight then, Oi'll leave yer to it an' see yer in the morning. If yer need anythin' jest give us a shout." Charlie started to leave again but turned at the door.

"Oh yeah, I meant ter say, don't be afeared o' noises yer might 'ear durin' the night. What with foxes barkin' an' owls hootin' an' badgers scufflin' about, there's all sorts goin' on at night. That's the country fer yer, but there's no 'arm in anythin' aroun' here, so don' go worryin' yer head none. You'll get used to it. G'night' Sam. Sam peered out of the window, but it was still too dark and misty to see anything.

"Well, it is November," Charlie said, clearly reading Sam's thoughts again.

"Yeah. It'll wait till tomorrow to take a look," Sam replied.

"G'night then, sleep well. Everythin'll look better tomorrow." Charlie closed the door on his way out.

Sam went to the bathroom, cleaned his teeth then returned to his new bedroom and was about to close the curtains when a movement outside caught his eye. Putting on the bedside lamp, he turned out the top light and went back to the window, peering out into the night. It was still misty but he could just see as far as the garden wall. I'm imagining things, he thought. Just beyond the wall on the right hand side, a pale, yellow light moved parallel with the wall heading towards the left. Sam guessed it would probably be about a metre or so off the ground. Then it disappeared. Then it happened again, and that one too vanished. He looked at his watch. At ten, and on a night like this, it

was pretty late for anyone to be about. He peered out again, yet a third light came into view and the pattern was repeated. He shook his head. Was the country air playing havoc with his mind? Or perhaps it was just that he was more tired than he thought.

It happened again and this time he was convinced; he was not hallucinating. He watched for a while longer but saw nothing more. Whatever was out there had gone.

Snuggling down under the covers, his mind working overtime, he decided not to say anything about the lights to Cathy or Charlie. They'll only tell me I must have been dreaming and anyway, Charlie said I shouldn't worry about noises but he didn't mention lights!

He heard the backdoor open and Charlie call the dogs. The door creaked closed again and he heard footsteps crunching on gravel fading into the distance. He was warm and comfortable and glad he didn't have to go out in the cold. He reached for his book, turned to the right page and promptly fell asleep.

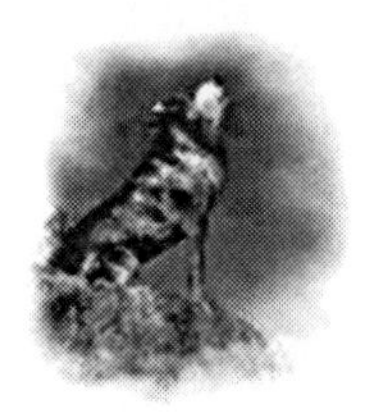

Chapter Thirteen

About the same time Sam left Nottingham, a dark blue Jaguar car sped away from Bristol with Mikey at the wheel. Jake sat in the passenger seat cleaning Mikey's dark glasses, as they were too smudged for him to see through clearly. Danny sat in the back looking very bored.

"How far is it to Winterne?" he asked.

"It'll take us about three quarters of an hour," Jake replied, "why? You in a hurry?"

"No, just wondered," Danny sighed.

Jake handed Mikey back his sunglasses.

"Dunno why you're wearing them, Mikey," Jake scoffed, "it's getting misty. Can you see where we're goin?"

"Shuddup!" Mikey barked.

Using his fingers to squeakily wipe condensation off the window, Danny tried to see through the thickening mist. "So what's the story with old man Atkins, then?" he asked in all innocence. "I don't know nuthin about him."

Instantly Jake swung around in his seat, the safety belt stretched across his neck.

"Mikey's brother or not, you show MISTER Atkins respect! D'you hear me?" Jake spat, his face set in a furious scowl.

"I'm...I'm sorry," Danny said quickly, scared witless by Jake's attack. He knew he was out of his depth with these men but Mikey had said everything would be alright and he had had believed him at the time, now he was not quite so sure.

"Now you listen to me, young feller, an' I'll tell you all about Mr Atkins," Jake said as he reached over wagging a finger in the younger man's face.

"Mr Atkins is a self-made man," Jake began, "'e 'ad some money an' an 'ouse left to 'im in a Will an' used it to started up 'is business, see. The house was in East London, 'Ackney, I think. Anyway, 'e managed to sell the place for a lot more than it was worth an' 'e's bin a self-made man ever since. 'E's 'ad a couple of business partners over the years an' 'im and one of them made a lot of money together, let's just say they was cuttin' corners on building materials, if you get my meaning." Danny did. "I don't know what 'appened to that bloke, do you Mikey?" Mikey shook his head. "Anyway Mr Atkins moved to Bristol an' set up a proper business, for appearances sake, on 'is own like, e, but 'e likes to keep 'is 'and in if you know what I mean, and still has the odd thing going on that none of his posh new mates know about." Mikey's head turned towards the rear view mirror, Danny knew Mikey was watching his reactions.

"Yeah! Like what Jake?" Danny was interested. He sat forward, keen to know more.

"That's none of your business but if you're around long enough you'll find out. That's all I'm sayin' 'an don't interrupt me again. Eventually he met Mrs Atkins an' they bought the estate where we're headed now. Seems like he's 'ad a few family problems, but that's none of our business. Me an' your bruvver 'ave bin with Mr Atkins for a long time now, me a lot longer than Mikey. We know to respect 'im and you'd better learn pretty quick. Speak when you're spoken to and don't be too obvious when e's about, know what I mean? Just do as you're told an' you'll be fine," Jake finished, and turned to face the front again.

Danny sat back. He wanted to know more about Mr Atkins, but was now too scared to ask. A couple of weeks ago, Mikey had bullied him into standing in for the missing Del but had refused to tell him why Del had gone away. Danny knew that meant Del was in prison and knowing that made him uneasy about joining them. None of them seemed to want this job but were too scared to try and pull out. *Just how much power did Atkins have?* Danny's stomach tied itself into knots. He tried to make eye contact with his brother in the rear view mirror, but it was impossible to see his eyes. All the same, he had the

feeling Mikey took his eyes off the road to look at him from time to time, but he said nothing and did not smile. The only conversation after that was between Jake and Mikey about which roads to take to get to Winterne.

Danny pulled up the collar of his jacket and sat dejectedly in the back of the car wishing he was anywhere else and staring gloomily out of the window. He noticed the hole in the knee of his jeans and picked absent-mindedly at a loose thread. At eighteen Danny had been in trouble with the police but only for minor offences, then he decided to get a job and behave himself. Trouble with the police got boring. Once you were known you always got picked up first, even if you were innocent and he wanted out. Now, thanks to Mikey, he was involved in the criminal world again.

As they approached Winterne Manor, the car stopped, Mikey opened the glove compartment and took out a remote control from a small black box and pointed it at a pair of large, black and gold wrought iron electric gates that slowly opened allowing the car entry into the long tree-lined drive. After the car drove through, the gates closed automatically behind them. The mist had now thickened to a dreary grey fog but the manor could just be seen on the left as they turned a corner of the driveway and Danny whistled at the scene. The sprawling half-stone, half-timber building took his breath away. He had never been so close to a place like this before. The lights of the house shone brightly through the haze.

"Ain't it posh!" he said, awestruck especially when through the haze he glimpsed the silvery lake through the trees. "It's just like a film setting, Mikey." Mikey didn't reply.

They took a turning on the right along a narrow lane that ran between a field on the left and woods on their right. The fog lay thickly on the fields.

"It'll be about another half mile," Jake informed them.

"I know where it is, I've bin 'ere before," Mikey snapped.

"I know you 'ave, but 'e ain't," Jake answered, jerking his right thumb over his shoulder at Danny, "an' I was talkin' to 'im."

"Is it always this quiet down 'ere?" Danny had resumed his sulk.

"Quiet! No!" Jake spun round. "It can get quite noisy. What with cows, an' owls, an' foxes, an' what else is there? Oh yes. There's bats,

they squeak sometimes an' there's the stables just up the lane so there's 'orses neighin' as well. Yeah, it can get really loud."

Danny sat back again in silence. The weather's rotten, I'm stuck doing something I don't want and it'll be borin' too even though the place looks nice. I can't wait to get this over, he thought despondently. The car pulled up outside the cottage and the three men got out. Mikey opened the front door of the cottage while Jake and Danny took the bags out of the boot. Mikey pulled his sunglasses down onto the bridge of his nose to look over the top and was pleasantly surprised by the clean, comfortable interior of the cottage. He turned back to Danny.

"Look, I don' like the countryside and I know you don't, but we're here for a while so let's make the best of it, alright?" Mikey was trying to be friendly for a change.

"Why are we doin' this again, remind me?" Jake shouted slamming the boot shut. Mikey pushed his dark glasses back up to the bridge of his nose.

"'Cos it's orders that's why, and you'll do anything Mr Atkins says!" Mikey shouted back. "Stop yer moanin Jake," he said under his breath.

"Yeah, I get it, but I don' like it," Jake grumbled again. Mikey turned back into the cottage.

"If I 'ear one more word," he muttered under his breath as he shook his head. Danny stood quietly to one side not daring to speak. The cottage was clean and warm and would serve as a good base for the five or six weeks Mr Atkins said they would be there.

"Hey Jake," Mikey called out, "if we're gonna be 'ere for a few weeks, we better buy a Christmas tree."

"Whaddya mean, buy? There must be one around 'ere we can uproot or chop down."

Mikey decided to check which bedroom he wanted and ran up the stairs two steps at a time. Although the bedrooms were clean and comfortable, there were only three, so with five in the group, four would have to share two of the rooms and he wasn't going to be one of them. I'm team-leader an' I ain't sharin' with no-one, not even Danny. A car pulled up outside and Mikey turned back to the front door. The other two had arrived. Henry got out of the car and waved to Mikey.

"Got the kettle on yet?" he shouted.

"Give over, we've only just got here," Mikey replied from the doorway.

Henry hurried over to Mikey and Jake. "We got everything 'e asked for, jemmies, pneumatic drills, masonry drills, sledge-hammers and even dynamite. I even remembered to get 'old of six miners' helmets, you know the ones with the lamps on."

"Six?" Chips queried. "Yeah," Henry barked, "well Mr Atkins'll want one if he comes down there with us won't he?"

Jake was holding his breath. He had gone an interesting shade of puce. "Dynamite? D'you know how to use that stuff? It's dangerous ain't you 'eard?"

Henry grinned back at him revealing a revolting mouthful of missing and broken teeth. "Nah, it'll be good, I've been lookin' up the instructions. No need ter bottle it, Jakey, old son. We'll be fine!" As Henry bent down to put a miner's helmet back in the bag, Jake and Mikey exchanged uneasy looks.

Mikey changed the subject. "I'm 'avin' the bedroom on the right upstairs. The rest of you can sort it out between yerselves," he informed the group.

Headlights appeared round the corner, and a beige coloured Mercedes purred into the cottage driveway.

"It's the boss! Mikey yelled. "Get them bags upstairs an' I mean now!" he ordered.

Jeremiah Atkins climbed out of the Mercedes and locked the door. "Can't take any chances these days you know; there's thieves about!" he smiled slyly at Mikey as he entered the kitchen.

No chauffeur today, thought Mikey, he's definitely keeping this under wraps.

"See you all arrived OK," said Jeremiah. "I've arranged to have this place well stocked with food and so on, and there's fishing rods and nets in the shed, so you've everything you need to look the part. There's hurricane lamps out there too, you'll need them in the caves. Now here's the map. Get everyone in here," he spread the map out on to the kitchen table.

"We're here…and this…is where you enter the caves," he pointed to a spot on the map, "and this is where you'll start looking," he pointed to another area further to the left.

"Hey look, Mikey," Danny said eagerly, "there's Wookey Hole. You remember, we went there when I was a kid."

"Yeah, I remember, Danny, it was good, weren't it?" Mikey replied with an unusually soft expression.

"If you two have quite finished reminiscing, do you mind if we get on?" Jeremiah barked impatiently.

"Sorry Mr Atkins," Mikey and Danny said simultaneously.

"I got just one question, Mr Atkins?" Jake put in. "Ain't no-one gonna complain about us bein' on their land if we gets seen? And ain't it Local Government land or somethin'?"

"I know you find it hard to count, but that's two questions, and I believe we have already discussed this," Jeremiah raised his eyes to heaven. "You remember," he said slowly and deliberately, "the land's up for sale and there's been no interest for some time, remember?" Jeremiah shook his head in disbelief. "I'm not going through it all again. Just trust me when I tell you there's no-one about to care about you being there. As you can see it joins my property and, if there is any silver, there'll be no-one to argue ownership." He looked up at the five faces studying the map. "This side of the hill's well away from Wookey Hole so you're not treading on anyone's toes and I don't want people taking too much interest in you and asking awkward questions. You'll take all the equipment there tonight and leave it inside the entrance. No-one ever goes there. I've kept an eye on this place for a long time. I don't even know if anyone knows about it except me, apart from you now that is. Inside is clean and dry so nothing will get damp," he nodded towards the box of dynamite. "I suggest you wait until after nine tonight before you head out there. It'll be still be misty and most decent folk will be home watching television in front of the fire and, don't forget you'll work at night. By my reckoning, it should be easy enough to find the silver ore. I have printed off details of what to look for." He handed Mikey a bundle of papers. The five men stood around the table looking at the map and nodding agreement.

"Do we leave the stuff there all the time then Mr Atkins?" Chips enquired.

"What did I just say?" Jeremiah cuffed Chips around the back of his head, then looked at his hand and reached out for the kitchen roll, wiping his hand with a contemptuous look at Chips, leaving the weedy little man very embarrassed. "Now pay attention. Don't you think it

would look a bit suspicious if you were seen carrying sledge-hammers and dynamite when you're supposed to be fishing, you idiot!" Chips looked down at the floor.

"Yes, Mr Atkins," he mumbled. The other four looked anywhere but at Chips.

Jeremiah continued, "Keep your heads down, don't attract unwanted attention, read up on local rivers and types of fish. If anyone asks you ought to know your stuff." He turned to leave then stopped at the door. He turned. "Just one more thing, watch out for my daughter, Meredith. You remember her Mikey," Mikey nodded. "She comes past here on her way to our stables further down the lane every day, at least once. Don't do anything to arouse her suspicions. She's no fool and has a good knowledge of local wildlife, including the fish in the lake. So if you see her watch what you say because she'll know if something's not right. So don't make me nervous. We could all do very nicely, thank you, with this little caper, and I want it to go right. So follow my instructions *to the letter,* and everything'll be fine."

"Yes sir, Mr Atkins, you can rely on me sir and the lads'll do as they're told," Mikey assured him as he walked Jeremiah to his car.

"They'd better. Now I plan to join you Wednesday evening but do not, I repeat, *do not,* tell my daughter if you see her. She mustn't know I'm going to be here, get that?"

"Of course Mr Atkins, she mustn't know you're gonna be 'ere," Mikey repeated.

"Now here's a mobile phone so we can keep in touch. I'll see you Wednesday," Jeremiah handed over the phone, got back into his car and drove away. He did not look back.

Chapter Fourteen

It was Sunday morning and the elves were troubled. Jimander had called a breakfast meeting of the Clan Council, over which he was to preside. Claptrap, Piggybait and Jerrill, sat with him, their faces sombre, while they waited for the assembled company of senior elves to settle down. Finally, Jimander called the meeting to order. It was a bitterly cold morning and the smell of smouldering peat blending with burning pine cones wafted through the chamber providing a warm, welcoming fragrance to cheer the anxious elves.

"We were seen," Claptrap began, "I'm convinced of it. I definitely saw someone at the window and I'm sure he saw us, so what are we going to do about it? I mean Jerrill was so scared he almost refused to cross the field. It was his first time on duty for a while and we had to make sure he went through with it."

Piggybait, having been deep in thought, came up with a possible solution. "If we keep the lanterns on until we get to the edge of the trees, blow them out to cross the field, then relight them at the other side, we should be alright. Our eyesight is excellent so I'm not really sure why we use the lanterns anyway."

Claptrap sat back on his snake-skin covered chair. He had found a shed skin of an adder last summer, kept it and lined the chair with it. "You're right. It is only when there's no moon or stars that we really need them," he said. "And, anyway, it's unlikely we would be seen anywhere else, especially not in the woods at night. See if you can manage without the lanterns when you and Jerrill go tonight. If you do find you need them, just turn them off when you go by the wall."

Jimander raised an eyebrow but remained silent. He was too busy crunching on an apple to speak. A general discussion broke out with twenty voices vying to be heard, making suggestions or disagreeing with them, in between mouthfuls of hazelnut bread, cheese, plums or

apples. While listening to the hubbub going on around him, Jimander leaned towards Claptrap.

"Let's hope there are no repercussions from last night. I have no wish to be caught up in the world of humans again, unless it's on my own terms. I fear my destiny is linked to humans, and it will be they who determine my future."

Claptrap felt an icy chill run down his back.

Chapter Fifteen

Sam awoke on Sunday morning feeling surprisingly relaxed but still intrigued by the strange lights and wanted to ask Charlie about them. He dressed quickly and ran down the stairs to the kitchen where he found Cathy already clearing away after breakfast. She and Charlie were used to getting up early.

"Morning Sam, can I get you some breakfast?" she asked. Sam shook his head.

"Not really hungry at the moment, thanks Cathy. Is Charlie around?"

"He's out with the dogs but they're only at the bottom of the field. You can get there through the gate in the garden wall."

Sam grabbed his fleece jacket that he had left draped over a chair the night before, and rushed out. It was a cold, clear morning and the ground was covered in a crisp frost that crackled under his feet as he ran to the gate. Sliding back the glistening bolt, Sam saw Charlie and the dogs at the other end of the field. Charlie turned, saw Sam running towards him and called to the dogs. On seeing Sam they dashed back up the field towards him, jumping up and almost tripping him up as they bounded around his legs, tails wagging and tongues flapping.

"They're certainly pleased to see you," Charlie laughed. Sam made a fuss of both dogs and he was just about to mention the lights when Charlie asked.

"Sleep alroight did you? I bet you 'eard all sorts last night, probably dreamt about strange things too. It's funny 'ow this place affects new people. It's got a strange 'abit of getting queer thoughts into people's 'eads."

Well, that answers that, thought Sam, If I say anything now, he'll just say I'd been dreaming and perhaps he's right, maybe I did dream it.

He decided to not to mention it for the time being. They continued their walk with Sam asking Charlie about the village and the residents while the dogs trotted happily along nearby, noses skimming the ground following every new scent they found or trailing behind a little, then bounding along, tails high, to catch up with the humans. After about an hour they returned to the cottage where Cathy greeted them with hot tea and toast for Sam.

After breakfast, Sam showered and dressed and got ready to go into the village with Cathy to get the Sunday papers.

"Are you ready?" she called up the stairs just as Sam appeared at the top. "Come on then, let's see who I can introduce you to." As she opened the front door, a large black cat who had been sleeping on the doorstep stood up, stretched and rubbed herself against Cathy's legs for a few moments, then walked regally, head and tail held high, into the cottage.

"Well, there you are, you've now met all family. That's our Frida. Been out on the tiles all night and now she's ready for a full day sleeping. Charlie'll feed her. Oh, morning Vicar," Cathy waved to the village Parson as he cycled past.

"Nice man, Mr Driver. Not too 'churchy' if you know what I mean."

Sam was surprised to find there was no pavement at the side of the road, just a grass verge on either side. On the other side of the grass, small brooks gurgled along on both sides of the road. Stone slabs spanned the brooks allowing residents of the cottages to cross over the small streams to their front gardens. Sam thought the village old-fashioned and pretty like the pictures on countryside jigsaw puzzles. Everyone they passed said, "Morning Cathy," "how are you?" or "nice day, considering." They even smiled and nodded at Sam, and none of them knew him. He found this very strange; city people rarely talked to strangers.

"That's how things are done in the country Sam. They're friendlier than in town, don't you think?" Sam agreed but his mind was on something else.

"Cathy, Charlie said the cottage was built around a well, but weren't wells outside?"

"Well, yes, normally they were, but the people who built our cottage built it around the well so they never had to go outside in bad weather.

It never freezes up. They were quite sensible really. Originally, most of the cottages here were quite small and over the centuries they have been added to. The main part of ours is about three hundred years old but the heart of it, the bit with the well, dates from much further back," Cathy added.

"Charlie said it's not safe, is that right?" Sam asked.

"Probably. I've never actually seen it. Charlie says the well-shaft is old stonework and thinks it may be dangerous to go too near so he keeps it locked." A grin appeared and her eyes lit up with amusement. "Frida's been known to open a door before, she swings on the handle, so Charlie thinks it best to keep it locked to stop her getting in there. He keeps some tools in the little room there and goes in occasionally, but always locks the door when he's going in or out. He might show you it one day if you ask and apparently there's still water in it, and it's pure."

When they stopped at the village general store and sub Post Office Cathy pointed to some people across the road. "You see that woman with the dark red coat over there? Well that's Sarah Richards and she has Jenny and Simon with her." Sam looked vague. "You know, the family next door? Come on, I'll introduce you."

Sam felt unexpectedly nervous but Mrs Richards smiled warmly as they approached and he instinctively, liked her. Sarah Richards was fairly tall and plump with fading blonde hair and rosy, apple cheeks that gave her healthy, fresh air glow. Her grey eyes smiled kindly at him. "So this is Sam," Sarah reached out to shake his hand before Cathy had a chance to introduce him. "I'm delighted to meet you. We were sorry to hear about your parents' trouble but we'll try to make your stay here a good one. This is Simon," she indicated her son. Simon was very tall; Sam guessed he was well over six foot. He shook Simon's hand and wondered if he had the same problem Charlie had with low ceilings. Then Sarah introduced her daughter. "And this is Jenny."

She's quite tall too, and pretty, thought Sam. He smiled shyly.

"Jenny's your age Sam, so she can help you with meeting the other young folk around here, can't you?" Sarah Richards asked her daughter.

"Uh, yeah, I guess so. Nice to meet you too," she said quietly. Jenny was blonde like her mother, but her hair was so pale in colour it was almost white and it fell, thick and straight, passed her shoulders,

but it was her eyes that took his attention. They were a warm, deep brown; an unusual combination with her hair colouring. Sam immediately felt that, although she seemed shy, he might have just made a friend and felt better still about staying in the village.

"Did you hear what that rotten little toe-rag, Jonah Atkins, did to Dad a couple of days ago?" Sarah asked Cathy, her previous amiability disappearing as she angrily described the incident. "Hit him with a pellet from that blasted rifle. He's got a horrible bruise on his neck. Mark my words, Cathy, that boy'll do some real harm one day."

"Hmm, yes, I heard," Cathy frowned. "They need to do something about Jonah but short of restraints I'm not sure what. How is Arthur?" Sam observed Jenny flinch and Simon scowl at hearing the name Jonah Atkins.

"He's better now, no thanks to the Atkins's. I know what I'd like to do to Jonah if I got my hands on him." Sarah's anger left Sam in little doubt of what she would like to do.

"So, you're starting at my school," Jenny cut in, changing the subject, "if it's alright with you Cathy, I'll take Sam around the village later. It'll be good for him to get to know a few people before he starts school."

"Is that OK with you Sam?" Cathy asked. Sam nodded quickly; he was more than happy at the thought of spending some time with someone of his own age.

"Thank you, Jenny," Cathy said, "Sam's free after lunch if that's OK for you and we'll see you later then. Bye Sarah, bye Simon. Sarah, give your parents my best wishes and tell Arthur I hope he feels better soon."

As they walked away, Cathy asked Sam, "How soon do you want to start school? Do you want a week or so to settle into the village or would you like to start straight away? Only I've got to phone Alan Davies, the Head Teacher, this afternoon to sort it out. He's a friend of Charlie's, so phoning him at the weekend's not a problem."

He thought for a moment then agreed that the sooner he got started at school the better.

In the shop Cathy introduced him to Mrs Askam and bought the Sunday papers while Sam looked around the shop. He picked up a film magazine and asked Cathy for some of his money to buy it. A few minutes later, they left the shop and Cathy pointed out the church, the

local pub and where the school bus stopped. As they headed home Cathy continued telling him about local people. "Mrs Askam's daughter, Susan goes to St. Merriott's as well. Her older sister's left the school now, that's Rachel who's doing her nursing training at Wells General Hospital but Susan's in the same class as Jenny. She's a nice girl too, you'll like her."

As she talked, Sam became aware of a number of boys, about his age, across the road. One of them, dark haired and wearing a smart black leather jacket and denim jeans, was leaning against the telephone kiosk. His hair was brushed back from his forehead and he wore a small gold earring in his left ear. He was staring at Sam who felt goose-bumps creeping over his neck and shoulders. The boy's attempt at intimidation worked even from a distance. He said something to the three other boys who stood a little behind him, without ever removing his gaze from Sam. Menace emanated from him and Sam felt chilled, until he saw the brace on the boy's front teeth and at once the spell was broken; he was just a boy with crooked teeth.

"We have a newcomer to the village," the boy said loudly, "we'll have to give him a proper welcome, won't we fellas?" but there was no welcome in his tone. He glared at Sam for a few seconds more before he and his group moved off in the opposite direction. Cathy, aware of the impending confrontation, took Sam's arm to move him away quickly but, looking back, Sam saw the boy turn back to stare menacingly at him as he walked away.

"Who was that? What a git! Sorry!"

"No need to apologise. You've just encountered Jonah Atkins who we were talking about just now. Do yourself a favour and stay away from him. His father owns the local mansion, farm and stables. Charlie works on his estate but, even more unfortunately for you, Jonah goes to St Merriott's. It's a pity he didn't go to a private boarding school as we were all hoping, but we're stuck with him. He's a nasty piece of work; very spoilt. He likes to bully and generally picks on girls or smaller children, and I heard he likes to play practical jokes on people as well and none of them are funny. Hurting old Arthur for instance, that was just plain wicked. Stay away from him if you can."

"So that's him," Sam understood now. "Yeah, I'll do that. Jenny looked worried when his name was mentioned, do you know why?"

“No, I don’t know of anything specific but none of the young people like him, in fact nobody likes him, which may well be part of his problem, but I can’t sympathise with bullies. He might’ve been picking on Jenny which would explain why she’s nervous, but she’ll probably tell you if there’s anything when she’s ready. Now, enough of Jonah Atkins! Let’s go home, you’re going out this afternoon and I’ve got to get lunch ready.”

When Jenny arrived the dogs went wild with excitement, barking and bouncing until Cathy called them off.

“Are you ready?” Jenny asked Sam.

“If it’s OK with Cathy, I am.”

“Of course, off you go have a nice time and be back about five-thirty for dinner,” Cathy told them. They were already at the front gate when Cathy called Sam back. ”Sam, I don’t want to worry you, but if you *do* see Jonah Atkins, don’t forget to stay out of his way. You never know, you might get to know each other better at school and perhaps things will be alright, but in the meantime…watch out for him…Jenny’ll keep you right. Won’t you Jenny?” Cathy called to her and Jenny nodded, her fingers crossed behind her back.

“Can you ride a bike?” Jenny asked. “Only I thought you could borrow Simon’s old one and we could get about a bit more while the weather’s still not too bad.”

“Yeah. I can ride a bike, no problem,” Sam told her. They took two bikes from the Richards’ shed and cycled through the village in an awkward silence until they reached the village green. Charlie and three other men were setting up a very tall Christmas tree in the middle of the Green; Sam guessed it was probably over six metres high.

“They’ll be switching the lights on tonight when it gets dark and it always looks lovely.”

It was the first time Jenny had spoken since they left the house and the ice thawed. Charlie saw them and waved, supporting the trunk of the tree with one hand, while his companions pulled it upright with ropes.

“That’s Susan Askam and her sister, Rachel over there,” Jenny indicated two red-headed girls standing outside the village shop watching the tree being raised.

“Isn’t Susan in your class?”

“Yes, she is…how did you know?”

"Cathy told me, and she said Rachel's studying to be a nurse." He grinned broadly, "See I'm getting to know about people here already.

"Jenny smiled back, "Well just let's see what else you know, smartie!"

"They live in the house next to the Post Office."

"Are you ready to move on?" Jenny asked. Sam nodded and they waved goodbye to Charlie and cycled on around the green, passed by the church and took the road towards Wells. Just after they passed the Three Horseshoes pub on their right, Jenny pointed out her father's dental practice a few doors down but, apart from a couple of antique shops, a butcher's shop and, almost at the end of the main road, a small red brick primary school, that was it; the village ended. Sam had never seen a place so small, no restaurants, no cinema, nowhere to hang out for people his age. A few minutes later they cycled past the last cottage and Jenny suggested they stopped to rest. Getting off the bikes they sat on a cold stone wall and watched a flock of sheep grazing in the fields beyond as the watery sun sank lower and the heavy grey clouds they had seen earlier crept closer.

"It's not bad here…but it's so small," Sam said leaning on the wall as he looked around.

"Villages are usually small so what else did you expect?" Jenny sounded offended

"Yeah, I know that…it's just that I've always lived in a city and it's so quiet here but it's alright though," Sam added hastily, not wanting to upset her.

"It's not that quiet you know. It's just that the noises here are different to what you're used to. She pointed towards the end of the next field, "You see that cottage over there at the bottom of the field?"

"Yeah."

"Well, if you want excitement, try going into that field or the orchard beside it."

"Why? What'll happen? Will the bogie man get me?"

Jenny ignored him. "That's old Ben Bragg's cottage. He's a weird one and he's scary. If you get too close he either sends the dogs at you or rushes out with his shotgun like he did at Simon and me when we were trying to get his piglets back into his garden after they'd escaped through a hole in the fence…he called us pig-thieves!"

"He shot at you!" Sam could not believe his ears. "You are joking!"

"Oh no I'm not," she said with a chuckle. "He said we were stealing them…scared me to death." She started laughing. "It's funny now but it wasn't then so, there's a warning for you, Sam Johnson. Stay away from stray piglets or you may get shot at!"

"He really shot at you?" Sam still found it hard to believe. He was beginning to see the countryside in a very different light. "It's a good job he missed you or who would show around?"

The sky darkened and the threatened rain began falling as a cold drizzle. They decided to head home before they got soaked. They were putting the bikes back in Jenny's garden shed when Sam plucked up courage to ask Jenny something that had been on his mind.

"What's the problem with that Jonah…Jonah…?"

"Atkins…" Jenny finished for him as she leaned her bike against the shed wall. Sam immediately felt a change in her mood. She frowned. "Why?"

"I had a sort of eyeball session with him earlier and he got mouthy but I dunno why.

He just looked like he wanted to prove something, him and his mates!"

"Yeah, sounds like Jonah," Jenny exhaled loudly. "OK, I'll tell you about him but let's get back inside first." She took Sam into the warm kitchen and poured out two glasses of orange juice which she set down on either side of the heavy rectangular wooden table; they sat down opposite each other now completely relaxed in each other's company, all previous shyness between them now long forgotten.

"OK, so where do I begin?" she looked down at her glass and ran a finger, pensively, across the rim. , She looked up and Sam fleetingly saw something in her eyes, a mix of hatred and fear and something else that looked almost like nausea. "Jonah thinks he owns everything round here…huh…well I s'pose his Dad pretty much does, so he treats everyone badly," she raised her glass to her mouth, but put it down again, wrapped both hands around it and stared down into it. "His father's never about, always too busy, his Mother's not well, she shuts herself up in her room and doesn't see anyone and he's got a sister, Meredith, who's OK but she's more interested in horses and he's only got friends 'cos they're scared of him. I stay out of his way if I can and while you're here you should too. He's bad news. St Merriott's would be alright if it wasn't for him and he bullies people into hanging out

with him by threatening to get their parents sacked or throwing them out of their home. He's selfish and mean. A real taker!" she paused for breath. "So, do yourself a favour, keep your head down at school and try not to get in his way. You're not going to be here long so he doesn't have to be your problem. So that's it. That's Jonah for you. Sorry to go on a bit, but you did ask."

"Thanks for the warning but it might be a bit late not to be noticed now," he grinned. "I guess I'd better get back next door but thanks for showing me around. I guess I'll see you in the morning at the bus stop."

"D'you want me to call for you?" Jenny realised he might be a little nervous about starting at the new school, especially as he probably had made an enemy already.

"Yeah, thanks. That'd be cool," Sam grinned. He was relieved. It would be good to have her company and not to have to get to the school bus alone.

"I've just thought," Jenny went on. "I took you out to meet people and you didn't meet anyone, did you? That's awful seeing as that's what we went out for."

"Doesn't matter," Sam smiled, "it was good to look around anyway."

The dogs barked a welcome as he walked through the back door and Agnetha made straight for his legs again, purring contentedly as he made a fuss of her until the phone rang and he rushed to answer it hoping it might be his Mum.

"Hi Mum, how are you? How's Dad? How was your flight?" As Charlie came in and Cathy signalled him to be quiet while she eavesdropped at the kitchen door hoping to find out if Sam said anything about how he felt staying with them but Charlie gently pulled her away and closed the door. "Let the boy have his privacy, m'dear," he chuckled. Eventually the call finished and Sam joined them in the kitchen. He looked relieved. "Dad's healing well and he's happier now Mum's there with him. She said the tests showed no permanent damage with his back, just bad bruising and torn muscles. His legs are going to take some time to heal though and they still don't know yet when he'll be able to leave hospital, so it looks like I might be here for a while."

"An' yer very welcome my lad," Charlie ruffled Sam's hair with his shovel sized hand. "You can stay as long as you need to. We'll be glad ter 'ave yer an' Oi'm glad to 'ear yer Dad's doin' alroight."

After dinner, as they sat in the living room watching television, Charlie looked up from the crossword he had been trying to finish.

"So what do you think o' the village, Sam?"

"Yeah. It's OK, I'm getting to like it here," Sam replied.

"An' you've made friends with Jenny then. What do you think of Simon?"

"I haven't really seen much of him. He's alright I suppose but I'm not sure we've got anything in common though."

"An' I 'ear you 'eard all about Ben Bragg today."

"Yeah. Don't think I want to meet him. He sounds mad but…but how did you know what we talked about, Charlie?"

"Oh, a little bird told me." Charlie winked. "This is quite a place you know, 'ave you ever 'eard the stories about these parts?"

"I've heard about King Arthur, but I don't think I know about anything else. Why?" asked Sam.

"Ah. So where to start then! Big on legends and stories around 'ere. There's lots of history with curses, bodies, tunnels, Merlin an' King Arthur, then there's the cave-dwellers. All sorts of stories about them, an' then there's the little people, although no-one really believes in'em. But no, my boy, don't you make the mistake of thinking nothin' ever goes on here. There's all sorts gone on an' still goin' on." Sam looked wide-eyed at the mention of curses and bodies. Charlie continued. "About a hunnerd years ago the local squire riled a farmer by tricking him out of his best fields. Seems the Squire got the parish minister involved in his plans too, so then the farmer had a grudge against both of them. Neither of them knew he had two aunts, both of them into the forces of nature and natural laws of magic, shall we say."

Sam was fascinated. "What, you mean they were witches? Like, real ones?"

Charlie continued his story as if he hadn't heard.

"Well, to cut a long story short, their curse was for a hunnerd years, and when the aunts died, the minister refused to bury them in the church cemetery, wouldn't have them on consecrated ground. So the farmer, 'e buried them in 'is garden jest next to the 'ouse, which is about five minutes from here. Of course the village's grown a bit since

them days and there's one o' them Yuppie types livin' in it now. They've extended the 'ouse roight over the aunt's graves. Mrs Jenks lives next door an' says if the Yuppie upsets 'er again, she's gonna tell 'im about the bodies. Nice woman, Mrs Jenks, knows all about 'erbs and stuff like that."

"I suppose they'd have burned her as a witch back in the old days Charlie," Sam innocently commented.

"No, course not…they 'anged 'er," Charlie replied absent-mindedly.

Cathy and Sam looked up at the same time, then at each other.

"What did you say, Charlie?" Cathy asked.

"They did what?" Sam looked aghast.

"Well, she says they did, in a previous life loike." Charlie grinned broadly and winked. Cathy and Sam smiled with relief; he was obviously teasing.

"What happened about the curse?" Sam was intrigued.

"The Squire's house is Winterne Manor that's now owned by the Atkins family but as for the curse, well first of all the Squire's cows stampeded over 'im, trampled 'e was. 'Is daughter an' 'er 'usband moved away when he got made up to Bishop an' she sold the manor, but no-one could never do anything with it. There were freak accidents, fires, people who lived there died young of all manner of strange illnesses, or those who did survive could never make enough money to keep the place going. It lasted until about twenty years ago an' which, funnily enough, he hunnerd years was up about around then. That's when the Atkins family bought it an' turned it around an' they've stayed, more's the pity. Funny though, it lasted exactly one hunnerd years! There's some folk think the curse transferred to the village instead with the Atkins movin' in."

Sam was totally enthralled. "And, is all that true?" he asked.

"O' course, my lad. Would I lie to you?" Charlie grinned.

"Charlie, don't go filling his head with your nonsense," Cathy scolded, then smiled at Sam. "It's going to be busy day tomorrow, Sam, starting at St Merriott's and everything."

"Yes, I think I'll go up now. G'night." He stopped at the door. "Charlie, got any more good stories for tomorrow?"

"Course Oi 'ave." Charlie nodded. Cathy shook her head good humouredly. Upstairs in his room, Sam turned on his bedside lamp then went to close the curtains. He watched the moon emerge from

behind a night cloud, its shafts illuminating the surrounding area quite clearly. He was about to pull the curtains closed when a slight movement caught his eye just inside the line of trees on the right. He pulled the curtains around him shutting out the light from the lamp and saw again a pale light moving inside the edge of the trees. Then it was gone. He saw a movement at the trees on the left as a light flickered on just inside the ring of trees. Again a light on the right, then off! After a few seconds another light on the left, then twice more. He hadn't been imagining it. The lights were real!

Chapter Sixteen

Later that night, when the moon was high, two cars arrived at the edge of the woods and parked behind a tall hedge: even though it was unlikely anyone would be about, the drivers made sure they had left them completely hidden from the lane. Henry began unloading equipment from the car boot. Heaving a bulky bag he held it out for Chips to take from him. "'Ere this one's for you."

There was no response. Chips was not there. Muttering something about "bloody idiots messin' about," Henry stuck his head around back of the car and switched on his torch. Chips was standing a short way off, staring into the sinister depths of the woods. In the torch's pale yellow beam, Chips' face was deathly pale, beads of perspiration shone on his forehead and top lip along the pencil line moustache.

"I knew you were sweatin'. I could 'ear yer," Henry said sarcastically.

"Can't 'elp it!" Chips retorted. "I always sweat when I'm nervous, you know that...an' I really don't like this job an' I don't like the look of in there." He pointed towards the dense woods. Even Henry felt there was something creepy about the trees, he shuddered, then told himself he was being stupid and was not going to let a few big plants scare him. He elbowed Chips.

"Don' think about it, just get on with it," Henry advised a little more kindly than usual. "Come on let's get a move on before the others see yer scared." Chips sullenly did as he was told.

"Hey Jake, 'ow d'you put this light on, then?" Mikey asked holding up a miner's helmet.

"If you get rid of them bloomin' shades you might see the switch!" Jake retorted, "an' keep yer voice down, there might be someone about."

Mikey made a show of looking around them, "Don't be daft. Who the Hell's gonna be 'ere at this time of night!"

Laying the map on the bonnet of Mikey's car, they used their torches to check which path they had to take and once they thought they had their bearings, Mikey folded it up, stashed it in his pocket and led the way into the uninviting wood.

"Right, follow me," he said, trying to sound confident but the density of the trees and the sinister atmosphere around them had him worried, "it's this way for a bit, and then where the path forks, we take the left one for another...bit...then we should see the rock covering the 'idden entrance!"

"Very precise directions, I don't think!" Jake scoffed. "And just when were you a boy scout, Mikey?" Mikey hissed an unrepeatable reply. "No well, we'll 'ave it your way, Mikey, you obviously know yer way 'round 'ere!" sniggered Jake. The other three exchanged nervous looks.

"You can take that look off of your face Jake Rumpsall, I know what I'm doin'…don't you worry about that," Mikey bluffed, "you just stay close, no more than ten minutes an' we'll be there, you'll see. Now keep quiet and stay close…an' turn yer 'elmets off. We don't wanna waste them batteries…don't know 'ow long we're gonna be down there tonight," Mikey ordered.

"'Ow we gonna see without the helmet lamps?" Henry asked. "It's dark in them trees."

"Is everyone goin' stupid tonight?" Mikey was getting angry. "What 'ave I got 'ere then 'Enry?" he shone his torch beam into Henry's eyes.

"Oh yeah, I forgot about those!" Henry said contritely. Turning on the hand-held torches they continued into the dark, forbidding woods, huddled close together. First Mikey then Jake immediately behind him, with Henry and Chips alternately moving in front of each other, while Danny, constantly looking behind, brought up the rear. He had the uneasy feeling the trees were closing up behind them as they moved along. An owl hooted somewhere and Jake's heart began thumping alarmingly.

"Ere, Mikey, ever 'ad the feelin' yer being' watched?" Jake asked in a whisper.

"Oh, grow up you lot, there's no-one about, alright?" He shone the torch beam in a full circle and the shadows between the trees flickered unnervingly. It was Mikey's turn to scoff now. "You can see there's no-one around…it's just yer imagination."

"I think he's right, Mikey!" Danny called from the back, his voice thundering in the silence.

"Be quiet, all of yer!" Mikey snapped in a loud whisper. He too had the uncomfortable feeling they were not alone but there was no way he was going to admit it to the others. The shifting mist and gloomy atmosphere chilled their hearts even though there were intervals when the sky cleared allowing the moonlight through, and they could see the numberless stars lighting up the heavens. A noise from just inside the dark line of trees made them jump.

"What was that?" Henry stopped dead, prickling goose-bumps crawled up his arms and neck.

"It's a bird you idiot!" Mikey sneered. "Now pull yerself together, all of you. Yer like a bunch of little kids scared of a ghost story. For Pete's sake! Whassat? Mikey stopped suddenly. Jake, who was right behind, stumbled into him, scraping the back of Mikey's heel with his boot.

"You clumsy idiot!"

"It's your own fault!" Jake yelled at him. "If you hadn't stopped…what the…I can 'ear it too. Shhhushhhh all of yer. All five of them stood deathly quiet, hardly daring to breathe as they peered out into the shadows, their torch-beams cutting through the dark between the trees.

"Hell's Bells! Whassat over there?" By this time even Henry was quaking with fear, Chips froze and Danny inched closer to Mikey.. Something large and dark moved across the beam of his torch. Quickly turning all the torches in the same direction they saw two pools of reflected light peering back at them.

"What is it?" Henry whispered. They grouped closer together.

"Sshhhh…keep quiet...it might not 'ave seen us…whatever it is," Mikey whispered.

"Oh, yeah. Why didn't I think of that? An' there was me thinking 'ere's us shinin' a bloomin torch, right in whatever it is's eyes, but it won't 'ave seen us?" He shook his head in despair. "Are ya stupid? For 'eavens sake…it's 'ardly goin' ter miss us is it?" Jake hissed

between his teeth. “Just keep movin’ nacheral like, an’ per’aps it won’t bother us…uh oh! Too late…it’s comin’ this way.” Adrenaline pumping, they wanted to run but were rooted to the spot as the shape advanced, increasing in size as it loomed closer.

“It’s flamin’ big…whatever it is,” Mikey croaked, barely audible from behind the tree where he was hiding.

“Tell us somethin’ we don’t know, will yer,” Jake’s teeth chattered. As the eyes loomed closer the moon re-appeared and a shaft of light fell directly onto…a stag.

“Ohhh…it’s just a deer,” Danny let out a sigh of relief and began breathing again.

“Yer see, I knew it’d be somethin’ like that,” Mikey stated, straightening up to his full height and putting his shoulder back, he stepped back out onto the path. “I dunno what all the fuss was about,” Mikey blustered and strutted off ahead of the others and missed the knowing looks exchanged by the other four. “Right let’s go. We got a job to do.”

They all felt very foolish as they the stag passed by them obviously far less concerned by their presence than they were of his and the embarrassing incident was never mentioned again.

At a fork in the path, they took the left track until they found the bush Jeremiah said concealed the rock at the cave entrance. Mikey pushed his way through while Danny and Jake, between them hauled the bulky rock that concealed the narrow cave entrance out of the way. It was now time to don the miner’s helmets as it was only a matter of minutes before they would be inside the caves.

After a short hesitation when no-one wanted to make the first move, Jake finally made a move towards the opening. Getting down on his hands and knees he crawled through, followed closely by Danny, then Henry, Chips and finally Mikey.

One by one, they found themselves inside a small cave that had a dry, sandy floor and a ceiling that was about a half a metre above six-foot Mikey’s head; what worried them was that it appeared to have no other exit. How were they to get to where Mr Atkins wanted them to go? . Mikey and Henry looked puzzled; Chips scratched his head and Danny just looked thankful.

“So what now?” Henry muttered.

But Jake had disappeared. Saying nothing to the others, he had noticed a draught coming from a gap at the back of the cave. While the others were looking perplexed he was already exploring, closely inspecting the back wall where he discovered a gap hidden by an outcrop of rock that had not been easily visible. He briefly wondered why Mr Atkins had not mentioned how to find their way through but decided it was just his little joke on them or more likely knowing him an initiative test which Jake was determined to pass. Examining it more closely, he realised it was just large enough for a well-built man to squeeze through. Jake was just such a man, so if he could get through, the others certainly could. From beyond the crevice he could hear running water and began forcing himself through the narrow gap with just one moment when he thought he was stuck. It had been uncomfortable and he would have a few bruises but the sight that met his eyes had been well worth the effort.

"Hey fellas, come and see this! Jake called. "It's fantastic!" One by one they joined him and found themselves in the most astonishing place they had ever seen. The vast cavern, illuminated by their helmet lamps, glistened in jewel shades of pink, cream and yellow, the ceiling reflecting the gentle rippling of the water in the underground lake below. Awestruck, they spread out carefully along the wide rock shelf encircling the water. Stalactites of all sizes, formed by mineral rich water seeping through the limestone, hung from the ceiling while stalagmites rose up from the floor like huge pillars. Jake whistled under his breath as he took in the incredible beauty of the cavern. Rock ledges with layers of solidified limestone ending in cement-like fringes were deposited around the cave walls. Most of them had never seen anything like it except in pictures.

"What a sight! I've heard of Wookey Hole before, but never realised the inside of a cave could look like this," Jake's voice echoed at them.

"We 'ave, ain't we Mikey," Danny answered. "It's just like lots of jewels all shinin' at us," Danny commented, his eyes wide with amazement. "It's just like when we came 'ere when we was young, ain't it Mikey?"

Henry, mouth agape, was so entranced grossed by the phenomenon he forgot to look where he was going and whooosh...thump! "Ow! That bloody 'urt!" he yelled as he landed on his back. Chips and

Danny sniggered but Mikey silenced them with a look. He had finally taken off his sunglasses and the expression in his eyes brooked no humour. He reached down to help Henry up and almost slipped as well. "You all watch where you're walkin', the floor's wet and slippery an' I don't want no accidents. Alright?" Mikey warned.

"You know," Jake began as he watched Henry brush the water off his trousers, "if my memory serves me right, these caves are where some river starts an' there's loads of underground lakes in these 'ills. There's divin' goes on in 'ere too and there's some legend about a witch an' her dog or cat. She got turned to stone or somethin' like that. Some of these caves are famous an' like Mr Atkins said, there'll be tourists an' that." A thought occurred to him. "Hey, I wonder if anyone's been in 'ere before. 'Ere what if we're the first people ever to see this place?"

"Yeah," Danny said, "we're explorers, ain't we Mikey?"

Mikey gave his brother a look of disdain. "We'd better 'ave another look at Mr Atkins directions now."

Chapter Seventeen

In the largest of the side chambers at the side of the elves' Great Hall, Jerrill was wringing his hands nervously, pacing the floor, his forehead screwed into furrows.

"I tell you, I know we were seen!" he wailed hysterically.

"Will you calm down, relax," Jimander said coolly, trying to soothe his fretful companion, "we don't *actually* know we were seen and, so what even if we were. What's the worst that could happen? The Chief can sort out any problems," he said, stroking his chin thoughtfully.

"Oh, please don't do that Jimander, you'll have Jerrill getting upset again," Claptrap implored, "and we all know you only do that when you think there's trouble coming. It makes me nervous too." He ducked as Jimander threw a pine cone at him that flew passed Claptrap, and whacked a snoring Piggybait, asleep in an armchair by the fire, right on the nose.

"Ow! Wha…?" Piggybait opened one eye.

"Go back to sleep Piggy. There's nothing happening here," Claptrap told him. Piggybait settled back into his snug armchair and closed his eyes, but he was awake and too interested in the conversation to sleep.

"Jimander, don't tell me that you aren't concerned," Jerrill continued, "even poor Saldor knows we have to look after the girls, but he's worried too. I wonder if we should move them nearer to here?"

"Saldor's always worried, when he not asleep. His nerves haven't been right since the pixies gave him those herbs, remember? His memory's never been right either since he regained consciousness, so his being nervous isn't unusual," Jimander answered not looking up. He was growing impatient with Jerrill's fussing.

“Well I’m going to play dominoes with Halmar and Rondo,” Jerrill stated grumpily. “Use your centuries of experience to come up with an answer to this, will you?” He flounced huffily from the chamber.

Piggybait opened one eye watching Jerrill leave. “I wonder what he would do if he had a real problem to deal with.”

Chapter Eighteen

Monday dawned bright and very cold. Sam had been awake from about five thirty unable to get back to sleep; tension had got the better of him. Before going downstairs he showered and dressed in a white shirt, black trousers and black 'V' neck jumper. He could smell bacon and coffee but his nervousness had stopped him feeling hungry and the aroma was actually making him feel quite queasy.

On entering the kitchen, Cathy had bacon, eggs and toast ready for him. She poured out a cup of tea for him and another for herself then sat down opposite him at the table. To be polite he managed a few mouthfuls and had to force himself to swallow but the butterflies in his stomach left little room or inclination for food.

"Charlie's already gone to work," she said, "he left quite early as there was some problem he needed to sort out at the Estate Management Office before going to help sort the post. He told me to tell you that he was sorry not to see you this morning but hopes you have a good day at school and said he'd see you tonight," she added. Under the table, attracted by the smell of bacon, the cats rubbed around his legs hoping for any titbits that might fall their way.

"Jenny's calling for me soon Cathy, is it going to matter that I don't have the uniform?"

"Bless you, no, Alan," Cathy said as she began to clear away the breakfast plates from the table, "Alan, that's Mr Davies of course, said you didn't need it as you'd only be here for short while. If you were staying it would be different, but you look very smart. You'll be fine as you are."

Frida jumped onto his lap and snuggled down covered by the table-cloth. "She's really taken to you…very unusual, she normally keep her distance."

“Yeah, she slept on my bed last night and it was nice to have her there…it reminded me of Portia.”

Sam helped clear the table and peered out of window every time he went by but tried to appear casual. He wanted to investigate the area around the back gate for any signs of who or what he had seen the previous night. “I’m just going for a walk in the garden,” he told Cathy, who assumed he was just walking off his nerves about starting at a new school, Jonah and what the coming day might bring.

At the bottom of the garden, Sam opened the gate and searched the ground by the wall for clues that would help explain the lights, but he found nothing out of the ordinary, no footprints, no litter, nothing.

Jenny was watching him, with a look of puzzled amusement, from her back door. “Hey, what are doing? It’s almost time for the bus, you ready?”

“Yeah, just coming.” He walked back up the path to meet her.

“What were you doing?” Jenny asked as they went back through the cottage to collect Sam’s bag and jacket, they called out goodbye to Cathy who was upstairs making the beds. Closing the front door they headed up the lane, unaware that Frida had decided to follow them until she sped up and ran alongside them.

“I’ll have to take her back,” Sam said, “we’re too close to the main road.”

“Don’t worry, she’ll stop here,” Jenny told him. “She never goes beyond the end of the lane. She doesn’t need to; she has the fields to hunt in.

Sure enough as they reached the main road, Frida sat down and watched as they ran for the bus stop.

“Anyway,” Jenny continued, “don’t change the subject, what were you doing in the field?”

“Looking for pixies, what else? Come on, race you!” he winked at her as he pushed past.

“Hey that’s not fair!” she complained laughingly but it soon became obvious Jenny was the sprinter as she overtook him and reached the bus stop a few seconds before he did, both of them out of breath. “You’re just a townie slow-coach, Sam Johnson,” she panted. “I’ll give you a head start next time.” Jenny laughed as Sam rubbed his side to ease the ‘stitch’.

Susan Askam was already at the bus stop, her face almost matched the colour of her hair when Jenny introduced her to Sam.

"Who is he? I saw you with him yesterday," she whispered to Jenny, "and he's gorgeous. Just like Chris Hemsworth, you know like Thor in the films." Sam overheard her comment and squirmed with embarrassment.

From the direction of the Green, two boys ran towards them, like Jenny and Susan, they were both in the maroon and grey uniform of St Merriott's. Sam recognised them as being two of the boys he had seen with Jonah the previous day. He was about to mention it to Jenny when she told him the larger one was her cousin, Ben Harvey and the other was his friend Ian Chadwick, so he avoided saying anything, but Jenny had not finished. "Ian always hangs around with Ben and does whatever he tells him. Ben makes the bullets and Ian fires them, if you know what I mean. Sam hoped they would not recognise him; as friends of Jonah's they might make the bus journey difficult for him and for Jenny. As the boys approached Ian nudged Ben and pointed at Sam. Ben slowed, glared at Sam, his walk became a swagger as he headed towards the group and he stopped right in front of Sam. Ian stood behind him; he obviously did not have Ben's bravado.

"I heard you were staying next door to Jenny," Ben remarked in a distinctly unfriendly tone, his face only inches away from Sam's. "How long are you staying?" his tone was threatening.

"Long enough," Sam answered staring back, eyeball to eyeball, not allowing himself to be intimidated.

"Back off Ben!" Jenny intervened. "I don't know what your problem is but Sam's OK and he's not here for long, so pack it in," she demanded, pushing her way between the two boys.

Ben threw Sam a filthy look before stepping back and looking away. Jenny, very aware of the tension, was relieved when the ancient green and brown school bus arrived and she pulled Sam into the seat beside her. They both ignored Ben and Ian's muttering about them from two rows behind, when they could hear it over the rumble of the bus engine.

"It's Jonah isn't it?" Jenny whispered. "You really have rattled him."

Although at times Sam could overhear some of the conversation between Ben and Ian, his ears pricked up on hearing Jonah's name

mentioned a couple of times, he also heard Polly and Megan, the two girls sitting in the row in front of them making comments about Jenny having a new boyfriend. That stopped when Jenny pulled Megan's ponytail sharply.

Looking round the bus, Sam noticed a boy with spiked sandy coloured hair sitting alone in the seat in front of Ben and Ian and knew that he was the third boy in Jonah's little gang as well and was surprised when the boy nodded to him and almost smiled until Ben nudged him in the back. Sam leaned in towards Jenny, "Who's that?"

"That's Jason Harris, he's OK and he'd be even better if he'd stand up to Ben a bit more but his Dad works with my granddad and his brother works on the estate as well so he has to keep in with Jonah," she scowled. "As for Ben, he's a pain and I don't like him much but as he's family, I have to put up with him."

The bus finally rattled to a stop at the school gates and Jenny led the way to the office through giggling groups of girls all asking her about Sam who found himself surrounded at time and found the whole episode very embarrassing.

"You're getting yourself quite a fan club," Jenny giggled as she grabbed his arm and managed to steer him away from the last two girls.

"Yeah, so it seems, but why?" Sam asked.

"Well you're not bad looking and you're quite tall, but most of all you're new, so everyone's interested," she told him finding his discomfort quite appealing, "but cheer up, by the end of the week you'll be old news, everyone will be used to you and the fuss will die down." Sam sincerely hoped she was right.

Inside the school, Sam's nose turned up at the distinctive stale cabbagey smell that mingled with the smell of fresh paint. Jenny told him not to worry about the 'Wet Paint' signs as the re-decorating had been done a week before and the paint would be dry; they just hadn't removed the signs yet. Turning right into a long corridor she pointed out a door with several chairs placed against the wall beside it.

"That's the office. You'll have to wait here to see Mr Davies then he'll bring you up to the classroom or arrange for someone else to." Sam felt a fluttering in his stomach, the butterflies were back. "Don't worry, you'll be fine, it's been arranged that you'll be in my class and I'll ask Mrs Wilkinson if you can sit next to me. I know Cathy's had a word with her..."

"She knows her too?"

"…Yeah, she knows just about everyone and those she doesn't, Charlie knows. Gotta go now but I'll see you soon." Jenny hurried off, but turned to give him an encouraging smile before disappearing around the corner.

Alone and curious about St Meriott's, Sam scanned the notice-boards on the wall. There were the usual football and netball fixture notices and dates of parent's evenings, but he was surprised by how many evening and weekend activities there were. There was even an Aikido club running on Saturday mornings. It's been a long time since I went to Aikido, maybe I should give it another go. An image of Jonah flitted through his head and he made up his mind to sign up thinking classes might come in handy.

He became aware of a clack-clacking sound and turned to see a thin, austere looking woman in a dark pin-striped skirt suit and plain white blouse quickly approaching and staring at him in a very unfriendly manner. Her dark grey-streaked hair was pulled back tightly in a knot at the back of her head giving her eyes a slanted appearance. Narrow, black framed glasses dangled from a cord around her neck and they bounced against her flat chest and she looked so surly that Sam sincerely hoped this was not Mrs Wilkinson. The woman stopped in front of him, put on her glasses and studied him for a few uncomfortable seconds, then spoke in a very brittle voice.

"Sam Johnson, I presume." He nodded. "This is most inconvenient you know, starting school at this stage of the term," she inhaled loudly as she pressed four numbers on the door keypad, "and for just a few weeks. I've never heard of such a thing and I hope you appreciate the trouble you and your family have caused. Come in, come in," she ordered, standing back to let Sam pass by her into the office, "I have a mountain of paperwork to get through today and you've just added to it." She sniffed contemptuously.

Infuriated, but too astonished by her attitude and response to his situation to complain Sam obediently did as he was told and entered the small office. "Well sit down, sit down," she commanded.

Sam looked around the office while she sat down, put on her glasses, opened her desk drawer and pulled out a folder which she opened and silently skimmed though the handwritten notes inside.

Three grey filing cabinets stood side by side against the left wall with a kettle, teapot and several floral china teacups neatly stacked upside down on their saucers on a tray on the middle one. The right wall was covered from floor to ceiling with bookshelves. There were so many books tightly crammed, in the shelves bowed in the middle.

"Now then!" she snapped, studying Sam over her glasses. "I am Miss Earnshaw, the School Secretary and you would be well advised to remember that I expect decorum and discipline from pupils in my school at all times. School rules must be obeyed and, when we have finished completing the necessary documentation, *I* will provide you with all the information you will require during your *short* stay at St Merriott's." She reached into her desk drawer again and pulled out several forms. "Name, date of birth, current address and the name of your guardian while you're are with us." Sam gave her the details. "And precisely how long do you intend to be here?" Miss Earnshaw asked irritably. "It's rather inconvenient going through all this paperwork when you're only here temporarily," she tutted again, not bothering looking at him, "and as if I don't have enough to do!"

Sam had not expected her to fall over herself with sympathy, but her manner was really offensive. "I don't know how long I'll be here and I'm sorry to inconvenience you," he replied frostily sincerely hoping that not all the staff at the school would be like her.

Receiving no response (she reminded him of Mr Gibbins), he tried a different, friendlier, approach. "You see my Dad's been hurt in a car accident in South Africa and Mum's gone to look after him until he's well enough to travel." Miss Earnshaw continued to glare. Sam was finding it increasingly difficult to be pleasant. "So until they're back I'm staying with my Aunt and Uncle. Is my being here a problem?" Sam asked acidly polite.

"No," she sighed impatiently, "I'm sure we can accommodate you under the circumstances, but I…"

Sam never did find out what she was going to say because the door opened and a middle aged man in a brown suit and trilby hat poked his head around the door.

"Good morning, Miss Earnshaw. And, hello, you must be Sam," he beamed, shaking Sam's hand roughly. "I'm Alan Davies, Headmaster. It's good to see you at last and I was so sorry to hear about your father,

nasty business. Still let's hope everything sorts itself out soon and he's home safe and sound. Have you finished with the lad, Miss Earnshaw? Right then, come on then, Sam," and he ushered Sam out of the room without waiting for a reply. Sam grinned with satisfaction at hearing an exasperated "Oooooh!" from Miss Earnshaw.

Mr Davies walked so quickly Sam struggled to keep up with him until he ushered Sam into his office a few doors down from Miss Earnshaw's and invited him to sit down on a small armchair beside a coffee table, then sat down opposite him.

"I must apologise for the smell of paint, it's still lingering even though it was all finished the other week. Magnolia again, the Council always use Magnolia."

Mr Davies opened a folder which, reading upside down, Sam could see had his name on it and while he read through the contents, Sam glanced around the room. The walls were festooned with certificates of past school successes, choir, football, netball, cycling proficiency etc. and the necessary Health and Safety Regulations. Mr Davies's professional certificates were displayed in silver frames on a shelf behind his desk and above them, on the wall were long school photographs in chronological order. The earliest was dated 1957. Somewhere a bell rang loudly and Sam heard feet trampling in the corridors as students rushed to class.

"Right then," Mr Davies began, "this disruption to your schooling could make things a little difficult for you, but we'll do what we can to help and obviously, you're welcome here for as long as you need. I know your guardians very well and they obviously wish for as little disturbance to your schooling as possible, as do we all. At the moment, we're awaiting an email from your school," he looked down again at the folder, "umm, oh yes, here it is,..Redlands, yes that's right," he said looking up at Sam again, "with details of your current curriculum. This will enable us to schedule time for your own work. However, if you're agreeable, we feel that spending time with classmates will help you settle in quicker and help you to socialise and make friends, what do you think?"

Again, without waiting for a response, Mr Davies stood up and walked to the door. The interview was obviously over. "Right, now that's settled, follow me, Sam and I'll take you up to Mrs Wilkinson

who's expecting you. Ready?"

Sam was not at all sure he was ready, but Mr Davies opened the door, ushering him back out into the corridor and leaving him no choice in the matter. They took the stairs to the next floor and stopped at Room Seven. "Of course, you already know Jenny Richards don't you. Nice girl Jenny. She'll help you settle in." Mr Davies opened the door, without knocking. The entire class stood up as they entered. "Good morning, everyone...please sit down again, I just want to have a word with Mrs Wilkinson." Sam searched the room for Jenny and found her in the middle row near the back of the room, she grinned and gave him a little wave.

"Morning Mr Davies," Mrs Wilkinson walked towards the door to meet them. "So this must be Sam," she smiled warmly as she moved forward to shake his hand. "I'm very pleased to meet you and I'm sure we'll have you settled in no time."

"I'll leave you with Mrs Wilkinson then, Sam and I'll see you later," Mr Davies said closing the door behind him. Sam had been too busy looking for Jenny to take much notice of Mrs Wilkinson, but looking at her now, she reminded him of Cathy, just a little taller and perhaps a bit heavier than his Aunt. Her short greying hair curled round her face and, like Miss Earnshaw, she wore spectacles hanging on a chain around her neck. Her beige twin set and brown skirt looked a little aged and, at first Sam thought she was rather plain, but then she smiled and her face lit up radiating a warm cheeriness that made Sam feel at ease and he instinctively liked her. "We've a desk beside Jenny who has volunteered to help you settle in.

Jenny winked at Sam and grinned widely until she was poked hard in the back with a ruler by a dark curly-haired girl sitting behind her. "Hey, he's cute," Sharon Sowerby said in a loud whisper, "Where've you been hiding him?" "Shhhh…they'll hear you!" Jenny replied out of the corner of her mouth.

"Now then Class," Mrs Wilkinson said, "this is Sam, Sam Johnson and he'll be staying with us for a week or two and I would like you all to make him welcome." She gave him an encouraging smile. "Sam's school is sending his work schedule to enable him to keep up, so there'll be times when he'll be studying separately, although he will join in with some subjects. I trust you'll help him settle in."

“I’ll help,” said Susan Askam, blushing.

“Right Sam, if you’d like to take your seat until everyone’s settled and then we’ll talk about what help you’ll need with your own workload. I’m sure introductions will be made as the day goes on.”

Sam walked along the row drawing admiring glances from many of the girls, which clearly irritated a few of the boys judging by their reactions, but Sam ignored it all. He gratefully sat next to Jenny; sitting down he was not so visible.

“How’s it going?” she asked him. “Are you alright?”

“Why wouldn’t he be alright?” An icy, venomous, voice came from behind them. Sam turned to see a pair of malevolent brown eyes glaring at them. Jonah Atkins!

“I’m sure you’ll settle in perfectly well, Johnson, seeing the fuss being made of you. Of course, if you don’t, my friends and I can always give you a proper welcome.” A shiver ran down Sam’s back. The friendly atmosphere of the class was gone. For some reason it had not occurred to him that Jonah would be in the same class.

A short while later Mrs Wilkinson asked Helen Blackwood, the class Representative, to take charge for a short while and beckoned Sam to the front of the class. He felt Jonah’s eyes boring into the back of his head as they left the classroom and followed Mrs Wilkinson to the library where Mrs Tansley, the Librarian, joined them to discuss his schoolwork.

Mrs Tansley was a thin, pale young woman, who Sam guessed was somewhere in her middle thirties. In her ankle length denim skirt, with a long sleeved floral top and lots of beaded necklaces and bracelets that rattled as she moved, she reminded Sam of pictures he had seen of a ‘hippies’ taken in the 1960’s.

Her abundant mousy coloured hair was long and curly and piled high onto the top of her head in a kind of twist kept together with, what looked like, four chopsticks. On greeting Sam and welcoming him to the school, she confirmed they had received the email from Redlands Academy giving the details of his curriculum and she offered to let him use the library for his studies whenever he needed and to look out any books she thought he might find useful and Mrs Wilkinson volunteered to tutor him in work for both schools.

Sam was now much more confident he would not fall behind with

his work for Redlands and the rest of the day passed enjoyably enough, although he watched out for Jonah. Thankfully Jonah appeared to have forgotten about him.

Chapter Nineteen

After the first two weeks, Jeremiah's five guests were wondering if the task he had given was a fruitless one as after several nights working in the caves, they had found nothing. True, they had not spent as much time there as Jeremiah would have liked, but as Mikey said, "What he don't know won't 'urt him."

One night, when Jeremiah paid them an unexpected visit, he almost caught them out; they had decided to stay in the cottage for the night and not waste their time looking for something that, in their opinion, did not exist. Luckily Danny saw the headlights of the car heading down the lane just in time to warn the others and, panicked, they hastily grabbed their bags and tools making it appear they were just about to leave. Thankfully Jeremiah was successfully fooled. But this visit was not a social one as he spent an hour berating them for having failed him, before storming off to his car and disappearing as quickly as he had arrived.

After a few minutes recovering from Jeremiah's rant Mikey persuaded them that they should go to the caves just in case he hadn't left and was expecting to catch them out. Reluctantly they agreed and twenty minutes later they drove off.

The next morning though, there was a completely different atmosphere in their cottage; they had finally found silver and Mikey excitedly tapped out Jeremiah's telephone number on his mobile phone while his four associates sat around the table, looking smugly pleased with themselves. After a few moments Jeremiah answered.

"Mr Atkins," Mikey said cheerfully pointing his thumb upwards at the others, a rare smile lighting his face, "We've done it, Mr Atkins.

We've found silver ore." He stopped to listen for a moment. "Oh, no Mr Atkins, we've done alright, honest, yeah."

Jake got up from the table and began hovering around Mikey began firing questions at him. "What's he sayin', Mikey? Is he pleased?"

"Shhhhhh," Mikey rolled his eyes and frowned. "No sorry, not you Mr. Atkins, it's just Jake's sayin' something. How many? We've got eighteen full bags, Mr Atkins, it's great." He waited for the reply again. "Oh, yeah, of course we're going' back again tonight." He made a rude gesture at the phone which Jeremiah, obviously, could not see.

Danny groaned and rested his head on his forearms on the table, Jake walked to the window shaking his head, while Chips and Henry just stared at each other in disbelief; after the success the previous night didn't they deserve a rest?

"Right OK, Mr Atkins. Yeah, yeah, don't worry I'll tell them. Yeah, bye Mr Atkins."

"Don't tell me we can't 'ave a night off," Jake grumbled.

Mikey shrugged, "The good news is, he said well done and the bad news is, we're to go back tonight."

"Well I reckon we should 'ave a night off," Jake repeated. His face was grey with exhaustion and he had deep black rings under his eyes. Mikey looked at the other three weary, disappointed faces, all of them were showing varying degrees of exhaustion. Only Danny, appeared to be unaffected; he was just fed up.

"Yeah well, Mr Atkins's going up to Birmingham tonight for a meeting early tomorrow, which means…" he waited to see if anyone was following his thoughts, but they just looked at each other, blankly, "…which means...anyone thinking what I'm thinking? I don't believe this, 'asn't any of you got any grey matter up there?" He tapped his forehead. "If Mr Atkins is in Birmingham tonight 'e's not likely to come bothering us, is 'e? So we can 'ave the night off anyway."

The transformation was immediate. With sighs of relief and smiles, the older three men appeared revitalised. Danny just sat back in his chair and grinned widely.

"Hey Jake," Mikey threw him the car keys and a wallet. "Take Danny and go and get us some beers and crisps and stuff, you know what to get. I think we've earned a rest no matter what Mr Atkins says."

Chapter Twenty

Sam found settling into village and school life much easier than he had expected and within a couple of weeks he was really enjoying his new and temporary life. Jane telephoned every two or three days reporting on his father's progress which had been so good Sam had been able to talk to him for a few minutes the last time she called. And the fact that Jonah had left him alone was a bonus.

In his free time Charlie and Cathy showed him around the area, taking him to Wells, where he saw the Astronomical Clock inside the cathedral, with models of knights jousting every fifteen minutes, they took him to the Bishops Palace where he saw the swans on the moat that rang the gatehouse bell when they wanted feeding and they went to the caves at Wookey Hole and Cheddar Gorge. One bright clear day, when the weather allowed, Charlie took Sam up Glastonbury Tor; the climb to the top was a long one and where Sam had thought he was fairly fit, he soon found that he wasn't and by the time they reached the top he was very out of breath and his heart was beating fast; Charlie, on the other hand, continued breathing at his normal rate and appeared untroubled by the climb. It was so cold and windy though that they only stayed for a few minutes but, during that time, Sam felt as though he could see the entire county from the top. The walk back down was much easier than the ascent but it made Sam determined to do something about getting fit again.

Cathy taught him how to use watercolours and gave him lessons in making pottery using the potters' wheel. To begin with he made a terrible mess but after a week or so there was a marked improvement, and even though he knew it would be a while before he made anything vaguely resembling a pot, at least he could keep the clay on the wheel. Cathy enjoyed his company and found his attempts at potting hilarious.

Charlie told him local stories and legends nearly every night including the rumours of tunnels running from Glastonbury Abbey to the Tor where, it was said, there were hidden chambers. "They say the monks used the tunnels as escape routes when the Voikings raided. The monks'd grab precious relics, crosses, gold cups, that sort o' thing and disappear down the tunnels before them Voikings knew what was goin' on."

Sam couldn't quite believe the monks knew enough about engineering at that time to have safely constructed such long tunnels, but they were good stories and Charlie had a wealth of them. He was now thoroughly enjoying his stay and most evenings he joined Charlie when he walked the dogs and they talked about all sorts of things as they walked through fields or woods, no matter what the weather. Often during these occasions the unpleasant subject of Jonah cropped up.

"No child is born bad, Sam, remember that," Charlie remarked on one of their evening walks. "It's their circumstances change 'em. I know it's hard feeling any sympathy for Jonah with all his nastiness, but deep down he's hurting, you remember that."

As Christmas drew nearer, Charlie and Sam became very close. Sam had no memory of any of his grand-parents and, as his father was an only child, having family in Cathy and Charlie made him feel part of something special. He spent as much time with Charlie as he could, but one day it occurred to Sam they always ended up talking about him as Charlie never mentioned anything about his past or about having any other family which made Sam wonder but somehow he never found the right time to ask.

In general, life was pretty good but just three things still played on his mind. The first was Jonah, of course. The second was that, after walking the dogs at night, Charlie regularly went out alone late at night and would usually be away for a good hour or so which Sam thought was a bit weird; Cathy never mentioned it either and Sam wondered just what Charlie was up to. His third worry was that the doctors looking after his father could still not say when he would be fit to travel and it was beginning to look as though he would spend Christmas in the village after all. Thankfully Mrs Wilkinson kept him busy with both sets of school work and, at Jenny's suggestion, she had roped him to understudy two of the lead characters in 'A Christmas Carol' by

Charles Dickens. He was given the 'Scrooge' and 'Bob Cratchit' parts to learn.

Unfortunately, Jonah had the part of 'Scrooge' which could have been a problem but, so far, all the rehearsals had gone smoothly even though Sam had the impression that Jonah was just biding his time.

On the upside, Jenny was playing 'Mrs Cratchit' and had the job of Assistant Stage Manager and their friendship grew stronger while she helped him learn his lines. Also, thankfully, although he was busy keeping up with work from Redlands, it had proved easier than he expected with the help of Mrs Wilkinson and Mrs Tansley who both gave him all the support he could ask for.

Luckily, Sam had made some good friends and when Jonah was not around he was fairly relaxed but he sensed trouble was just around the corner and a showdown was probably inevitable so he joined the Aikido class to refresh his skills. His main worry was that Jonah would ambush him when he was alone, so he kept his wits about him and avoided places where it could happen. When the time came he wanted to make sure the odds were on his side.

About a week before the play, the entire cast were rehearsing during their lunch-break and everyone was there, except Jonah. Mrs Wilkinson was annoyed; she knew he was in the school somewhere.

"Jonah did know there was a rehearsal today?" she asked the assembled group.

"I'm sure he did, Mrs Wilkinson, it was arranged at the last one," Susan called from the wings where she checking the lighting panel, "and he was there then."

"Well, we'll carry on without him for now." Mrs Wilkinson was angry. "Sam can you read his lines please?" Without Jonah, the rehearsal went really well, no bad atmosphere, no tension, and Mrs Wilkinson was delighted. "If you perform that well on the night, you'll all deserve Oscars, but the best I can do will be hot chocolate and doughnuts." The session ended fifteen minutes before afternoon lessons and, as they left the hall, Jenny began rummaging around in her bag.

"Oh, no! I've left my copy of 'As you like It' in my locker. I'll have to go and get it. You go on to class and I'll catch you up," she told Sam.

Some of the class were waiting outside the room when Sam arrived and, before long, everyone was there except Jonah, Ben, Ian and Jason...and Jenny. Sam glanced at his watch. It should only have taken a few minutes for her to get to the locker room and back. A hideous, sinking feeling in the pit of his stomach told him something was very wrong. He had to find Jenny!

"Hey! Sam, where're you going?" Brian shouted after him. "Miss Shaw'll be here in a minute." But Sam had already turned the corner and was running down the corridor ignoring the puzzled stares.

At the girl's locker room, he was unsure whether he should go in, it was the girl's room after all, and he hesitated before opening the door but he had to check.

He opened the door and was about to call Jenny's name when he heard male voices but he was too far away and the rows of lockers muffled the sound making it difficult for him the hear anything clearly. The voices grew louder as he approached. He was sure one of them was Jonah. Standing on a bench by the row nearest the voices, he tried to see over the top but, with two rows standing back to back he could still see nothing. Then a stifled squeal sent a chill through him. Jenny! Steeling himself not to act rashly, he edged his way behind the lockers until he reached the end of the row. What he saw made him feel sick. How could Jonah be so cruel, so brutally vicious?

Jenny was seated, pinned against the back of one of the benches while Ben, her own cousin, was behind her holding her arms very tightly. Her legs were tied at the ankles to the bench with school scarves, while Ian Chadwick covered her mouth with another to stop her calling for help and Jason Harris was gripping her left hand tightly stopping her from pulling away. Angry, terrified tears brimmed from Jenny's brown eyes and slid down her cheeks like raindrops on a window pane. She struggled, tried to kick out but the scarves around her ankles were tied too tightly. She wriggled, attempting to pull her hand away from Jason but he would not release his grasp. As he drew closer Sam saw blood on the fingertips of her left hand that oozed out from under her fingernails. Fury replaced nausea as he realised what was happening. Jonah was holding something thin and metallic in his hand and he watched in horror as Jonah lifted Jenny's right hand and stared at her fingers. Bile rose in Sam's throat again as he now fully understood Jonah's spiteful intentions. He swallowed hard. Stay calm,

he told himself, stay in control, there are four of them and one of you; one mistake and you'll blow it but he knew he had to get Jenny out of there before Jonah hurt her any more.

"You heard Jenny Richards ask me to go out with her, didn't you?" Ben nodded. Jonah sniggered. "You see, Jenny, Ben heard it." He looked up at Ben. "And then she let me down," he looked back at Jenny, "and started hanging out with someone else."

Jenny squirmed again. "Now, be a good girl," Jonah mocked. "I have my reputation to think of and my girlfriend shouldn't be going around with anyone else so…so…who agrees with me that she needs punishing?" Jonah's eyes narrowed as he lifted Jenny's fingers higher. "Don't you think she needs another lesson, fellas?" No-one spoke. The look that passed between Jason and Ian showed their unease. Sam thought Jason especially appeared distressed.

Jenny struggled wildly, her eyes widening with terror as the needle moved closer.

"Giving lessons on how to treat girls are we, Jonah?" Sam appeared from between two rows of lockers, a metre or so away from the bench and almost laughed as Jonah jumped with shock, but there was no humour in this situation. "You really know how to win over the girls. Nice line in chat up," he smiled coldly. It's quite a technique you have there. Remind me not to use it!"

With their focus shifting to Sam, Jenny found her opportunity, wrenched her hand away from Jason, pulled the scarf away from her face and swung round to bite Ian in one swift movement.

"Yeeoow! She bit me," Ian shrieked, shaking his wounded hand where red teeth-marks appeared at the side of his thumb. Jenny had bitten hard and blood had been drawn.

"And I'll do it again much harder if you ever come anywhere near me again, Ian Chadwick, or you Jason Harris and especially you, Jonah Atkins," Jenny yelled tearfully, untying her legs. She tried to stand but her trembling legs would not support her and she sat down again for a moment to gather her strength. "And…and as for you, Ben Harvey, you just wait till Uncle Bill hears about this. I know you're more scared of him than you are of *him!*" She nodded towards Jonah. "I hope you're proud of yourself!"

Sam moved in front of Jenny, his face just inches away from Jonah's, the air between them crackled with menace. Jonah smiled, the

metal brace across his teeth glinting in the winter sun that streamed through the windows.

"So you're here to play the hero are you, Johnson? Well not this time! Jenny Richards is my girlfriend. She was before you arrived and will be after you've gone away again. So stop interfering and go away," Jonah sneered.

"In your dreams, Atkins!" Jenny swayed as she got to her feet, but rage and pain gave her strength. Enraged, she slapped him with such force he reeled backwards onto the bench behind. White finger-marks appeared on his cheek which slowly turned red as Jenny stood over him. "I never agreed to go out with you, no matter how many times you asked me or how many times you told others I was your girlfriend! It never happened. It's all in your own head! You may think you own the village, or your father does, but you don't own me and you never will!" she said furiously, anger helping her to forget the pain in her hand. Sam moved to stand beside her, gently lifted her injured hand and checked her wounded fingers where continued to blood seep out from under the nails.

"What makes you do things like this?" he asked Jonah who had pulled himself up to a sitting position on the bench, his cheek a flaming crimson, with four distinct white lines.

"What's wrong with you?" Sam said with controlled anger. "I really do think you must be mad." Putting his hand through Jenny's arm he led her away. "Come on, let's get this seen to."

Jonah remained silent but his gaze flickered alternately from Sam to Jenny then, for the first time since Sam appeared, he looked at his companions. Someone was missing! Jason had gone, and neither Ian nor Ben would meet his eyes. Was it shame or he saw in their faces? Jonah knew if he did not do something quickly, he would lose them as well and he had to show he was still on control. Jenny and Sam had reached the end of the bench and were heading for the door when Jonah lunged at the back of Sam's head. Jenny cried out but Sam had caught the movement at the corner of his eye, and dodged to one side as Jonah sailed by him slamming into the wall.

Jonah howled with rage and humiliation. Sam had made him look stupid. With his right hand bunched up in a fist, Jonah swung at Sam's face but Sam simply side-stepped to the left, leaving Jonah still moving forward carried along by his own impetus. Sam grabbed Jonah's right

wrist, pulling it back with his own right hand, and pushed hard against Jonah's elbow with his left, taking full control of Jonah's arm he moved his right leg out of the way and there was nothing to stop Jonah from falling. Down he crashed onto the hard tiled floor. Sam and Jenny left the room without looking back, and Jonah glanced up just in time to see Ian and Ben shaking their heads as they followed Jenny and Sam out of the door, leaving Jonah alone and bewildered. He had lost everything, including his pride. Sam Johnson caused all this, he thought, as hot tears welled in his eyes.

He was still sitting on the floor when the afternoon bell rang in the corridor outside. Picking himself up, he brushed the dust off his trousers and headed towards the door. "I'll make him sorry he ever started this," Jonah muttered to himself, "and I'll get those three. How dare they walk out on me! Cowards, that's what they are! Turn their backs on me! I don't think so! They'll be sorry too when their Dads get fired." He checked in the wall mirror for signs of swelling or redness where Jenny had slapped him and, satisfied he had just enough of a mark to play for sympathy, he headed for the door.

"I'm going to get that fat oaf of an Uncle of yours fired, Johnson. Are you listening? I can do that. *My Dad will do whatever I want him to do!*" Jonah yelled at the empty room. "I came in here with three friends," he said to himself, "and I'm going out of here on my own, but I'll show them. I don't need anyone!" Head held high he walked out into the corridor.

Chapter Twenty One

"We're going to see Mr Davies," Sam told Jenny as they left the cloakroom; he was very concerned about her hand and the pain she was in.

"No! No, we're not!" Jenny argued, holding back tears. "I'll put plasters on my fingers and if anyone asks I'll say I caught them in a door. I don't want anything said. Promise me! It's only English and we're reading passages today so it's not like I've got to write or anything but I need you to do something for me. Miss Shaw keeps a First Aid kit in the desk behind the curtains on the stage. Can you get some for me? I'll soak my fingers in salt water later, but now we've got to go on like nothing's happened."

"But why?" Sam retorted angrily. "Why cover up for him? It doesn't make sense." He was angry and could not believe she was letting Jonah get away with what he had done.

"Sam, look," Jenny pleaded, "I want to get him back for this but I've got to think about my family who work on the estate and I know I told Ben I'd tell Uncle Bill, but I won't. I just wanted to frighten him. If your relatives depended on the Atkins family for their home and jobs you'd understand. Please?" Jenny was frantic and he knew he would stay quiet, for the time being anyway.

Sam went to the hall, found the drawer and helped himself to four plasters. As the afternoon wore on Jenny winced a couple of time but tried not to show it; her courage impressed him. Her fingers must have been very painful but she gave no sign of it. Jonah eventually joined the class, excusing his lateness on losing his watch, but he stayed well in the background. Some of their classmates wondered if he was feeling

ill as he was unusually quiet. Ben and Ian were nowhere to be seen and Jason, claiming he had a headache, hid in the medical room for the afternoon.

Occasionally Sam caught Jonah's eye, but for the first time Sam saw uncertainty there and it was Jonah who broke eye-contact. At three-thirty Jenny sighed with relief when the bell rang for the end of the day. Sam was worried she had left it too long before attending to her wounds.

As they headed to the bus stop with Susan Askam, Jenny's wounded hand in her coat pocket, she gave Sam a slight shake of her head; Susan must not know what had happened.

"Got all your Christmas presents yet, Sue?" Sam asked trying to make conversation. Jenny smiled gratefully at him.

"Not quite finished yet. Mum's meeting me outside and we're going to Wells to get the last of the Christmas presents. How you doing? Are your Mum and Dad going to be back in time?" Susan asked.

He shook his head. "It doesn't look like it. Dad's still in hospital and not able to travel yet, so it's not likely."

"Shame," Susan replied, "Still I suppose that means you'll be having Christmas here then. I'll have to get some mistletoe," she said shyly, blushing again. "Oh, there's Mum. Bye." "She's got a bit of a thing for you," Jenny said as they reached the bus stop.

Sam frowned but did not answer.

"Hey, wait up you two Jason Harris ran up to them.

"What d'you want?" Jenny growled. Jason looked down at his feet.

", I'm really sorry...you know for what happened in there...but...but you know what he's like," he spoke quietly, so quietly it was almost a mumble.

"I didn't hear that," Jenny said angrily wanting to humiliate him. "I said I'm really sorry." He looked up and faced her this time. "I should never have let myself get caught up with him but, well you know what he's like. I just didn't think he would go that far." This time he spoke loud enough for some passing pupils to turn and stare. He ignored them.

"Honest, Jen, I didn't realise what he was going to do until it was too late, and I know I should have stopped it but," he stopped to look at

his feet again, "I was scared of him," he ended weakly. "I can't speak for Ben and Ian but they feel bad about it too, they think he's gone too far this time and I don't think they'll hang around with him anymore."

"You never used to be like this Jason and, yeah, I do know what he's like. She sounded more sympathetic than Sam would have expected.

"He said my Dad and brother would lose their jobs if I didn't do what he said. He likes people to think he's got mates, but no-one really likes him and I've had enough. I'm gonna tell me Dad when he gets home."

"No Jase, please don't," Jenny pleaded. Jason looked startled at her reaction and three girls waiting at the bus stop turned at her raised voice. He looked questioningly at Sam.

"Yeah, I know. She's told me not to say anything too."

"Look, if you tell your Dad my folks will hear about it too and it'll just cause more trouble that could backfire on my grand-parents and they could lose their home."

Sam still didn't like it, but he understood her reasoning, and Jason agreed not to say anything to his parents.

"OK Jen, I owe you that but don't go thinking Jonah will forget it." He frowned and turned to Sam. "Y'know, you're alright, so just to warn you, watch your back now you've shown him up, in front of other people. You had him down twice, floored him, without a fight back and he's angry."

"Luckily I remembered an Aikido move."

"Well whatever it was it worked, so watch out. If it's any comfort, I'll keep an eye on him and I think the others will too and I'll speak to some of my mates, but we can't be around all the time and I'd guess Jonah's about as dangerous now as he's ever gonna be as far as you're concerned."

"Thanks Jase," Jenny said gratefully, but she looked worried.

"Yeah, thanks Jason." He shook Jason's hand. "I appreciate it. It's taken a lot for you to face Jenny and perhaps we'd better help each other. I can't imagine you'll get a Christmas card from him this year."

Jason grinned, "Am I bothered?" He grinned. "Yeah, well to be honest I am a bit."

The three of them sat together on the bus home talking now like old friends which was made easier as there was no sign of Jonah. "Where's

Susan?" Jason asked. He'd been looking around at the queue at the bus stop and now Jenny realised why.

"See you tomorrow," Jason said getting off the bus outside the Askam's shop and trying not to be noticed as he peered through the open doorway. Jenny smiled.

"Thank you for not saying anything today," she said to Sam as they walked up the lane towards the cottages. "I just need to keep it from Mum now. Come in with me?"

"Hi Mum, I'm home," Jenny called up the stairs.

"I'll be down in a minute," came the reply.

"How d'you think you can hide that from her?" Sam asked in a whisper. Mrs Richards was on her way down the stairs.

"Don't know yet but I'm going to try."

Instinct told Sarah Richards that something was wrong; they were both far too cheerful after a long day at school. "OK, what's going on? What've you two been up to?"

"Nothing, just talking about homework. You wouldn't believe how much we've got." Jenny turned away from her mother and hid a wink at Sam.

"And just about every s…s…subject," Sam stuttered.

"Well, that's good then," Mrs Richards replied turning away to the sink.

"Good! How can you say it's good? It's nearly Christmas! We should have a break!" Jenny retorted.

Mrs Richards turned to her daughter, a cross expression on her face. "It's good because I know you, young lady and you can't hide anything from me so what's going on?

They looked at each other uncomfortably but Sam, unable to stay silent, blurted out, "Jonah hurt Jenny today!"

"Sam, you promised!" Jenny wailed.

Ignoring her, Sam poured out the story and why Jenny wanted to keep it quiet.

"He hurt her hand badly, Mrs Richards." Sam could see Jenny was upset with him, but her hand needed attention, and he didn't think she would be able to hide the pain much longer.

"Let me see," Mrs Richards said to Jenny, who flinched as her mother tenderly pulled off the plasters.

“Damn that boy!” Mrs Richards exclaimed. Blood was still seeping out from under Jenny’s nails. With eyes full of anger, she filled a bowl with hot water and antiseptic. “Right, put your hand in there and steep your fingers and make sure your nails are completely covered. When Jenny’s hand was under the water, Mrs Richards took a closer look at the damage. A single thick dark line went halfway down into the bed of each nail and the tips were swollen. She shook her head in disbelief.

“What on Earth did he do to you?” What did he use?” her voice rising with anger.

“Did you see this, Sam? Why didn’t you stop him?”

“He’d already done this before I got there,” He explained, hurt by her accusation.

“Mum, it’s not Sam’s fault. If it hadn’t been for Sam it would have been a lot worse ‘cos he stopped Jonah. He saved me so don’t have a go at him. And it was like a darning needle, like the one you use for darning socks,” she finished quietly.

“Ye Gods!” Mrs Richards banged her fist on the kitchen table, her face and paced up and down the room.

“I’m sorry, Sam, I shouldn’t have taken it out on you, but I’m just so angry. First Dad and now this…but he’s gone too far this time!”

“Mum, you should have seen Sam. He was great. He made Jonah squirm with the things he said, and when we were leaving Jonah went for him but Sam was too quick. He never laid a finger on Jonah, but he went down all the same and looked stupid,” Jenny smiled at Sam, “but that’s probably made Jonah worse. Jason helped Jonah but he apologised as we left school.”

“Well I should think he would. Really brave aren’t they? Proper heroes aren’t they, two boys onto one girl.”

“No Mum, there were four of them. Ben and Ian Chadwick were there too.

“What, our Ben?”

Jenny nodded.

“I don’t believe it. It just gets worse! Just wait till your grandfather hears about this. He’ll tell Uncle Bill and he’ll sort young Ben out. What was he thinking of?” She stopped at the sink to check Jenny’s hand and passed her a dry towel. “Right, now dry them off and then I’ll put some antiseptic cream under your nails.”

“Sam, I’m sorry if I shouted at you when I should’ve been thanking you for helping her. It took courage to take on four of them on your own but watch out for Jonah now. We’ll try and sort it out so things don’t get worse and I’ll talk to Jenny’s Dad and Simon about this tonight but you watch yourself. Jonah’s very good at holding grudges and you’ve made him look daft in front of his mates, you’ve made an enemy there.”

“I don’t think they’re mates anymore, Mum,” Jenny interrupted. “Jason said the others had walked away as well. Jonah’s practically a ‘Billy no-mates’ now.”

“Well if that’s the case he won’t be likely to get any help, but he’ll blame Sam for that as well and, if what I hear is right, he won’t face you fair and square. He’ll be a lot craftier now if he’s got no help and he’s only tough when he knows he has back-up, like all bullies,” Mrs Richards stated.

“That’s the second time I’ve been told that, Mrs Richards. Jason said he’d watch my back, so that’s something and he said he thought Ben and Ian would help too, but none of them will be around all the time.” Sam frowned. He wasn’t at all sure how confident he felt about being on his own anymore.

Chapter Twenty Two

It was the seventeenth of December and after the successful dig a few nights before, Mikey and his crew were convinced they were onto a good thing and after taking a night off to celebrate, they knuckled down to digging and drilling again.

Jeremiah, delighted at hearing of their find, had rushed down to Winterne the following day and collected all eighteen bags of silver taking them as he said, to 'put them somewhere safe'. As Mikey and Jake helped Jeremiah load up his car, they exchanged significant looks. They were beginning to wonder whether Mr Atkins could be trusted after all, but neither of them voiced their doubts.

After having had two unrewarding weeks, that one successful night encouraged them to face the cold nights and return to the tunnels with renewed enthusiasm but, since that fortunate find their luck seemed to run out again. For the next couple of mornings they trailed back to the cottage worn out, cold, empty handed and disheartened.

"Let's 'ave another look at that map Jake," Mikey said as he finished his toast. Jake, who had been washing up the breakfast dishes, picked up the map that had been left on the top of the refrigerator and threw it over. Mikey scowled as wet bubbles of washing up liquid slid into his mug of tea. "Cheers Jake! You might as well wash that up as well now, it tastes soapy."

"Whaddya want the map for?" Henry asked without looking up from his crossword. "Four down, a lump of metal, five letters…space, 'n' 'g', space, 't'. Whaddya think that could be, then?" Henry scratched his head with his pen.

"Ingot, you idiot," Mikey snapped. "Dunno why you do crosswords, you've never finished one yet," Mikey sneered.

"Not my fault," Henry protested. "I bet you couldn't finish this one either."

"Already 'ave…I got that paper too," Mikey mocked. "Anyway, Jake come 'ere and let's 'ace another look at that map."

Jake, wiped his hands on the tea towel, leaned over Mikey's shoulder. "Well, what bit are you lookin' at then?"

"I was thinking, if we moved a bit further along 'ere," he traced a line on the map with his finger, "we might 'ave a bit more luck. Whaddya think? With what we've found already maybe we've cleared that area, and there's more to be 'ad somewhere else."

"Why not? We're stuck down 'ere anyway and might as well do somethin' with our time," Jake agreed. "I just 'ope that, if there are tunnels further in they're big enough for us to get through."

Chapter Twenty Three

Later that evening, the senior elves were having a well-earned rest from the hectic Christmas preparations when Jimander, who was resting his feet on a root footstool reading Claptrap's 'Elfland Chronicle', felt the tremor before anyone else. It started with the tips of his ears trembling slightly then, as the vibrations increased in intensity, the points of his ears quivered furiously.

"What under Earth is that?" Jimander roared, getting to his feet, holding both sides of his head with his hands. Jerrill ran in to find Piggybait and Claptrap steadying the older elf as they helped him back into his chair. By this time his ears were pulsating wildly.

And he was not alone. All the elves were suffering with ear vibration in varying degrees. Unfortunately Jimander, who was reputed to have the most sensitive ears of all the Somerset elves, was suffering dreadfully. Elf ears work in a similar way to radar and some elves are more vulnerable than others to the effects of shock waves.

Ellien ran to her father and, as Piggybait, Claptrap and Jerrill waited by his side for the episode to pass, the others crowded around. After a few very worrying moments Jimander's ears stilled.

"Do you realise what that was?" he asked, his ashen face contorted with rage. "I should have paid more attention to the humans in our tunnels and they're not here just to explore." A ripple of panic ran through the company and Ellien looked as if she was going to faint but Halmar moved to her side for support. "But what is it they want?" she asked her father.

“Don’t worry my dear, we’ll get this sorted out. Halmar, take Ellien to Primola and ask her to make her some camomile tea.” Halmar nodded and lead Ellien away.

Jimander turned to Jerrill, “We have to get rid of them before they do any real damage. Jerrill, whatever worries you had before are insignificant compared to the problem we now face.”

He turned to the anxious elves. “We’ve been so busy with Christmas preparations we’ve neglected our security and allowed humans to get too close again.” As Piggybait and Claptrap moved to his side, a worried look passed between them; Jimander appeared drained, his pallor ashen and several wide streaks of white had appeared in his hair; he was ageing before their eyes, when he turned away on them for a moment, Piggybait mouthed to Claptrap, “He’s been weakened.” Claptrap nodded in agreement, just before Jimander headed back towards them.

“This is my fault,” he told them sadly. “It’s no good me expecting anyone else to share the blame. I let my guard slip.”

“You can’t blame yourself,” Piggybait protested. “We’re all responsible for the safety of the clan and…and everything else.”

“Thank you for your support, Piggs old friend, but as leader, this is my responsibility. I have allowed the clan and Christmas to be put at risk and I have to do something about it fast. Alfheim alone knows what would happen to Christmas all over the world if these…these…whoever they are find the transit cave. I can’t bear to think of it.” His brow furrowed into deep worry lines but he took a deep breath, pulled himself straight and said, “Who’s coming with me to see what’s going on?” Piggybait immediately volunteered and, to give Saldor something to do, they asked him to join them.

On arriving near in the area where the intruders were working, Jimander and Piggybait, with Saldor following close behind, edged their way along a narrow tunnel that steadily widened allowing them to look down on the humans as they hacked, drilled and dug at the ground; the elves were appalled by what they saw. Jimander pointed out hammers, drilling equipment and a quantity of well-filled heavy bags stowed by the entrance.

“Can you hear what they are talking about over that racket, Piggy?” Jimander asked.

“No. Not from here I can’t but I’ll get closer. You stay here and make sure Saldor doesn’t follow me. I won’t be long.” They had passed a pot-hole a short way back that he guessed would probably lead to near where the men were working. To keep Saldor entertained while they waited, Jimander played Five Stones with him with pebbles of similar size and shape they found on the on the tunnel floor.

From his vantage point Piggybait saw two men stop digging and sit down. One, short and balding, unclipped a water bottle from his belt and took a swig before he pointed out something on the wall to his taller, dark-haired companion. They were talking and pointing to the wall. Piggybait had heard enough. He turned and scampered back to his companions.

“Silver, that’s what they’re looking for and I heard one say something about, ‘after the last lot. They should be looking harder as there must be some more down here.’ They were discussing possible deposits,” he smiled, “at Saldor who was trying to interest him in a couple of the prettier pebbles he had found. “Oh, yes, and another thing, they’re fed up with being down here most nights.”

Jimander’s eyebrows knitted in a deep frown. “Are they indeed? Then they’ve probably been coming in longer than I thought.” Jimander stroked his chin. “And they want silver.” The corners of his mouth turned upwards and he chuckled. “Thanks Piggy, that explains a lot. Come on, we’d better get back and explain what’s going on to the others.” He turned to go back up the tunnel, but the way was barred by a now sleeping Saldor who could nod off at the drop of a hat. Jimander grinned. “Seems a shame to wake him but it’s time to go.”

He was about to give Saldor a shake when something occurred to him. “My instinct tells me Jeremiah Atkins is behind this. I’ve had dealings with him before and, when he’s after something he won’t let anything get in his way. He’ll get it, one way or another but we have to stop him…and them.” He indicated the men in the tunnel below, “before it’s too late. Just think what would happen if they explored further and discovered the Christmas cave or the ladies, Alfheim forbid! I need to think this out.”

Piggybait had overheard quite a lot of the intruder’s conversation, had not told Jimander everything as he was still trying to make sense of it himself. He thought, but was not certain: he had heard the word *dynamite* and was hoping his usually reliable hearing had let him down

this time. If he had heard correctly, Jimander was right. They had to be stopped and got rid of soon.

"Right, let's go," Jimander urged. "I can think better at home and I have seen more than enough here." He gave Saldor's shoulder a gentle shake.

"Wha's goin' on?" Saldor cried, disturbed from his slumber, promptly tried to nod off again.

"OK Snoredor, time to wake up. We're going home."

On the way back, Jimander and Piggybait discussed strategy while Saldor laboured to keep up, occasionally nodding his head and agreeing as if he understood exactly what they were talking about. On arriving back at the hall, they found most of the clan waiting for them. Jimander settled himself at the dining table as the other elves assembled waiting to know what they had found.

"They've come for silver," he informed the group, "and they are dangerously close to our own tunnels." He took a sip of the reviving wine, then another while his audience waited for him to continue, "and unless we do something about it, they may find more than silver and, of course, there's the amount of damage they will leave behind them and, by the way, I believe Atkins is behind this. It's just like something he would do." A collective rumble of concern broke out in response to his words.

"Quiet please, quiet!" Jimander called above the hubbub of voices. "Piggybait overheard some of their conversation and it seems they have had some success recently, but none for a few days." He regarded the sea of faces, all looking to him to find an answer to the problem. "I think we should give them some more."

"Give them some?" Why? I don't understand," Piggybait thought he had gone mad.

"We have silver, lots of it. In fact, we have so much we can't ever use it all no matter how many centuries we live. It's mostly used for bells and decorating the leather trappings anyway and think of the number of our chests that are full of the stuff hidden away, never looked at, like our gold." He stopped talking as a horrified expression crossed his face. "Oh! Thank the Lords of Alfheim they don't know about the gold! Look, I don't like the idea of giving Atkins anything but if we have to sacrifice some silver to get rid of them, then so be it. If they think they've found silver in one of the tunnels and if, they find

enough to keep him happy, it's just possible they'll give up looking for any more. Piggy heard them say they were sick of being down here." He began pacing again. "We also have one other advantage. We visit them in the night and once they're asleep we whisper into their ears. We tell them the ore is exhausted and they'll wake up believing it. Remember, suggestions placed into human dreams are often taken as reality, and I think we'll have them where we want them. They'll give Atkins the silver we provide them with and, considering how many unsuccessful nights they must have had, they'll be only too pleased to tell him the supply is exhausted and, if the Lords of Alfheim are with us, he'll be convinced," Jimander paused waiting gravely for feedback.

"It could work," Piggybait said thoughtfully, "but what if they're not fooled? What if Atkins isn't fooled?"

"If I know Atkins," Jimander replied, "he'll suspect something's amiss, *but* he doesn't like getting his own hands dirty so it's unlikely he'll rush in here to start digging himself. If they're convincing enough he might be satisfied with what he has and go," Jimander pulled a face. "Let's hope so, eh?"

The surrounding elves stood in silence while Jimander looked around. "Anyone got a better idea? No-one spoke. Jimander urged impatiently. Finally he called all the male elves together and outlined his plan and how it was to be carried out. "We give up a generous portion of our silver and make it look as if the seam peters out into a dead end. I hope you all agree that, to protect everything we hold dear and the caves, being parted from a tiny amount of our wealth is a small price to pay. Do you want to take a vote on it?" The elves all shook their heads: there was no questioning Jimander's wisdom. "And now," he continued, "if you will excuse me, I need to rest and so should you all. Today is going to be busy."

Later, over a light breakfast of mushroom omelette, Claptrap asked Piggybait whether they should ask the Chief what he thought of Jimander's suggestion.

"There's no need for him to be involved if we can deal with it ourselves." Piggybait was itching to do get on. Jimander had said it would be a busy day and they were all still waiting for him to get up. He still hadn't mentioned the dynamite to anyone but he was worried that, if the men were unable to find any silver easily that night, they might well use it. A cold shiver ran down his back as an image of

tunnels collapsing and their home being destroyed flashed before his eyes.

He knew there were only a few hours left until dusk when the men would return. Would that give them enough time for all they needed to do? He was relieved when he saw Ellien head up the stairs to the sleeping quarters and return a few minutes later with Jimander who still looked tired and drawn; his rest did not seem to have refreshed him at all.

"I know, I know, I'm late. I'm sorry," Jimander began. "I really should have woken earlier than this. I don't know why I'm so tired," he yawned. We could do with finding a way to hold these men up to give us a little more time." He sat down at the long table and helped himself to some apple juice and a pear. Piggybait racked his brains trying to think up some delaying tactics. How do you stop the men getting to the cave? Then an idea popped into his head. Jimander, Jerrill and Claptrap were pondering the problem when Piggybait startled them. "I think I may have an idea," he was clearly keen to head off.

"What have you got in mind? Claptrap enquired.

"Wolf."

"Wolf?" repeated Claptrap.

"What can he do?" Claptrap's eyebrows shot up.

"We get Wolf to wait near the entrance tonight and, when they arrive, he can spring out and scare them off. They'll run a mile when they see him and hear that awful growl of his. We know he's just a big pup," Jerrill looked doubtful, "but he can look really vicious when he wants, and he'll be delighted to help out. He's not too keen on humans so he'll enjoy himself and it'll give him a break from guarding the ladies, plus the exercise will do him good." Piggybait searched their faces impatiently. Jimander's face lit up. Encouraged, he went on, "I'll keep an eye on things and make sure he knows when to stop and he'll disappear into the undergrowth and head home. It won't keep them away for long, and from what I hear, they're more scared of Atkins, so they'll come back anyway when the big, scary doggie's gone, but it might just buy us some extra time to lay enough silver around to make it credible. We only have a few hours to make a decision, yes or no."

"I like it," Jimander grinned. "You go and see Wolf now, while I explain the second stage of the plan to the others. Piggy, wait a moment

please, I'd like a word before you go!" He took Piggybait to one side. The others wondered what was going on, their faces full of puzzlement and curiosity as Jimander and Piggybait huddled together. Claptrap and Jerrill tried to eavesdrop.

"…they'll get their own special broadcast," was all they heard Jimander say as Piggybait grinned, nodded and left. Jimander returned to the inquisitive group, but told them nothing of the conversation with Piggybait. "Tomorrow, during the day, while they're sleeping after their hard night's work, we pay our unwelcome guests a visit to plant thoughts into their dreams.

"But that means moving about in the daytime. It'll be light then!" Jerrill went very pale. "Aren't you worried we'll be seen?" Jerrill looked for support from the others but received none.

Jimander frowned. "If you're really scared you can stay here."

"No, no, I'll come too as it is really necessary," Jerrill replied weakly.

"You worry too much my friend," Jimander reassured him. "We'll cloak ourselves, stay close to the hedgerows and be invisible to human eyes and we'll have a lookout just in case," Jimander pulled up a seat. "Now, here's the plan. When they go to bed we each choose one and whisper into their dreams that the silver lode is empty, that they'd over-estimated and have exhausted what was only a very small seam and the 'ancients' used most of it up then we get out. When they awake they'll believe there's nothing left and hopefully, if they're convinced Atkins will believe it too. We could scatter remains of trinkets the ancient ones made thousands of years ago. He knows about them and might see these items as a personal bonus. He's too greedy to share them." When he finished talking, he searched their faces waiting for a response. "It may not be the best solution but it's the only one I've come up with at short notice…so come on…what do you think? Only we've got to move quickly."

Claptrap stood up. "I'll get the silver. Who's coming with me? I need four or five helpers."

Jerrill, who had finally stopped complaining, decided perhaps he should get involved. Rondo and Rondina also volunteered. Jerrill stopped to collect Halmar on the way and Saldor, not really understanding what was going on, trailed along as well. Six is better than five, thought Claptrap.

An hour later, Jimander went into the chamber where the television was kept, allowed no-one inside and was heard talking to himself.

Chapter Twenty Four

The following day, disheartened and tired after another unproductive night, the men were preparing for their next hours in the cave. They had still only had one successful night and might have been more enthusiastic if there had been a good rich deposit to be exploited but, not having found anything that looked remotely promising, felt they were wasting their time and that Jeremiah was wrong.

Mikey was annoyed; the moon was up and the others still weren't ready. He yelled up the stairs.

"Get a move on. We ain't got all night yer know!" Walking into the kitchen he felt a strong impulse to watch the news and switched on the television. It was the local programme:-

"We are interrupting this bulletin to notify local communities of a warning issued by Quarantine Officials in Bristol. Anyone residing in the areas of Farnshall, Winterne and Cairnstow should be especially vigilant after a large wolf-like animal escaped from its holding pen at Bristol Docks earlier today. It was en-route to a private zoo near Winchester..."

"I thought you were..." Jake began as he entered the room. "Listen!" Mikey snapped.

"... and injured a veterinary surgeon during a routine check prior to the transfer to the zoo. The vet is now recovering in hospital and is awaiting results of rabies testing. Police and Quarantine officials have stated that attempts were made to tranquilise the animal, but Police marksmen were unable to get a clear shot on the target.

The animal was last seen heading south east and sightings have been reported in the vicinity of the villages mentioned. Once again, people are warned to be vigilant and, under no circumstances, should anyone approach this animal. Sudden movements or loud noises may also provoke an attack. Please keep all children indoors until the

animal is recaptured. In the meantime, if anyone is bitten or scratched by any strange dogs they should seek medical advice immediately. We repeat, any sightings of this animal should be reported to the authorities. Do not try to capture it. This report is being simultaneously broadcast on all local radio and television stations."

"But that's round 'ere," Jake sounded nervous.

"Shut up!" Mikey said threateningly, turning the television off. "I don't want them 'earing this. It won't take much to spook them, so you stay quiet, y'hear!" They heard footsteps on the stairs.

"Well?" Mikey caught hold of Jake's collar pulling him close, their faces inches apart.

"Yeah, yeah! Mikey. No need ter get rough!" Jake pulled away as the others entered the kitchen.

Chapter Twenty Five

A pale grey dawn was breaking as five exhausted men made their way back to the cars. Tired though they were, they seemed unusually alert, looking in all directions as if they were afraid of something. They carried the results of the night's work in large bags, some attached to their belts, others in their hands. The bags looked heavy and they were having trouble managing them all. They should have been pleased with themselves but something was worrying them.

"I was scared that flippin' dog or whatever it was, would still be out 'ere," Chips said to Henry as he turned to look behind.

"You're always scared of somethin' an' it's probably long gone, leastways I 'ope so." Henry, who had somehow managed to get a nasty bruise on the side of his nose, sounded unconcerned but his gaze kept darting around the immediate vicinity.

"See, I told you we'd find silver," Mikey said loudly. The others straggled along behind him.

"Shhhhh…someone'll hear yer," Jake warned. He was still annoyed Mikey had stopped him from alerting the others about the radio broadcast.

"Who's gonna be around at this time of the morning?" Mikey retorted. "Look," he pointed upwards, "even the bats are still out."

"Yeah, well, I was just sayin'," said Jake looking around. "Anyway, we're lucky to get what we did. I didn't think we was gonna get in there, that flamin' wolf-thing, or whatever it was. It scared me to 'alf to death it did."

"Yeah," Henry heard their conversation, "an' my legs are still scratched from the brambles. 'Ere, look, me trousers are torn. I 'adn't noticed that before."

"Must 'ave bin a good hour we was tryin' to get away from that' animal," Chips said, adjusting the weight of one of the bags to make it more comfortable to carry. "I was all for packin' it in for the night, but the cave was nearer so it made sense to keep going."

"It's a shame for you lot you're all knockin' on a bit, 'cos I was up the nearest tree before it got anywhere near me," Danny grinned. "I was a bit scared when it kept jumping up and growling though, but luckily it saw Henry and chased after him instead," he sniggered. "Ow!"

Henry cuffed him round the ear and the others made several rude remarks. Reaching the cars, they checked the area once more, packed the bags in the boots, and drove back to the cottage gratefully.

After unloading the cars, Mikey plonked himself down onto one of the kitchen chairs, kicked his boots off and left them lying under the kitchen table. "Oh, that's better," he groaned. "Well, it was a good productive night last night, animal or no animal, and I'm ready for a cuppa and some breakfast before we kip an' I want some peace and quiet now, so stop the bellyaching…all of yer. It's over and done with." He looked over at Henry. "They're bound to 'ave caught that reject from a dog's home by tonight. Funny 'ow it just walked off like that, wasn't it? It was almost like someone had called it away, funny that, innit?" He stretched his legs, "'ere Danny, put those bags in the cupboard over there, there's a good lad and then we can get breakfast sorted out."

After they'd eaten, Jake went to lock the door before they went up to bed for the day.

"Hey Mikey," called Jake, "the boss's daughter's snoopin' again.

"You know, yer getting' paranoid in yer old age, Jake. What's she doin' then?" Mikey hid behind the curtains making sure Meredith couldn't see him.

"She's always goin' down this lane, ain't she?" Jake said over his shoulder. "Think she's keepin' an eye on us?"

"Yer daft you are. She ain't watchin' us, she's on 'er way ter the stables. Remember, Mr Atkins told us she runs the business an' she's got 'er own 'orse there. Don't you remember nothin'?"

"Yeh, I suppose yer right, said Jake, "but just bein' 'ere still gives me the creeps. All this countryside…it's not natural really is it? There's too many trees an' 'edges an' birds an' insects and stuff an' I'm not 'appy bein' underground so much, nor are the others, it gives them the creeps too. D'yer know, I could 'ave sworn we was bein' watched last night. I'm sure there's somethin' down there. It gives me goose-bumps it does. I'll be glad when we've finished and gone back to Bristol or better still, London. I know what I'm dealing with in a city."

"Well that's a shame Jake m'boy, 'cos Mr Atkins wants us ter finish this job for 'im and finish it we will. All of us, alright! I don't want any more complaints about somethin' givin' you the creeps. I don't want ter 'ear it alright! An' that goes fer the others as well. As far as I'm concerned, after the silver we found last night we must be onto to a good seam an' we'll stay until Mr Atkins says we can leave."

Jake backed down. "Alright Mikey, we'll stay…but…but you mark my words, there's somethin' down there and it don't want us there! The others know it, an', if er 'onest, so do you."

"Yeah, yeah! I'm worn out with diggin' all night, and I need some sleep. I'm off to bed," Mikey yawned. "I'll get me breakfast when I get up."

As they snored comfortably in their beds, several small figures crept close to the garden hedge, their green and brown outfits blending with the surroundings. Checking there was no-one about, they scuttled across the lawn and with a sideways movement of Jimander's hand, the window lock clicked sideways. Then, as he raised his hand, the window opened sliding silently upwards, giving the elves the run of the house.

"We must be quiet. Now, you all know what to do. Pick one human each and say precisely what we rehearsed into their ears. When they wake later they'll all believe exactly the same thing. There's only one seam of silver which they've used it up and there's no trace of any further deposits."

"I only hope they can persuade Atkins," Claptrap worried, "but I'm not convinced."

"I know, I know, but I can't think of anything else to get rid of them before they bring about a cave-in," Jimander frowned, "not without doing them some real harm."

Chapter Twenty Six

Jake was the first to wake up that afternoon. It was four pm and already dark outside. Scratching his head and yawning sleepily, he went downstairs to the kitchen. He was starving hungry so he headed straight for the fridge having a hankering for a cheese omelette.

"What rotten so and so's finished up all the eggs?" he said irritably. "It'll 'ave ter be a cheese sandwich, I suppose." He looked for the cheese. "That's gone as well! Some selfish swine's been down 'ere while the rest of us 'ave been sleepin' an' 'elped 'imself. You wait till I find out who it is! I'll sort 'im out!" He was angrily clattering about making tea when he saw headlights in the lane, heading towards the cottage.

"Oh 'ell!" He dashed back upstairs, banging loudly on the bedroom doors. "Get up, quick...come on *up*! Mr Atkins is 'ere!"

There was a scramble of voices and scurrying movements in the rooms as Jake ran back downstairs hoping to meet Mr Atkins at the door. He was too late. Jeremiah was already in the kitchen and he looked unhappy.

"Evenin' Mr Atkins," Jake said lightly, "did you 'ave a good journey down?" Jake smiled shakily, trying to make small-talk.

"Where are they?" Jeremiah growled.

"Just sortin' themselves out upstairs and they'll be down in a minute. You'll be pleased ter know we've found the silver, just like you said we would."

Jeremiah's eyes lit up. "Show me!"

Jake opened the cupboard door to reveal the bags of silver stacked inside but his smile slipped when he saw the look of disappointment stamped on the boss's face.

"Well I suppose it's not bad, but I'd hoped to see twice as much. You're not holding out on me are you?" The expression on his face almost scared Jake to death.

"No…no…I assure you, Mr Atkins, none of us would do that. You've already 'ad eighteen bags, so add these to them an' surely that's not bad. Look Mr Atkins, we work for you…I've bin with you fer years…and I…we wouldn't con you. We've worked 'ard to find that lot, Guv'nor and we think that's it," Jake said nervously.

"You think that's what?" Jeremiah stared at him as if daring him to repeat what he had just said.

"It's the end of the seam. There's no more silver, Mr Atkins, and that's the truth," Mikey entered the kitchen behind Jeremiah.

Jeremiah swung on his heels and glared at Mikey. "Is that right? That's it huh? Mikey opened his mouth to speak but closed it again when Jeremiah snapped at him.

"No! Not possible!" He rushed at Mikey, his expression thunderous and threatening.

"I'm not saying you're lying to me, Heaven forbid, but I believe you're," he moved away then spun on his heels, "shall we say, mistaken."

Mikey's face paled. "No. Honest, Mr Atkins! We spent ages looking, just like Jake said. To begin with mostly we found bits of old tools, iron or bronze an' we know there was people living in there thousands of years ago. I been readin' up on the history an' that," he added boastfully. "Then we found bits of jewellery and a few old coins, Roman or something. They should fetch a bob or two. We brought them back for you as well. They're there in the bags. We searched for ages to find another seam of silver, used everythin' but the dynamite, didn't we, Jake?" Jake nodded gravely. "Honest, Mr Atkins," Mikey continued, "we think these people what used ter live in the caves used most of it up and then, what with all the silver minin' around 'ere, it's all gone. Even the minin' stopped ages ago. They gave up, probably 'cos everyone's already 'ad what was there. We just found a scrapin' of what was left."

By this time the other three had come into the kitchen and were following the argument in front of them nervously. They all hoped Jeremiah would take their word for it; the silver ore was at an end.

He sat down at the table, “Get me a coffee someone, not much milk, strong, no sugar.” With his elbows on the table he leaned forward and rested his head on his hands.

“Mr Atkins,” Mikey said as he sat down opposite Jeremiah, “the lads all feel the same. There’s nothin’ left worth ‘avin down there. It’s time to go ‘ome. You’ve already ‘ad one lot and this is the last of it.”

Jeremiah cast a sideways glance at the five weary faces. “Where’s that coffee?” he demanded. “I’ve had a long drive.”

Henry topped the kettle up with water and flipped the switch. It didn’t take long to heat up as it had not long boiled. Jeremiah sat cradling his coffee mug silently contemplating and the longer they waited for him to say something, the more nervous they became. He stared into the cupboard. Just twenty bags. That wasn’t enough, not nearly enough.

“You got jewellery you say?” he asked Mikey.

“Yes sir, Mr Atkins, it’s all there, everythin’ we found, we can melt it down.”

”Melt it down!” he roared. “Don’t be stupid! It’ll make much more on its historical value than scrap,” he looked around at them all, trying to read their faces, “but you all agree there’s no more silver to be had?”

“Yes Mr Atkins,” Mikey spoke up for them all. “Judgin’ by what we’ve seen in there, there’s no more.”

Again, silence while Jeremiah thought. No-one breathed.

“No, *no!* I’m not having it,” he finally declared. Disappointment and disbelief showed on all their faces.

“There’s more silver to be found here and you’re going back. You’ll have to prove to me there’s nothing else worth taking from those hills. You know I’m good for my word and you’ll get your share. The more silver you find the larger your shares will be.” Over his coffee mug, Jeremiah observed the mutinous and miserable looks exchanged between the five men but he had given them no choice. They would do as they were told and go back to the caves. “And this time I’m going with you, but not tonight. I’ve done a day’s work and I’m tired. Mikey, I’ll take your bedroom.” Mikey resentfully agreed. “Tomorrow night I want to see for myself,” Jeremiah went on. “Is the dynamite there already?”

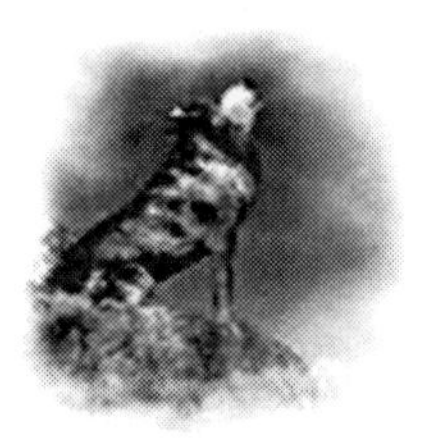

Chapter Twenty Seven

The sun had set and night-time clouds were scudding across the sky when Meredith and Wilmot closed up the stables for the night. She made one last check that all the horses were settled, and they began the walk home. It had been a long day and the temperature had dropped considerably. Meredith shivered in her navy waxed coat and wrapped her scarf tighter around her neck and her woollen hat further down over her ears. Wilmot ran alongside, the chill air not bothering him at all as he sniffed at every scent along the way.

As she approached the cottage where her father's guests were staying, she spotted a third car outside that was not quite concealed behind the hedge. It was her father's Mercedes! Why was he here? There had been no message to say he was coming home and, if he was home, why wasn't he at the manor?

She crept nearer to the cottage, staying close to the hedge. Thinking they were playing a game, Wilmot bounded over to her and she softly ordered him to lie down. Thankfully this time he obeyed but lay there wagging his tail waiting for the game to begin again. With her head low, Meredith edged her way around the side of the cottage towards the back door. The light was on in the kitchen and she could hear voices so she dropped down to peer, unseen, through the window and, keeping her head low could just see over the window sill.

Her father was sitting at the table with his back to her. The five men who she had seen around the cottage were standing nearby. From the position of his head, her father appeared to be staring at a coffee mug in his hand.

She could see the tall cupboard door was open and there was something bulky on the floor. She craned her neck to get a better view and saw a number of beige-coloured cloth bags piled up on the cupboard floor. They looked heavy. What was going on? Had they done a bank job or something? The thought terrified her. Surely her father would never go that far? Was he letting a bunch of criminals use the estate as a hide-out? Was he helping them or, worse still, was he behind it all?

Meredith jumped as a wet nose pushed at her face. Wilmot! "I told you to stay, you stupid dog!" she whispered loudly. Anxious she might have been heard she peeped cautiously over the window sill and breathed again. No-one appeared to have noticed. They were all talking now and looked upset. She tried to catch some of the conversation while attempting to keep Wilmot still. With the door blocking out most of the conversation she learned very little but a chill ran through her when she heard, 'I'm going with you, but not tonight,' and 'dynamite.'

Chapter Twenty Eight

Unable to sleep, Sam threw back the covers, put on his dressing gown, and went to the bedroom window. The night sky was the colour of blue ink. There were very few stars and the moon kept sliding behind thick rain clouds. Or were they snow clouds?

The back door creaked open and light from the kitchen streamed out into the garden. He heard Charlie tell the dogs to stay. He was going out without them again! It was almost eleven o'clock and bitterly cold. Where *was* he going? Sam peered from the curtains as Charlie headed down the garden path, through the gate and disappeared into the night.

Even when the moon crept out of hiding from behind the clouds, it was difficult to see anything clearly beyond the wall but at the creak of the garden gate, Sam made up his mind. This time he would investigate.

He threw his fleece jacket on over his jumper, grabbed his trainers, quietly opened his bedroom door and tiptoed down the stairs avoiding the middle of the eighth and ninth steps down, as they groaned squeaked loudly. Downstairs, in the sitting room, Cathy was nodding off in an armchair by the fire, her tapestry work in her lap and a half-finished cup of cocoa on the coffee table beside her.

She had been decorating the room with green and gold Christmas garlands earlier and the room was now festooned. An enormous tree stood tall in the corner of the room, twinkling lights flickering on and off rhythmically. Benny lay curled up in a huge basket to the left of the fireplace, while Bjorn slept by Cathy's feet. He didn't move his head, but twitched an ear as Sam peered into the room. Benny wagged his tail gently and Bjorn yawned and stretched but, neither of the dogs took any real notice of him. They had already had their evening walk and were happy to be settled in the warmth of the cottage. Cathy slept on.

Sitting down in the kitchen to put his trainers on, Sam hoped Charlie was still near enough to be easy to follow and, carefully lifting the latch, he stepped out into the shadowy night. The cold air almost took his breath away and he pulled up the zip on his fleece. A frost had begun to settle on the trees and hedgerows and the ground crunched loudly beneath his feet so he tiptoed to avoid making too much noise. When he reached a point half-way down the path he heard the Richards' back door open and ducked down. Jenny's father, Joe, came out of their cottage and went into the wood-store for logs, stocking up for the morning, then went back into the cottage, shut the door and turned out the light.

Sam stood up and, out of the corner of his eye caught a flash of light in the trees. He wanted it to be Charlie. At the end of the garden, he opened the gate quickly; it creaked; the noise strident in the silent darkness. He closed it behind him slowly. This time it made no sound.

There it was again; another flash of light. That was the way he needed to go. He realised he was holding his breath.

"Come on, relax." Charlie had told him there was nothing around that would do him any harm and now he needed to believe it. Charlie hadn't thought about Jonah when he said that.

At the edge of the wood he hesitated, nervous about going any further. If he went back he could surround himself in the warmth of his bed; he would have no need to chase puzzling lights and even more puzzling uncles, but then he would have no answers either. Even so, it was very dark and there were strange noises; rustling leaves and animal cries. Should he go on or back? He had to choose. For the first time he wished he had remembered to bring a torch but it was too late to go back for it. Now or never?

Now! He plunged into the shadows. The night breeze rustled the tops of the trees and Sam heard the high pitched bark of a fox somewhere in the distance. He picked up what looked like a path and guessed Charlie had gone the same way. He wished he'd been in the Scouts, then maybe he would know how to track signs of animals or people, but then, he realised, he would still have needed a torch! Cold seeped into him the moment he stepped into the dense woods. Pulling his fleece closer for warmth, he bitterly regretted not bringing his gloves and a scarf or a thicker coat.

A few yards into the woods the trees cleared a little and moonlight broke through. He had been losing his nerve a little, but the moonlight cheered him as it was now easier to see ahead and he felt he was still going the right way. He had no idea where he was going or where he was but it was too late to head back; now he was out there he had to see it through.

There! A flicker of light in the distance. Picking up his pace, partly to keep warm and partly to get closer to the light, he sped along the dark trail. "Ow!" He tripped over a tree root and fell to his knees. An owl, perched in the branch above him, hooted indignantly and flapped its wings in annoyance at being disturbed by his yell. It looked down its beak at him clearly very disgruntled.

"Sorry," Sam called up to the owl as he picked himself up. "Couldn't see where I was going. It's alright for you with your night vision." He felt something cold and wet land on his cheek, then another and another. It was snowing! That's all I need, he grumbled. He brushed the dirt off his knees and palms and winced as he felt a sore place on his right palm; it was scraped and felt warmly wet. Not being able to see much in the dim light, he tentatively touched the area and felt a large flap of loose skin and warm blood.

"Aww. Hell! This night just keeps getting better!" The snow was falling more thickly, in large feathery flakes that covered the previously murky ground with a thin carpet of white and settled on the branches of the trees.

With his good hand Sam felt around in his pockets and found a large unused tissue in his pocket and wrapped it around the wound. The snow fell heavier, faster until it was almost a blizzard; it became difficult to see in any direction; it was in his hair, his eyes stung with cold, and he realised just how much danger he was in. He had heard of people dying of exposure when their body temperature dropped too low and he had no intention of that happening to him. "*I'm not going to die out here in this*." But only the owl heard.

Sam couldn't see more than a metre ahead as the snow continued to fall, faster, heavier. Everything was covered in a deepening blanket of white. Why hadn't he stayed indoors? It was all Charlie's fault. If he had had stayed at home, he wouldn't have been following. Then he cried out in desperation, his shout shattering the silence.

"*Please let the snow stop so I can see where I'm going.*"

Immediately, and as if by magic, the snow lessened to a few defiant flakes and he was able to see clearly ahead. On the ground, the spaces between the trees were now illuminated by the pale, eerie glow of moonlight reflecting on the glistening snow making the path easy to see and he realised that since it had snowed, he actually felt warmer. He wondered why everything had become so very unreal. The owl still eyed him crossly. "It's alright, I'm going. I'll try not to disturb you any more tonight." It stared down its beak at him, blinking alternately and hooting disdainfully, then flapped its wings and flew off, but as Sam had already turned away, he missed seeing a clump of snow dislodge from the branch as the owl launched itself into the air. It landed on the back of his neck and slithered down inside his fleece.

"Yeuk!" he shouted as the cold, wetness slid down his back. "Can this night get any worse?" He thought of Cathy sleeping comfortably by the fireside and envied her the warmth. She would worry if she checked in on him and found him missing, so he convinced himself she would go straight to bed and assume he was tucked up in bed.

Deep in the trees, noises of the night surrounded him making him jump but, where the moonlight shone on the snow, the path was easy to follow but as he had not seen the light for quite a while, he was unsure which way to go.

A rustling in the undergrowth stopped his breath. It grew louder and ferns fronds nearby began a rippling movement as whatever it was approached beneath their foliage. His blood ran cold. A fox broke cover and froze, both of them surprised by the other. The silver moonlight reflected in the fox's eyes as they stared at each other; the fox suspicious and Sam captivated. He guessed it was probably quite young and expected it to turn tail and run, but it stood its ground.

"Well…who are you? It's nice to have company tonight that doesn't have a go at you," he said, thinking of the owl. Backing up little by little to a large fallen tree trunk a few paces back, he sat down. The fox's eyes stayed focused on his, watching for any sudden move and prepared for flight but slowly, very gingerly it took a few steps towards him, backed away, sniffed at the air, then it hesitantly padded towards him again. It stopped just a metre or so away from him and, to his astonishment, it sat down, pricked up its ears and opened its mouth, panting slightly.

“Are you smiling?” Sam sat very still not wanting to scare it away. “Was it you I heard earlier or maybe a cousin or something?” Cautiously, he put out his good hand and leaned tentatively toward the fox wondering if the wary but curious animal would get close enough to let him stroke it. His hand was just about five inches away from its face, it held back, hesitant, although its eyes flickered constantly between his hand and face. Without warning it sprang forward, gently nipped his fingers, almost as a warning that he was too close. Sam was startled but before he had time to think about what had happened the fox vanished into the undergrowth as silently as it had appeared. By the light of the moon he inspected his fingertips. No break in the skin, no harm done, just an overwhelming feeling of exhilaration at the encounter.

What an experience, Sam marvelled. He could have bitten me but he didn’t. Thunderstruck at the privilege of being in such close proximity to a wild animal, he almost missed the flash of light that appeared further down the path until its flickering caught his attention.

Snapped out of his daze, he bolted down the path, now absolutely sure he was going in the right direction, the fox almost completely forgotten. Bright moonlight kept him on the path, but after what seemed like an eternity, he was still trudging along the same path and had lost all sign of the mysterious light. He wondered, miserably, how much further he had to go and how much time had elapsed since he had left the cottage, having lost all sense of time. His right hand throbbed painfully and his left now tingled where the fox had nipped his fingers, his feet ached and he was chilled to the bone. Weary, and now scared, he knew he could not go on much longer. Brooding, dark thoughts crept into his mind. Maybe I could die here. Perhaps no-one would ever find my body. I could be eaten by animals and crows and all they would find in the end would be my bones. *No. Stop thinking like that. I can’t think like that!* He took a deep breath, straightened his back, flung back his shoulders and moved on but made the decision he would only give it a few more minutes before turning back and prayed he could find his way to the cottage.

Large shadows moved between the snow-covered trees and Sam dropped down behind another fallen tree. Goosebumps crawled up his skin and the hair stood up on the back of his neck with yet another terror. Dropping to the ground to hide, he crawled to the nearest tree,

the cold damp seeping into his jeans and socks; he wished he was in a warm shower. Putting all thoughts of comfort out of his head for the moment, he stood up using the tree to hide behind and held his breath as a number of dark shapes moved towards him, the bracken rustled as they loomed nearer. A chill ran down his spine that had nothing to do with the cold air. Two startled pheasants flew out from ahead of the shadowy outlines and his heart missed several beats; his palms were sweating even in the chill night air.

The ghostly shapes waded through the undergrowth towards him; terrified to move Sam's feet were rooted to the spot.

The moon appeared from behind a cloud just as the shapes came into view and he stifled relieved laughter as a small herd of seven deer, one a large stag trudged across the path.

The stag lifted his head, stopped and sniffed the air regularly, clearly cautious and aware something smelled different. He nudged his family along a little quicker, keen to get away from possible danger.

As they moved on, Sam picked up the path again and went back to wondering what Charlie was up to, the deer pushed to the back of his mind as he wondered whether Charlie's nocturnal activities were entirely legal, but dismissed the idea as unlikely. Surely Cathy would not be married to a criminal?

The trees had become less dense in the part of the wood in which he found himself and soon he reached a clearing where the ground rose steeply into a line of small hills. The moon disappeared behind a cloud again and Sam peered into the darkness. He wondered whether it was time to go back, but could not see where he had emerged from the trees. He walked back the way he thought he had come but everything looked so different from how it had a few moments before. He searched but there was no sign of the path. It was as if the trees had closed up after he left the wood. But that was stupid! It was just his imagination playing tricks again. "If I'd had any sense I'd have brought that torch." Again he cursed not thinking things out properly before he left the cottage. A soft movement behind him made his skin crawl. Too terrified to turn round he froze.

"You've been following me."

It was Charlie. Sam turned, relieved.

"Now, what are we going to do with you, young Sam?"

That sounded threatening and Sam wasn't sure if his relief was a little hasty.

"Hi Charlie. What...are you doing out here so late?" He tried to control the tremble in his voice.

"I could ask you the same thing and I believe there's a saying. How does it go, now? Oh yes, I know." Charlie glared at him. He did not speak. Sam shuddered. The strained silence that seemed to last forever was unnerving. Then Charlie spoke, his thundering voice echoed through the still air. "If I told you I'd have to kill you." It was an old jokey saying but Charlie wasn't smiling.

Sam stiffened, rooted to the spot. He felt colder than he had ever known before; icy fingers ran up and down his spine as the hair on the nape of his neck stood to attention.

"It's alright...Ch...Charlie, sorry, I'll go back." Fear almost closed his throat; it was hard to speak. He straightened his legs, his knees forced rigidly back to control the trembles, he took a deep breath. "I haven't seen anything. I don't know anything, honest!" He hoped this was a dream, a nightmare. He would wake up in his own room and his mother would be at home; everything normal.

Charlie frowned and shook his head gravely. "I'm sorry, Sam."

"No Charlie, I promise I won't...," Sam cried out in terror, backing away as the huge man moved towards him. This wasn't happening. Charlie wouldn't hurt him...would he?

Charlie looked down at him sternly. "As I was saying, I'm sorry if I scared you but I told you before there's no harm in these woods for you. You weren't frightened of me were you? Why on earth would you be? No, not my style at all and why would I go to all the trouble of making sure you saw my lantern if I didn't want you to follow me. Took your time though didn't you?"

Charlie gave one of his enormous smiles and put his arm around Sam's shoulders. At once a warm calmness spread through him; he was no longer cold or afraid.

"Seeing as you were inquisitive enough to follow me, I suppose it's time for explanations. You'd better come with me. I trust you and I've got some people I'd like you to meet." Charlie led the way across the clearing and upwards, through the undergrowth of ferns that grew in thick clumps. Sam was curious about where he was going but no longer felt any anxiety. Wherever they were going he trusted Charlie.

"It's time we got you out of the snow and got that hand seen to." Sam did a double-take from his hand to Charlie. How did he know about that? He had said nothing about having hurt his hand.

"Who am I going to meet Charlie?"

"Some very special friends of mine and meeting them should explain a few things. It might be as well to prepare yourself for a bit of a shock though. What you're about to see, the people you're going to meet, will come as a…a…revelation and I'm asking you to give me your oath you will keep this to yourself...it has to be our secret. I'm placing all my trust in you because I think you're worthy of it so please, please don't let me down."

Sam raised his face to look his uncle in the eye. "I promise. I won't tell a soul," he said gravely. Something else struck him. There was something very different about Charlie but he had been too scared at the time for this change to register properly. It now occurred to him that it was the way Charlie was speaking. His accent was different. Charlie's usual broad west-country accent had disappeared and, in its place was what Sam could only describe as faintly Eastern European. Certainly Charlie's way of speaking did not sound like any British accent Sam had ever heard.

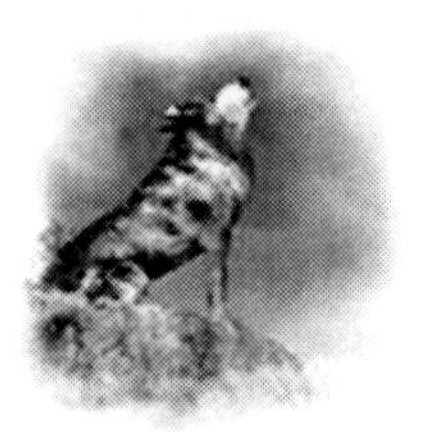

Chapter Twenty Nine

After what to Sam felt like another hour of struggling through dense shrubbery trying not to trip or fall again over raised roots and thick stems, Charlie stopped at a huge rock. He inhaled deeply, reached out his arms and said something Sam didn't understand then reached out and pushed the boulder aside with one hand revealing a small but dark and sinister cave.

Sam could barely believe his eyes. "But…but that rock's colossal. You couldn't move it with…with just one hand but I saw you do it. You did…with one hand. How?" Charlie smiled and tapped the side of his nose.

"All that breathing and posturing was just for show. Anyone can move that rock and many others around here. I'll explain sometime but that was probably the least surprising thing you'll have to take in tonight. You're about to see some things that'll make you question everything you've ever known, but I want you to accept what you see just as it is." He laughed, crinkling his eyes, his beard parting to show large perfectly white teeth. "Come on, follow me."

"We're not actually going in there are…we?"

"Oh, yes, my boy. There's something fascinating in there."

Sam doubted it. It was far too small for someone the size of Charlie to get into; even he would have to duck to go inside.

Charlie grinned again. "You know, people have been conditioned over the last century, yes, that's the right word, conditioned, to believe the world can't possibly hold things we cannot explain with logic. Very few people believe in natural magic, elves or fairies and if they do they're regarded as strange, fools, madmen or, if we are being kind,

eccentric. You're about to enter a very different world to the one you know and," Sam was about to interrupt but stopped as Charlie held up his hand, "I, and some special friends of mine, will answer all your questions as we go along. Stay close...and don't worry about the space in there," Charlie chuckled, "there'll be room for us both. Have faith, my lad."

Charlie approached the low cavern and Sam stared in wonderment as the entrance stretched increasing in height and width until Charlie could enter without stooping. Open-mouthed Sam followed, stunned by the puzzling and mysterious place in which he now found himself. He wondered if he was going mad or hallucinating.

"It's real enough. You're definitely here, you're not dreaming," Charlie assured him. "If you think this is strange, just you wait."

"But the tunnel's expanding and closing up again behind us. I...I don't get it."

"You will, my boy...you will." Charlie boomed, his voice echoing around them.

They had gone a short way inside when Charlie stopped to pick up a lantern. He opened the glass door and gently blew into it creating a bright yellow flame that flickered and grew, illuminating their way ahead and forming their shadows on the walls, Charlie's obviously much larger than Sam's.

Ahead of them the tunnel walls were strengthened by tree roots and instead of being straight, there was a bend and another tunnel that led to the right. There was a smell of damp earth mingled with a faint odour of vegetation that, strangely, Sam soon found quite pleasant but soon he thought he could smell bread baking. He shook his head. It was hardly likely but it did seem to be getting stronger.

"Not far now." After turning two more corners a faint light glowed in the distance. There was a sound of talking, laughter. Who could possibly live down here? Sam was even more confused.

Charlie stopped and laid a hand on Sam's shoulder. "Right, we're here. Remember what I said about natural and ancient magic. I hope you're prepared for a surprise." They emerged from the tunnel into a huge cavern full of small people, light, music and a huge table full of food. Sam blinked then blinked again. This was not a dream.

"What under Earth?" Claptrap grumbled. As the humans emerged from the tunnel into the great hall, he scuttled away into one of the

small chambers where he could observe the newcomers without being seen. There was something about the smaller human that seemed familiar. The others turned to see what the commotion was about and stared.

"No, I'm not awake…I can't be," Sam closed his eyes. When I open my eyes again I'll be in bed, he thought. He opened his eyes. He was not in bed. He looked up at Charlie, his eyes full of questions. "OK Charlie, just who are these…people?"

But Charlie was already surrounded by a throng of tiny people who parted to let someone approach. He too was laughing.

"Not again, Klaus," he chuckled, "surely not again!" Jimander took hold of the big man's hand and shook it vigorously. The tense atmosphere in the chamber vanished. "So this is the young man you told me about," Jimander stared at Sam as if trying to read him.

"Yes, this is he," Charlie replied, his face glowed with warm pride.

Sam stared opened-mouthed into the vast room in front of him, his eyes popping out of his head. A number of these small people dressed in various shades of brown and green had gathered around him. They seemed as surprised to see him as he was to see them.

"It's OK everyone, settle down. This is Sam, my nephew. He followed me here tonight and I thought you might like to meet him," Charlie spoke quietly, "but I'd give him a few moments to get used to this. I think he's a little… bewildered."

Their arrival had interrupted the evening meal which was just about to be served. Four elves, two females and two males were carrying a large tray between them, containing what looked like an enormous omelette, a delicious cheesy, herby smell drifted Sam's way.

It was then Sam noticed a silver-haired elf, wearing a monocle and a maroon coloured jacket, slip out of a side chamber and mingle with the group. On seeing Sam, he stared at him for a moment before sidling up to another of the elves standing at the back of the crowd. They turned away and whispered furtively, casting anxious looks back at him. The second elf glowered at him for a moment, shaking his head vigorously at the first who was whispering in a very agitated fashion. Charlie appeared not to have seen their animated discussion.

"I'm guessing one or two of my friends have 'found' some extra goodies for their dinner this evening," Charlie whispered, indicating the omelette which was now being cut into portions.

"I heard that, Klaus," Jimander looked sheepish. "We found the eggs and cheese...honest we did. They were just lying around in a refrigerator we came across. No-one was using them...at the time, so we thought we'd find a good home for them." Jimander's face was a picture of innocence.

Charlie smiled and sat down on a wooden seat which was much larger than the others. Sam guessed it had been made especially for him. But...who was he? Clearly not just his uncle or Cathy's husband! *He was someone else as well.* He thought he knew his uncle but now he understood, he knew nothing about him at all.

The vast hall with its bright decorations reminded him of fairy grottos and Toyland pictures he had seen in children's books about Father Christmas. His mind raced. A painful tingle in his hand suddenly reminded him of his injury but when he looked at his palm there was no sign of the wound. His hand was no longer bleeding, there was no longer a flap of bloody skin; it looked exactly as it should and the pain had stopped. Now I know I'm going mad!

Charlie's voice broke into his thoughts. He was still talking to the one he had called Jimander.

"Yes, he's a good lad and he has courage. Look how he followed me through the wood tonight. There's very few that would take a chance like that in these woods, as you know." Charlie said pointedly. Jimander nodded. "I've learned a lot about him and I'm very proud of him. You'll like him too when you get to know him." Sam listened to Charlie's introduction, how highly he thought of him.

The other elves chattered amongst themselves, still gawping curiously.

"Sam, I've introduced you but I owe you an explanation. These people are my oldest friends. They are of the ancient folk of the woodlands. To be precise, they are Elves."

Sam's mouth dropped open. He didn't believe in fairy tales but here they were; exactly as they were shown in story books. "Charlie, I think it's time we had a talk."

"Yes, you're quite right but before that there are a few things I want you to see. Claptrap, Jimander, Piggybait will you accompany us?" Surprisingly the two elves who had been talking about him joined them at the tunnel mouth. The one in the maroon jacket shot him a withering look but the other one seemed more relaxed.

As they passed one of the smaller chambers leading off from the main cavern, Sam spotted an old television, working perfectly well, showing that evening's episode of EastEnders, but with no aerial and no electricity to power it. He blinked and shook his head in disbelief. After everything else he had seen he wondered if he could ever be surprised again.

"*That's* none of your business," the unfriendly elf hissed. Sam hurried to catch up with Charlie and Jimander. He stayed close as they collected crystal lanterns from a ledge behind the fireplace. Bright yellow flames lit up the dark passageway.

"Could we talk, please sir," Claptrap had caught up with Charlie. He was clearly unhappy.

Charlie halted and looked down at his small friend. "Claptrap, have I ever done anything to cause you or the clan any harm?"

"No, sir."

"No. I haven't and I've no intention of doing so now. I'm aware of your concerns about humans crossing the boundary into our world, particularly with regard to Sam, of whom you are still somewhat suspicious but please don't worry."

"But…but he…"

"I'm aware he watched you from the window, but that was over a few nights and he said nothing to anyone, I know because he never even mentioned it to me, you have my word on that. Sam has also assured me he'll keep everything he sees tonight to himself. And…let me finish…you will recall I said there'd be changes coming and he's one of them but, he isn't going to be a change for the worse. Give him a chance Claptrap, have faith. Jimander is content no harm will come of this and if he believes, then please trust me, just as you have always done."

Sam watched Claptrap's shoulders lower, but he still gave Sam an unfriendly, sideways glance before turning back to Charlie. "It shall be as you say, sir. Just as you say."

Klaus? thought Sam, recalling Jimander's greeting. Did I hear

right? Klaus? But he's Charlie, not Klaus!

"Charlie, did I hear that…Jimander, is it, call you Klaus?"

Charlie sighed then smiled.

"Um, yes. That's another thing we need to discuss, but…um…all in good time. First, just around this corner I think you may find the answer to some of your questions." Charlie smiled encouragingly. "Oh yes, I forgot to tell you, you have Jimander to thank for healing your hand."

Sam mouth gaped open, "But how…how did he..?"

"All in good time. All in good time."

Around the next bend Sam found himself on a wide ledge halfway up a vast cavern. Looking up he guessed the roof was at least twelve metres high and it glowed in the light of a hundred of flaming torches. Then he saw conveyor belts and scores of elves scurrying around, small quad bikes that raced in from one entrance while others rushed out the other side hauling loaded trailers. He stared at the scene below utterly bewildered. One elf, his hat pulled down over his ears, waved up at them. Charlie and Jimander waved back.

"Hello Corporal," called Piggybait.

"Corporal?" repeated Sam. "Why's he called Corporal?"

"Sad case that one," Piggybait replied, "he's mad about the army so we nicknamed him Corporal."

"You've got an army?"

"Of course, haven't you?" Piggybait stopped, frowned and scratched his head. "You know after all this time, I can't remember Corp's given name." He shook his head, "No…completely gone. Isn't that funny? I've known him almost all his life…but anyway, back to my story. Corporal always wanted to go into the Elfantry but he failed the medical."

"Why, flat feet?" Sam thought he was joking.

"No! And it's not funny you know," Piggybait replied indignantly. "Flat ears!" a smile curled the corners of his mouth.

Sam laughed again. If this was a dream he might as well enjoy it. "Flat ears! You're joking, right."

"No, not at all. You see our ears work like radar, they're very sensitive and we pick up all sorts of sound waves and messages through the tips. Sadly, Corporal was born with the tops of his ears completely flat, both of them. They don't work properly so he can't be an Elf soldier. It's very sad really," Piggybait explained, "because his ears are almost as flat as yours.

Sam reached to feel the top of his own ears. "They're not flat, they're…sort of…rounded."

"Compared to ours they're flat..."

Their conversation was interrupted by loud chuckles. Sam turned to find Charlie and Jimander had been listening and had found the whole thing very funny.

"Oh, I get it. He's been winding me up hasn't he?" Sam saw the funny side himself.

"No," replied Jimander, he was no longer laughing. "Look over there." He pointed to an elf, dressed in a black leather jerkin and trousers and a green shirt, who was loading one of the trailers. "He has a similar but less noticeable condition and he manages very well but with Corporal's, it's actually a disability." He led Sam back to where the others were waiting.

Piggybait continued speaking as if Jimander had never interrupted. "There's quite a few of us that are known by names that fit either our personality or some instance in our lives…I believe humans call them nicknames. We rarely use our given names. I can barely remember my own given name, Claptrap over there never uses his either." Sam changed the subject. "I thought you elves were all tall and slim. No offence."

"None taken, but you've been watching too many movies. That lot all went off to Noozieland, or somewhere like that." Piggybait grinned then added, more seriously, "anyway we're underground dwellers, it wouldn't do for us to be tall, now would it? Perhaps we're more like those small big-footed creatures."

Sam was convinced Piggybait was teasing him, but thought it best not to say too much in case he did cause any offence.

Charlie and Jimander were deep in hushed conversation but Sam overheard Charlie say, "So do you think it's been taken care of?"

"Yes, I believe so, Klaus. We're still on guard but there should be no further cause for concern."

Deep furrows appeared on Charlie's forehead before he noticed Sam watching him. A quick knowing look passed between Jimander and Charlie they both smiled and walked across to where Sam stood watching the bustling scene below.

"What is all this, Charlie? Those look like Christmas wrappings," Sam asked.

“So the penny’s finally dropping is it?” Charlie teased. “Yes, they’re Christmas presents. My team of elves make, obtain and pack presents then transport them to depots all over the world for me where I collect on my rounds.”

“Hold on a minute! This is getting surreal. What do you mean your team of elves and your rounds?”

“In the past, the sleigh used to carry dolls, train sets, apples, oranges and so on but times change...”

“Sleigh? You did say sleigh?”

“I’ll take you to see it soon but…as I was saying…today’s presents are personal computers, laptops, iPads, tablets, mobile phones, games consoles and so on. There are children who still like their train sets, books, football team strips and dolls and such like but a lot of the presents are bigger than in previous years; apples, oranges, jigsaw puzzles, clothes, colouring books and pencils, and the sleigh can only hold so much at a time. We set up hidden depots across the world where I can load up again without being seen.”

Sam’s face was a picture of disbelief.

“Are you alright my boy? I expect it’s all a bit much for you to take in but it’s your own fault, you would follow me tonight,” Charlie winked at Jimander.

“The poor boy’s overcome, Klaus. It’s just like last time.” Jimander stroked his chin.

Charlie cast a troubled look at Jimander who inclined his head questioningly. Charlie nodded. Some silent agreement had been reached.

“I think it’s time for me to explain a few things,” he said taking Sam by the shoulder and leading him to a smooth flattened ledge on the cave wall that looked remarkably like a seat. “Sit down, my boy.” Sam waited for him to speak. Claptrap, Piggybait and Jimander turned away to watch the goings on below trying to be discreet and pretending not to listen.

Sitting beside Sam, Charlie leaned back against the wall and took a deep breath. “Where to begin?”

“How about the beginning, Charlie?”

“Ho, ho. Right back that far? This could be a very long conversation.”

For one brief moment Sam thought he glimpsed sorrow but then Charlie turned to him and gave a warm smile.

"You must have realised who I am by now. I have several names. Around the world I am known as Father Christmas, Santa Claus, Saint Nick, Sinterklaas…amongst others…"

"Have you brought anyone else here? I thought Jimand…"

"Ah, yes. Yes I have. I have brought two other young people here and that was many, many years ago and just as you are special to me, so were they. They kept faith with my friends and never told anyone what they had seen here. They're both long gone now and now it's your turn to keep the secret. I am putting my trust in you.

The face that Sam stared up now was no different to how it had looked before but everything had changed. Although he had been aware he was in the presence of something, someone, magical, now that Charlie had put it into words, his uncle had now taken on a legendary identity and everything Sam thought he knew was in question. He looked across to where the waiting elves were now looking at him, waiting for a reaction. But how was he supposed to react. He didn't believe in Santa Claus, that was always just a story for little kids, wasn't it?

He turned back to Charlie, examining every line of his face, who waited for him to speak. Looking into Charlie's eyes, he realised he was not really a different person, the old Charlie was still there, he was just far more than Sam had ever thought possible.

"What does Cathy know?"

"Ha, she just thinks I'm a bit eccentric and makes allowances for me. We have a good, happy life together but she knows nothing about my other life and that's how it should be. Can you imagine what life would be like for her if it was known she was married to Father Christmas? Everybody would be hustling at her for the whole year, every year? You see it all the time with people close to celebrities constantly being asked for introductions and favours. No, she's better off not knowing."

"But how do you get out on Christmas Eve without her knowing?"

Charlie chuckled. "Have you ever noticed Cathy drinking wine or sherry or any form of alcohol come to that?"

"No, I don't think so. Why?" Sam shook his head.

"It makes her sleepy, even just one glass. Two sherries and she's absolutely sound. Sleeps like a baby all night so it's easy for me to get out. The dogs are there to look after her so she's perfectly safe. They act like daft mutts but there's more to them than anyone realises. They watch over her for me. They understand."

"You said you've brought two other young people here but how long ago? And whatever happened to you living at the North Pole? You have to tell me everything now."

"I've lived through centuries and life can get very lonely. I have been married twice before. Unfortunately while my life goes on, it's not so for my wives who are mortal and when their time comes they leave this world just like everyone else. I've been in existence, in one form or another, for almost two thousand years."

Sam almost choked. He knew Father Christmas had been around for a hundred years or so, but what he was hearing now shook him to the core.

Charlie continued. "Over the last couple of centuries I've become the embodiment of Christmas...Father Christmas, Santa Claus, as some call me. I was born in Myra in Turkey, in the Fourth Century. When I died, as a reward for my good deeds, I was returned to the Earth and became flesh and blood again but, as time went on, I grew lonely although I've had good strong friendships with these wonderful people here," he indicated the elves nearby "but they have their own warm, loving families that I can't be part of. The children I spoke of before belonged to the two women I married. They both had a child each and they were both widows. My first marriage was in the year seventeen ninety five, the second was around a hundred years later. I was never going to have children of my own, but I was allowed to foster these special young people, to be a father to them to the best of my ability. Now I'll be an uncle to you in exactly the same way. You're every bit as special as they were and have become just as precious to me."

"But what happens to you when your wives die?"

"I've led the most wonderful life Sam, and I've met the most amazing people. Cathy is the pride of my life. She is talented, warm, kind and generous and I don't believe she has a bad word to say about anyone, except the Atkins family that is. The biggest gift she has bestowed on me is to allow me to share her life. In time, she too will leave this world and I can't change that, although there's nothing I

wouldn't sacrifice if I thought I could. I'll be there to watch over her and comfort her when the time comes and then I'll be left alone once again, grieving for a partner so perfect the world can only offer one like her in a century, even though there are millions of other ladies in the world. Then I must go on doing what I've always done. I'll always look the same, I can't age and the people I know always see me as somewhere between fifty and seventy and that's also part of the problem. If I'd met Cathy when she was eighteen, she would probably never have loved an old man or even if she'd been twenty-five or thirty. It's only the more mature lady that could take on an old codger like me, and that's probably as it should be but I consider myself very privileged to have known the warmth of family life instead of being on the outside looking in." Charlie's eyes had lost their joyful twinkle. Claptrap and Piggybait sat silently nearby, while Jimander's face was wet with tears as he recalled his own sadness.

"As for the North Pole," Charlie lifted the mood, "you know about satellites, polar exploration and global warming. These things make it virtually impossible for us to continue as before. We now have a series of tunnels across the world allowing us to move underground. The tunnels, as you saw earlier, are able to expand allowing my girls to travel underground with the sleigh as well as by land or air, as required.

"So what about Lappland?" Sam was testing Charlie now. "What about all those people who pay good money to take children to Lappland and the kids think they're seeing the real Santa?"

"And they are," Charlie replied, "as I said, with our speed of travel I can get there, see my guests and be back the same day, easy," Charlie looked over at Jimander and winked.

"This very hard to take in Charlie. I never believed in the existence of fairies."

Charlie grimaced. Jimander cleared his throat and looked away. Piggybait exhaled loudly and moved away to investigate some shiny, grey substance he had seen gleaming in the cave wall.

"Fairies! Who are you calling fairies?" Claptrap scowled.

Sam apologised.

"Please don't take offence at what Sam said, Claptrap. In the human world you are just myths and generally all rolled in together. We're asking a lot of Sam, expecting him to take all this in so quickly so

please have a little consideration and give him some time to adjust," Charlie implored.

"I'm not asking him to do anything!" exclaimed Claptrap huffily, turning his back on everyone.

"I'm afraid Claptrap can be a little tetchy sometimes, Sam," Jimander said, putting his hand on Claptrap's shoulder to placate him. Stubbornly, Claptrap turned his face away again and stuck his nose in the air which Jimander found more amusing than bothersome and left Claptrap to his sulk. Joining Sam and Charlie where they sat he squeezed himself between them on the narrow ledge seat. "Don't worry about him," he nodded towards Claptrap who seemed determined not to turn around. "He can be a little peevish sometimes, but he'll come round. It's not in his nature to stay grumpy for long." He wriggled trying to make himself more comfortable. Sam took the hint and stood up. "You see many years ago humans respected us," Jimander continued without commenting on Sam's courtesy. "They never saw us, weren't entirely sure about our existence but believed we'd make life difficult for them if they insulted us and sometimes they were right." He stopped talking and a pained look crossed his face as if some memory had returned to haunt him.

"You were saying," Sam prompted him.

"Ah…yes. Where was I? Oh, yes. People would leave us gifts, food and so on…to ensure 'the little people' would befriend them and mostly we did." He looked away, eyes glistening in the torch light. He obviously had something on his mind and Sam thought he was about to tell them but the moment passed. "Unfortunately, it's all different now. Humans who believe in 'little people' are thought to be…eccentric and they're treated as fools. Very few humans show respect to our folk now. That's why Claptrap and many others in our clan are suspicious of humans and appear hostile. Some will have nothing to do with humans at all but if you are true to us, he'll come round. Just be patient with him." He looked at Charlie. "Sorry to have interrupted you Klaus, please continue with what you were saying." Jimander pushed himself up onto his feet returned to where Piggybait and Claptrap, who was no longer standing with his back to them, were waiting for him, his expression less sulky, possibly moved by Jimander's words.

"You know about space exploration don't you?" Charlie asked Sam.

“Yes of course. There are space stations, satellites and so on…why?”

“So you know your stuff then. Ever visited the Space Centre in Leicester?”

“No. Not yet but maybe…one day. Perhaps when Mum and Dad get back…why d’you ask?”

“So what d’you think they’re looking for?”

“Bacteria, planet make-up, asteroid movements…um…life.”

“So do you think there’s life on other planets?” Charlie looked very serious. “Perhaps life as we know it…or do you think it might be like you’ll have seen in the films and television programmes, you know little green men with big heads and eyes and no ears?”

“Yeah, well maybe,” Sam started to see where the discussion was going, “but no, probably not little green men from Mars or anything like that, but yes, there’s probably some alien life forms out there.”

“OK, let’s think about this logically. If you agree there are life forms we’ve got no idea about out there…why shouldn’t there be life forms we don’t know about here? What’s the difference? If you’re open-minded enough to accept one without having seen it, why is it so difficult to accept another when you’ve met them face to face?”

“I’ll have to think about that one, but I guess you don’t want me to ask anyone else for their opinion?”

“I’d much rather you didn’t if you don’t mind.” Charlie returned the smile.

“Going back to the dogs being part of this, you’re not going to tell me the cats are involved too are you?” Sam laughed. So did Charlie.

“No, not the cats. Mind you they’re intelligent enough it’s just that they’re very spoiled and very lazy, well one of them is anyway. No they’re just our pampered pets but…um...there are some other animals you might be interested in though.” Charlie looked at Sam from under his bushy white eyebrows. “Would you like to meet them?”

It took a few seconds for Sam to register what Charlie meant, then he twigged and understanding lit up his face. “You’re joking! You’re not talking about reindeer are you? Are you telling me Rudolph and the others really exist?”

“Of course they do…but…um…don’t take the red-nose bit seriously. When he gets a cold, he sneezes and his nose goes red, just like anyone else.” Come on, I’ll take you to meet them.”

Chapter Thirty

Wolf had told the story of his escapade for over an hour this time. His audience, the reindeer, were now thoroughly bored and sceptical especially when the number of men involved increased with each telling.

"Did I mention there were ten of them? And you should've seen me chasing first one, then the other. They were scattering around, running for their lives. Well, apart from the youngest one who scrambled up the nearest tree and stayed there. You should have seen the terror on their faces when I started foaming at the mouth from the sweet Piggybait gave me; their screams were amazing. I haven't had so much fun in ages. Did I tell you about the big one? He was running away from me, looked behind to see where I was and smacked straight into a tree. I couldn't chase him for laughing and did I tell you about…?"

"Oh yes, I'm sure you did," Prancer stifled a yawn. "Is he ever going to let up?" she whispered to Donner, in the byre beside her.

"You really are a brave wolf aren't you?" Dasher raised her eyes to the ceiling. "D'you think he'll stop before Christmas Eve, Dancer dear?" she hissed.

"What was that Dasher? Did you want to ask me something?" Wolf asked hoping to relate more of his tale. "Of course, it was difficult to keep going as I was laughing so much, especially seeing Piggybait in the next tree along from the young one. He was having so much fun and struggling not to laugh he almost fell out of the tree. I was disappointed when he told me to stop but I just I slipped off into the undergrowth leaving them wondering where I was but I hid so I could watch what happened." Wolf noticed the jaded looks on the faces of the reindeer.

"You did very well, dear," Vixen told him, "and I think we get the idea of what happened. I'm so pleased you're our own little Wolf, so

brave and we're lucky to have you protecting us," she said before turning to Comet. "Perhaps flattery will work."

Wolf was so proud of himself he strutted around the cave, head held high. If he detected any sarcasm from the reindeer, he didn't show it.

The door opened and two people walked in. Wolf knew straight away who the big man was but he usually came with the elves, not with another human. He backed away into a byre and hid in the hay behind one of the reindeer, growling under his breath.

"Hello, my girls. Are we almost ready for the big night? Not long now." Charlie approached each reindeer in turn and softly stroked their ears or neck as they inclined their heads towards him for the affectionate pat. A soft snuffling noise showed their pleasure at seeing him. "Ladies, let me introduce you to my nephew, Sam. Sam's likely to be around for a while so it would be nice if you made him welcome. He introduced Sam to each one of the reindeer in turn. "These are my girls and we're very fond of each other, aren't we ladies?" With his hand on Sam's shoulder, he led the stunned boy, who reminded him of a rabbit caught in the headlights of a car on the dark night, over to the far corner to the last byre. "Now, this young man is Rudolph, Vixen next door is his mother and, for some reason, trying to hide behind Rudolph is Wolf. Just pretend we haven't seen him." The growling stopped, but Wolf did not come forward to be introduced preferring to remain concealed, his hackles raised and eyes narrowed in suspicion. Charlie stroked Rudolph's neck and the young reindeer, moved closer and lowered his head, blowing softly down his nose. "You try it, Sam." Reaching out gingerly, Sam too stroked the reindeer's neck. The woolly coat felt coarse and thick.

"You can open the door, Sam, he's very friendly and Wolf will stay where he is. No danger." Rudolph came halfway out of the byre, rubbed his head against Sam's chest and pushed gently with his nose.

"Hey careful fella, you'll have me over," Sam laughed. "I think I have a new friend Charlie. Hey wait a minute! Can I still call you that? What do I call an uncle who's Father Christmas?"

"No matter what other people call me, you'd better stick to Charlie."

Rudolph stood still, happily being made a fuss of but his mother Vixen frowned as she watched the stranger so close to her son. Her master seemed at ease with the young human but she was a little

reluctant to relax so easily and moved closer to keep a watchful eye on her son.

The outer door opened as Jimander, Piggybait and Claptrap joined them. The latter, by this time, had just about forgiven Sam for the remark about fairies and the atmosphere had become a little more positive if not yet actually amiable.

Piggybait explained about life working with Santa Claus and some of his stories were so entertaining, including one about a boar that had chased him that Sam laughed until it hurt so much his ribs felt bruised. After speaking to Donner and Blitzen for a while, Charlie appeared at Sam's side.

"As we've got this far, I think you'd better see everything," Charlie said gravely and led Sam back towards the cave entrance. Reaching his hand out to a piece of rock jutting out of the wall, he pressed his palm hard against it. A grinding noise came from beyond the wall, and slowly a section of the wall moved sideways, like a sliding door, revealing an adjoining cavern. Charlie lifted down a glass lamp with a brass frame and handle, lit it in the usual fashion and extended his arm as an invitation for Sam to go through. In the lamplight Sam's eyes opened wide in bewilderment, his mouth fell open. Hanging on rails in front of him were a number of white edged, red outfits, some long robes with hoods, others were suits of hats, jackets and trousers and, beneath the rails, neatly paired were ten pairs of black shiny boots.

"I wish you could see your face, it's a picture. Pity I don't have my camera with me," Charlie chuckled, thoroughly enjoying Sam's reaction. "But that's not all. A short while ago I made you a promise." Behind the rails was a floor to ceiling deep red velvet curtain. Charlie took hold of one side. Sam watched in wonder as it slid on a smooth curtain track.

"Oh wow!" On a platform in the centre of a small room was an enormous sleigh. Painted black, with plush red velvet seating, it was the most magnificent vehicle Sam had ever seen. The runners were silver, so were the guard rails at the back which could be pulled upwards to act like a cage and stopped anything falling out during flight. Black leather reins, stamped with silver patterns and strung with silver bells, lay folded across the railings at the front.

"Can I?" Sam was so excited he was like a very young child all over again.

"Yes, my boy, of course," Charlie invited Sam to sit in the long bench seat at the front. "Well, what do you think?"

But Sam was speechless.

Later, as they made their way back home, Sam pinched himself, "I thought I might've been dreaming," he said as Charlie beamed down at him. "You know, something's just occurred to me. What about pot-holers? How do you stop them and cavers finding you?

"That might be a problem in the future, but it isn't now. There is exploration of the caves going on but they've only reached about twenty miles or so in total and a lot of that is underwater.

At Wookey Hole, for instance, divers have been able to get to what they call Chamber Twenty Five, but not in dry space. We're keeping an eye on how they're doing, and you have to admire their sense of adventure and tenacity." Charlie smiled, "I don't think I'd have the courage to explore underground waterways, would you? Not knowing where you're going or whether you'll find your way back out?"

Sam shook his head. "No, I don't think so."

"Anyway, the elves are keeping an eye on what's going on and so far, in Chamber Twenty Five, the divers have got to about two hundred and fifty feet down after managing to break through a gravel blockage and now they're working their way back up. It'll be some time before they manage to break through to the surface and then they'll blast through to open up the chambers for people to visit, but that'll be a long while off…hopefully." He gave a kind of half-hearted smile.

"But how far away are they from the elves home?"

"Don't you worry about that either. There's over two hundred miles of cave in here and we're a long way from the exploration, they won't find us."

"But the pot-holers, they get into the narrowest tunnels, how have you stopped them finding you?"

"If it looks like they're getting too close, the tunnels close up; they just come to an end. Anyway, we have other ways to keep them out. You don't have to worry about us staying hidden. I'm not concerned, yet. The last time someone came close to finding our location was about four hundred years ago and since then our cave just…um…disappeared,"

They walked on in silence for a short while with Sam now completely satisfied with the security of the elves' world. As they reached the garden gate Sam turned to Charlie.

"Don't worry, Charlie, I don't know how I'm going to do it, but I'll keep all this to myself…and anyway…who'd believe me?" A thought struck him. "I hope Cathy hasn't checked my room on her way to bed. She'd probably be worried if she finds I'm not there."

"I wouldn't worry about that. I think you'll find she's still asleep in the front room. There's a lot less time gone by than you'd have thought."

Sam checked his watch and was astonished to see that only half an hour had elapsed since he left the cottage. This was all very strange!

That night he dreamt of little red-nosed green men who rode on quad-bikes and awoke the next morning with a headache.

Chapter Thirty One

Meredith's mind raced with worrying thoughts about her father being at the cottage. Why hadn't he let anyone know he was there? Did she hear right…dynamite? Just what devious plan was he up to this time? She decided to have it out with him when he came home but that thought went straight out of her head as she headed towards her room.

Dorothy was shouting. It could only be something to do with Jonah, again!

"Jonah," Dorothy shouted through the door, "you will not throw food at the staff again! I'll be speaking to your father about this when he comes home next. I'll add it to the long list of things I need to discuss with him but, for now you're confined to your room and, to make sure, I'm locking the door!"

Meredith ducked through an open door to keep out of sight as Dorothy stormed passed. She had no wish to get involved in the fallout from Jonah's behaviour again tonight.

"That boy!" Dorothy grumbled as she passed Meredith's hiding place. "Any more of this and I'll leave anyway. I don't need this, Harriet or no Harriet."

Meredith sighed. As if there wasn't enough for her to worry about.

Passing Jonah's room she heard him throwing things and stamping about. It's probably time he saw someone, she thought, someone professional. Dorothy had left the key in the lock and, for a moment, she considered going in to talk to him, but decided it was probably not a good idea. He might be her little brother, but his unpredictability scared her and he was obviously in a foul mood, not that that was unusual but this sounded worse than normal.

So she called in on her mother who wanted to know what all the noise was about but avoided telling her the truth. You just didn't upset Mummy; she couldn't cope with any unpleasantness.

There was no sign of her father at all that night and, in the morning, Jonah was allowed out of his room to get ready for school. He appeared to have calmed down but Meredith thought his amiability was a little forced. He reminded her of a dormant volcano, bubbling away and building in pressure until it exploded. She was scared he might be planning something awful and wondered how long it would be before he erupted.

After breakfast, she headed off to the stables to check on Angelo, but first she wanted to see if her father's car was still there. It was no longer at the front of the cottage but she thought she ought to check, so she scouted around the back. Just inside the line of trees behind the cottage she saw the car hidden in the dense bracken. No-one would have seen it from the lane as the hedge would have obscured their view of the lower part of the trees. What in Heaven's name was he up to?

Chapter Thirty Two

Getting through the last day at school was a nightmare. Ben and Ian kept glancing at Jenny and Sam and then looking round to see where Jonah was, as if they were expecting something to happen at any moment. Jonah kept quiet all day but stared darkly at them whenever they were close. Jason on the other hand, stayed with them as much as possible ignoring Jonah and trying to keep up a cheerful mood. It was his positive attitude to the day that helped Sam and Jenny keep their spirits up, even though they were both very much aware a storm was brewing, and Sam knew it was going to blow in his direction. They were both relieved at the end of the day when the school bus came to pick them up and nothing awful had happened.

At home later that evening, Jason went to his room to check his e-mails. There were several waiting to be opened. One was from Jonah. Expecting it to be some threat, he put off opening it while he attended to the others.

His mother called him for dinner and Jonah's email remained unopened while he watched the Yeovil versus Scunthorpe United game on the television, but the thought of it nagged at him and eventually, curiosity aroused and he decided he could put it off no longer. As he guessed, there were nasty comments about Jenny and himself but the main threat was aimed directly at Sam. It was obvious Jonah had every intention of doing Sam some harm, if not worse, and Jason knew he had to get a warning to him before it was too late. He ran downstairs, grabbed his jacket and shouted to his mother as he darted out of the door.

"Just going out," he called "won't be long." He hurried down the road towards the Nowell cottage but as he passed the woods a movement close the cottage caught his attention. Someone was

hunched over and moving low to the ground by the back wall of the Nowell and Richards' gardens, occasionally bobbing up to look over the wall before dropping low again.

Whoever it was appeared to be watching something inside the trees. Jason pulled his jacket closer and ducked down behind the hedge. He was unable to see clearly who it was but, as the moon emerged from behind a cloud, he recognised what looked like a black leather jacket and knew instinctively it was Jonah. What the hell was he doing snooping around near Sam's at this time of night? The figure slipped furtively into the woods with Jason following, staying well out of sight. Nothing good ever came of Jonah being around.

Chapter Thirty Three

An hour or so earlier, Sam had left the cottage saying that he was visiting friends. Cathy was very pleased that he had settled in so quickly that he had friends to visit. Of course, his actual intention was to pay another visit to the elves, especially as he was now confident about finding his way through the woods. He knew they observed everything that went on around them and would keep an eye on him and not let him lose his way.

Just a few metres away from the boulder, a noise from somewhere in the darkened trees behind him made him jump. He spun round but the silhouettes created by moonlight through the shadowy tree branches revealed nothing to worry him; probably another deer or fox, nothing suspicious; he felt secure, safe. He had friends in these woods and anyway it was only a short way to the boulder.

A few moments later a sound like the snapping of a twig made him look round again. This time the hair on the nape of his neck stood on end; a tingle of fear ran through him. Perhaps there was something wrong. His senses told him that if it had been a deer he would probably have seen them by now if they were close enough to have been heard. This was something else. He slipped behind a large oak and ducked down into the undergrowth. A crouched figure slipped between the trees near to the path a glint of a gold earring reflected in the moonlight.

Sam's skin prickled, his senses alert. His stalker was Jonah. "Why can't he bloody well leave me alone?" He felt both furious and terrified. He knew he couldn't allow Jonah to follow him but it would look very strange if he just doubled back.

Just at that moment, six men joined the path a little further ahead of where Sam was hidden. He sucked in his breath. “This place is really busy tonight,” he muttered.

As the last two men exited the trees and joined the others on the path he noticed they carried a box very carefully between them. He watched in horrified surprise as they opened another cave entrance he knew nothing about but very near the one he was going to use. Charlie had mentioned the entire area was riddled with caves and tunnels and there were underground rivers flowing through some of them carved out by the River Axe. Over thousands of years some of the tunnels had dried up while others had been excavated by the relentless flow of water into massive caves. He had further explained that many of these caverns were still unknown even though exploration of the underground waterways had started in the 1930s and now many of the caves were used for training divers for rescues and testing new equipment. Sam wondered if these men were divers but thought it unlikely as it was so late at night. A strange time for exploration!

From his vantage point, Sam watched as they stopped to put on miner’s helmets and switch on the lights before entering the tunnel and he waited a few moments after they had disappeared, not wanting to move too soon in case he was seen but needing to get in before they closed the entrance. He looked over his shoulder to see where Jonah was, hoping he was too far back to have seen the group of men approach. He didn’t want them to see Jonah or himself and he couldn’t double-back too soon either without Jonah realising he had been seen and was being led away.

The moon’s rays lit up the rock face and he saw his chance; the entrance was still slightly open leaving just enough space to slide through. Perhaps inside he would find a route to lead Jonah away and get him lost amongst the tunnels before he could retrace his steps and visit the elves.

He held his breath and counted to sixty, all the while keeping an eye on where he had last seen Jonah. Confident the men were far enough inside not to hear him, he coughed to make sure Jonah knew he was there. He was relieved there was no school the next day as it looked as though it was going to be a long night.

****

Jason had never been in the woods before even in daylight; he had heard far too many worrying stories about things that happened in there, but he took a deep breath and plunged into the shadowy moonlit woods after Jonah. Trees took on mysterious shapes, leaves rustled, bats screeched, owls hooted and some way off in the distance a fox yipped. Jason's heart skipped a beat at every sound, every spine-chilling movement.

In the tightly packed undergrowth of ferns, the quivering fronds cast slithering silhouettes in the irregular shafts of light when the moon emerged from behind the night-time clouds.

Trying to keep up an eye on Jonah was difficult to say the least as he constantly vanished behind trees and wearing dark clothes made him difficult to spot but, just every time he was about to give up, Jonah would appear ahead of him again.

Several times, Jonah looked around as if he knew he was being followed; once, before Jason had found the time to duck, it seemed that Jonah looked right at him but he just turned and moved on.

Eventually, after a nightmare of a trek, Jason saw Jonah crouch down amongst the ferns clearly not wanting to be seen. He was at the edge of the trees and watching someone head towards a gap in the rocks. Sam!

His earlier fears forgotten now there was something real to worry about, Jason dropped to his hands and knees and crawled through the cold, muddy brush towards Jonah, never losing sight of either of them until Sam slipped through the gap and disappeared. Jonah stood up slowly just as Jason saw a faint glow of light appear within the space where Sam had last been seen, then he scuttled across the narrow grassy approach to the opening and slipped inside. Jason stood up, leaned against a tree, trying to decide what to do. There was going to be trouble and he wasn't at all sure he wanted to deal with it alone.

****

Sam strode up to the gap in the rock, made an exaggerated show of looking around to ensure Jonah would believe he was up to something and squeezed through into a kind of lobby area where a number of tunnels ran off in different directions. A flickering light moved at the

far end of the first tunnel on the left. Sam did a quick calculation and guessed that it would lead the men away from the elves.

Soft footsteps approached. Jonah! Sam couldn't move away too quickly or Jonah might not see him and he needed Jonah to follow him. Wait. Wait.

A hand holding a torch reached around the rock at the entrance. OK, time to go. Sam turned on his own torch, chose the first tunnel on the right and hurried along its snaking path checking at each turn that Jonah was following. If he thought he had been scared when he first followed Charlie into the woods, it was nothing to the way he felt now. The tunnel ceiling was low; at times he had to stoop, the darkness and the smell of warm dank earth made him slightly claustrophobic and he had no idea where he going or how far the tunnel went. The last thing he wanted was to be cornered by Jonah. He could only hope the elves were watching over him.

Weighing on his mind was also the worry that the group of men might still come upon the elves' home. Although they appeared to be going in a different direction it could still happen. It also occurred to him that, if he was uneasy about being below ground, perhaps Jonah was. Perhaps he had given up and gone back. Turning a corner he looked round only to see the beam of a torch flickered against the muddy floor. His heart sank. Jonah was still there.

Chapter Thirty Four

Chips and Henry struggled to walk side by side through the narrow shaft as they held the box of dynamite very carefully between them. Jeremiah urged them to walk faster, eager as he was to get to the silver. Mikey followed Jeremiah, closely tailed by Jake, and Danny nervously brought up the rear again, trying hard to remember the way back. He wondered whether anyone would notice if he slipped away, but was too scared to try.

"Come on, come on! Stop lagging you lot!" Jeremiah badgered.

Mikey turned to Jake. "He's gone nuts," he whispered. Jake nodded agreement. After all the years of working for Jeremiah Atkins, Jake had recently seen a worrying change in him. This was not the man he knew; this was a man obsessed. The Mr Atkins he had always known would never have got involved personally in the past.

They reached the mouth of the tunnel where the silver had been found. It branched off into three separate passageways, one quite wide, the other two large enough for one person to walk comfortably, but narrower than the first.

"Which way, Mikey?" Jeremiah demanded to know.

"Er…I think it's that one, Mr Atkins," Mikey said, pointing to the smaller tunnel on the left.

"You're sure?" In the torchlight they could see Jeremiah's eyes had a strange, glazed appearance. He turned away towards the tunnel Mikey had indicated. Shining the torch into the small tunnel, Jeremiah disturbed a colony of bats. He ducked, clapping his hands over his head as the mass of panicking bats whizzed past his head, squealing shrilly. The others ducked in alarm as the bats narrowly missed their heads, fluttering frantically in their haste to get away from the intruders.

"What's the matter with you? It's only a few bats. Let's get on with it!" Jeremiah's voice echoed.

"I 'ate bats," Jake said, still shaking as he tried to smooth his hair back over his head.

"'ave they gone, Mikey?" Danny cowered against the tunnel wall. "Were they vampire bats?" He was as white as a sheet.

Fleetingly, an exasperated look appeared on Mikey's face as he stared at his young brother, then his expression softened. He moved closer.

"I want you to get out of here as soon as he's not looking. I want you safe. No questions, just get out. I shouldn't 'ave got you involved in this. Do yerself a favour an' disappear." Danny's already white pastiness turned a shade ghostly, but he looked relieved and nodded. "I'll find you, Dan. Don't worry. Afterwards…I'll find you."

Peering over Mikey's shoulder he watched Jeremiah examining the walls closely then studying the ground, talking to himself and emitting strange little giggles. Aware something was going on behind him, he swung round catching Danny looking at him from over Mikey's shoulder. Jeremiah knew Mikey ignored Danny most of the time and seeing them close together made him uneasy.

"Anything wrong, lads?" Jeremiah asked in a hideously pleasant tone, fixing his eyes on the brothers.

"No, nothing wrong Mr Atkins, just 'aving a little chat with me brother," Mikey was noticeably nervous.

"Well don't do it on my time," Jeremiah growled. "As for the rest of you, get digging. We've got silver to find. Oh and Mikey, don't get any silly ideas about Danny leaving us will you?" Jeremiah patted his jacket pocket significantly. Mikey, Danny and Jake were rooted to the spot. Henry and Chips set down the heavy box, moving closely behind Jeremiah.

"Why not try 'ere, Mr Atkins?" Henry asked, sounding unnaturally cheerful. "I think this is it."

"Bring the box, Henry!" Jonah snapped again leading the way toward the widest tunnel.

"We got to do somethin'!" Jake hissed to Mikey. "He's gone nuts! He's gonna kill us all. I just know that's a gun he's got!"

"I know!" Mikey replied quietly. "Danny, you get out anyway…don't worry about anythin' you 'ear, just go. Wait fer me outside," Mikey smiled at his young brother. Danny nodded, disappearing without a second glance.

Jeremiah, inside the large tunnel, missed Danny's departure, but Henry and Chips, hauling the heavy box into the tunnel, had seen him go but said nothing.

"I still don't think there's anything left Mr Atkins," Henry said tentatively. Jeremiah scowled. "If we can't dig it out, we'll blow it out! Pass me a stick of dynamite."

"I don't think we should use it, Mr Atkins, I really don't," Henry said. Jake and Mikey nodded their heads in agreement.

"You cowards!" Jeremiah roared, "I'll show you! I know what I'm doing!" He snatched a stick of dynamite from the box and held it up in front of them, threateningly. "Don't any of you think about getting out of here…where's…that boy, Danny?" As soon as he realised Danny was missing his eyes blazed furiously. Putting his hand into his jacket pocket he pulled out a small gun pointing it towards Mikey.

"Thought you'd fool me did you?" Well, just for that you can set the dynamite, Mikey." Mikey paled. His eyes darted from face to face appealing for help. Henry moved quickly and quietly behind Jeremiah and, thud! Henry had picked up the lid of the box and brought it heavily down on Jeremiah's head, knocking him to the ground. Jake picked up the gun and all four of them dashed out of the tunnel, running as fast as they could in single file towards the exit. But Jeremiah was only stunned and recovered within a few minutes, but those minutes gave them time to get away without anyone being hurt.

"Run out on me will you! I'll show you. I don't need any of you," Jeremiah screamed down the tunnel. "I'll get the silver and I'll keep it all myself!" He looked down at the stick of dynamite lying on the floor. Picking it up, he laughed softly. "It's OK. I know what I'm doing."

Chapter Thirty Five

Sam knew time was running out. Jonah appeared to be closing on him and he had to think quickly. There would be a confrontation, there was no way to avoid that but he needed an advantage. On and on he went along the seemingly endless tunnel that turned and twisted, climbed and descended, slipping a couple of times where the ground was wet.

Eventually, after what seemed like hours, the tunnel descended again and widened. Sam listened for sounds behind him. Jonah was still there, breathing hard and grumbling, the sound of his voice carried along the tunnel. That'll teach him to get out of PE so often.

Wondering how much further he would have to go, Sam moved on and followed the tunnel as it wound round to the left, in the distance an eerie green light glowed. At first he thought he had come across another of the elves' caves but soon he found himself gazing around a massive cave with a huge crystal-clear lake. The green tinged glow seemed to radiate from algae that fringed the rocks circling the water.

Sam also recalled Charlie explaining that a number of the caverns had their own natural light that radiated from an algae existing in the water and on nearby rocks. It was not bright enough to read by, but it would certainly allow a person to find their way about.

Sam stood opened-mouthed gazing at the mystical scene he had just found; it was just as Charlie described.

He was on a ledge approximately a metre above the water and about three metres wide that seemed to border the entire lake. The base of the ledge was crowded with stalagmites that rose up in columns of various sizes to meet the stalactites above them. Some met in the middle as the limestone enriched water trickled down from the ceiling. Many of

these columns were as much as a metre wide; massive limestone pillars in hues of yellow, cream and white.

At the far end of the cavern, more tunnels honeycombed out in different directions and he wondered which way he should go. Which of those would be a way out? Placing his feet carefully along the slippery ledge, he edged his way toward the tunnels but a gasp behind him made him turn. Jonah had arrived.

On finding himself at the same place Sam had a few moments before, Jonah too was also transfixed by the grandeur before him. For that one brief moment both boys felt the same awe, the same feeling of being overcome by the magnificence of Nature, both of them stunned into silence and united in wonder.

Seizing the moment, Sam asked, "Can't we find some way to sort this out?"

"You humiliated me," Jonah spat, unprepared to yield.

"No. I didn't humiliate you Jonah. You did that all by yourself. You could make real friends but instead you bully people into being with you. The fact they're frightened of you doesn't mean they like you," Sam tried to make him understand, "but they could, if you tried. What you did to Jenny isn't going to make her want to go out with you, but she doesn't hate you. She hates your cruelty, just like everyone else. I haven't been here long, but I've made friends already because I don't bully anyone and there's some really good people here. I've learned a lot since I've got here and I…I really like it. It's not too late to make some real friends you know." He was surprised that Jonah seemed to be listening.

"Yes it is," Jonah replied sadly. "*It is too late!*" He sat down on a piece of rock jutting out from the cave wall. "My dad doesn't like me…none of my family do. The staff at the house don't either. They only put up with me 'cos they're paid." He gave a sad little laugh. "I suppose I can't blame them." He looked up at Sam, misery in his eyes.

The fact Jonah was talking and opening up to him, gave Sam hope that perhaps things could be settled amicably but then Jonah's tone changed.

"Yes, people like you. Jenny likes you…even stupid Jason likes you." He stood up. "You spoiled everything when you came here. This was…*this was my village*," his voice rose to a shout, "and you took over!" He moved closer. Sam stood his ground. He saw Jonah slowly

and deliberately put his hand into his jacket pocket, all the time watching for Sam's reaction. He pulled something out, holding it in his hand and moved closer, he was just about two metres away when Sam saw the glint of something metallic in Jonah's tightly clenched fist. Oh God, I knew it. He's got a knife! He was in grave danger and froze with terror.

"No Jonah! Don't do this!" Sam begged.

"Scared are you Johnson. Chicken?" Jonah's face again twisted with fury, the green shimmer altering his features into some malicious spirit driven by vengeance. Sam's heart sank into his boots. This wonderfully peaceful place had been ruined by Jonah's hostility. Even though he expected Jonah's attack he was not prepared for how quickly it happened. In a second Jonah was on him and they fell to the ground with Sam struggling to avoid the knife. He didn't want to hit Jonah. He had seen his vulnerable side and now surprisingly felt sorry for him, but he was terrified of the knife.

He twisted away from Jonah and sprung to his feet, his Aikido training returning just when it was needed. In preparation for Jonah's next move, Sam moved his right foot, placing it in front of his left and slightly to one side; his right hand forward of his left, he was now in position to move either way. Jonah lunged again. This time Sam twisted out of the way knocking the knife out of Jonah's hand. It landed with an echoing clatter within easy reach of them both. They stared at each other, trying to judge when the other would make their move. Sam darted towards the knife a split second before Jonah, reaching it a heartbeat before Jonah and threw it into the lake, heaving a massive sigh of relief.

"*Noooo!*" Jonah landed heavily on the ground, watched the knife slide slowly under the water. Lying motionless he laid his head on his forearm and whimpered. Sam sat on a broken stalagmite while he caught his breath. It was several minutes before either boy moved.

Jonah pulled himself up into a sitting position and wrapped his arms around his knees. There were tears in his eyes and his expression was pained but Sam knew he hadn't hurt him. Jonah looked up at him, defeat etched on his young face. After all he had done, Sam could only feel sorry for him. He held out a hand to help Jonah up but Jonah refused his help, remaining where he was on the cold damp ground.

"I can't beat you. Even with a knife I can't beat you!"

"Good," Sam replied. "I don't really think you wanted to use it and it's not too late to sort this out. It's nearly Christmas so stop so being mardy. Think about it, peace and goodwill and all that."

Jonah stood up, walked towards the edge of the ledge. He turned towards Sam and smiled thinly. "You don't really believe that do you. Are you so…so…decent that you honestly believe that people…"

A thunderous rumble stopped him in mid-speech. The floor of the cavern shook violently and Jonah lost his footing. Sam reached out to grab him but he too tumbled away in the opposite direction. All around them pieces of stalactite were falling, crashing to the ground. Jonah tried to stand but was knocked to the ground again by a large chunk of the ceiling that crashed into his shoulder pushing him backwards towards the edge of the shelf. As he tried to steady himself, the ledge beneath him crumbled and he lost his footing, slithering downwards into the icy water. The once peaceful lake was now a seething whirlpool of waves angrily bubbling, reaching up to suck Jonah down into the icy water.

"Help me!" Jonah screamed. Sam struggled to keep his own footing, but he inched his way towards where he had last seen Jonah, swerving wildly to avoid the limestone rocks raining down from the ceiling.

"Hold on! I'm coming!" He was about a metre away from Jonah and could see the tips of Jonah's fingers gripping the ledge. "I'm almost there."

One of the widest stalactites Sam had seen broke off and landed with a crash in front of him knocking him off his feet. Another landed alongside it but Sam managed to steady himself. "Jonah! Are you alright?" Sam called out.

"Yeah. Just help me!" But there was no way through, the stalactites blocked Sam's way.

"I can't get to you. I've got to go for help. Hang on!" Sam turned to go but Jonah screamed again.

"No! Don't leave me! Please don't leave me! I'm going to die here! I can't hold on much longer my hands are too cold. Please don't leave. I'm…I'm scared. *I don't want to die!*" All around them the ground shook, the cave roof was collapsing and the water was rising fast.

"OK, hang on. I'll try to get round this lot." Half climbing, half slipping, Sam crawled over the crumbled stump of the big stalactite and stretched out as far as he could to grab Jonah's hand.

"You came back for me," Jonah cried. Sam remembered his jeans had a belt. He took it off and lowered one end to Jonah. The water had now reached Jonah's waist and his legs were freezing. "I'm so cold. Please help me."

"Grab hold of the belt. I know you're cold but reach round with your other hand and hang on. I'll pull you up."

"Hey. I'll help." A voice behind them made Sam turn. Jason! He had found his way into the crumbling cavern but he too was struggling to keep his feet.

"No Jason! Go back! Go and get help! You'll help more that way," Sam screamed over the crashing din. "Just get out, now!"

He saw Jason unsteadily run back out the way he had come.

Jonah had managed to grasp the belt while Sam held on. With one hand gripping the belt and Sam pulling, Jonah was able to get a foothold on the slimy rock and push himself further out of the water. Shivering and barely able to talk his teeth chattered loudly as he rested while he caught his breath, even though their position was still precarious. The tremors eased, began to subside and the bubbling and frothing of the water lessened to rippling waves.

Jonah's hold on the belt though was precarious as his cold, wet hands kept slipping and he found it difficult to hold on but Sam stretched further and grabbed one of his wrists and held on fast. With Sam's support Jonah heaved himself up over the edge and onto the slippery and unsafe ledge. With more cracks appearing in the cave ceiling and more rocks beginning to fall, they needed to get out in a hurry but Sam, fleetingly, had a terrible dread that the tunnel might not now be passable but as Jason had not come back he hoped it was a good sign. Now Jonah was safe from the water but he needed medical attention. Sam stood up and helped Jonah to his feet and pushed him ahead of him towards the exit. He was about to follow when a noise above made him look up.

Part of the ceiling directly above him, weakened during the tremors, had broken away and Sam watched in horror as a large piece of stalactite fell. The broken stalactites on the ground surrounded him blocking his way; he had nowhere to go. He twisted his body to avoid

a direct hit but received a glancing blow to the side of his head. The last thing he remembered was hearing Jonah screaming, *"Look out!"*

Chapter Thirty Six

A door opened and closed somewhere. Voices spoke in hushed tones. Sam tried to sit up but his head throbbed unbearably. Lying down again he tried to turn towards the sounds but a searing pain shot through his left arm and shoulder.

"About time you decided to wake up," said a deep voice from somewhere far away. Then he heard sniffing. Slowly and stiffly he opened his eyes, his eyelids felt as though they were weighed down with lead.

Cathy sat on a chair beside the bed, dabbing her eyes with a white handkerchief as she leaned in towards him and reached for his hand; Charlie stood at the foot of the bed, a huge grin on his rosy-cheeked face.

Cathy was crying and laughing at the same time. "Oh, Sam. Thank goodness… bless you." she smiled through her tears, "we've been so worried about you."

Again he tried to sit up but pain mingled with nausea and dizziness and he flopped back onto his pillow. There was no point in struggling against the weakness so he stayed where he was.

"I'll get the nurse, Charlie, you stay with Sam." At the door, she turned and smiled. "We're terrible guardians. I'm so sorry, Sam," her eyes welled with tears again, "we should have been looking after you better." Sam and Charlie exchanged meaningful glances. "I'll be very lucky if your mother ever forgives me and I couldn't blame her," Cathy said at the door, she was still dabbing her eyes, "I'll get a nurse." Through the open door Sam, could see a white corridor with people in blue or grey uniforms and one or two in white coats. She closed the door behind her leaving Sam alone with his uncle who quickly slipped into the chair Cathy has just vacated.

"She's taken all this pretty hard you know," Charlie explained.

"Yes, but I don't understand. What happened? Why am I in hospital?"

"The docs said you might not remember straight away 'cos of shock and concussion an' all that?" Charlie explained he was in hospital in Wells, that he had been unconscious for the last two days and it was Christmas Eve. He told Sam in detail everything he knew about the explosion in the caves, about Jonah's father being responsible for the cave-in by setting off dynamite and that the reverberations had brought about the tunnel collapse, causing the tremors and that the beautiful water-filled cave had been destroyed but the elves were hoping they could repair it

Bit by bit, as the story was related, Sam remembered. "What about Jonah? Did he get out OK?"

"Yes, Jonah's fine. He was in a ward here overnight, but they let him out the next day as he was only in for observation. He asked me to pass on a message to you. He said you showed him real friendship when you went back for him and he'll never forget it. He's asked if he can come and see you when you feel up to it and that he's already been to see Jenny and told her how sorry he is for how he's treated her. He said he doesn't expect you to want to be a friend to him after what he's done but he'd be really chuffed if you do. Young Jason got out too. He's a good lad that one. He said he'd gone looking for you to warn you about Jonah. He's been in to see you a couple of times as well. It seems he and Jenny will be OK with whichever way you decide on how things go with Jonah in the future."

"What about the elves? Are they OK? The explosion must have affected them. Piggy, Claptrap...?" Sam asked.

"Aah, now that's another story." Charlie turned away. Clasping his hands together, he sat forward looking down at the floor. Emotion made it hard for him to speak, he swallowed, looked up at Sam then down at the floor again. Sam waited until Charlie felt able to speak. Bad news caused pain.

"The explosion didn't hurt any of them directly," he began, "the elves' home is safe...everything continues as normal...*nothing* can stop tonight's journey, nothing!" He took a deep breath. "But we did have one casualty. Jimander *was* my dearest friend. His loyalty to me could never be questioned. He was brave and could be a merciless enemy, as some discovered, but above all he was a strong leader." Charlie looked

up at Sam and continued; his eyes glittering, distress clearly etched on his face. "I have lost many people over the years who were dear to me...but...but, somehow, I'd forgotten the time would come when I'd lose Jimander. We'd been together so long we were almost like brothers. No, we were much closer than that. We were there for each other's joys and heartbreaks and trusted each implicitly," Charlie looked down at the floor again. "In all the time I have been on Earth I understand the Circle of Life, it has to go on."

He paused. "But sometimes people you love leave a gap in your life when they go, and nothing is ever the same without them. We'll come to terms with this someday, but he'll never be forgotten. The only consolation his daughter, Ellien, and I have is to believe he's gone to the place where Malliena waits for him. Jimander was the most trusted and cherished of friends, and I relied on him more than I knew. Now Claptrap, Piggybait and Jerrill will take on the duties Jimander carried out." He turned his moist gaze to Sam again. "You see what I mean, Sam? As good as they are, it will take all three to manage what he did alone, and that's only as far as his official role is concerned. I can never replace him as a friend."

Charlie stopped, swallowed hard, wiped his eyes and was in control again; his public face was back.

"What happened to him?" Sam asked quietly. He was mortified to see his uncle reduced to tears and wanted to offer some comfort, but had no idea where to start.

"You remember the conversation you had with Piggybait about Corporal about elf ears being very sensitive to vibrations. Jimander had the most sensitive ears I've ever known. The tremors in the caverns and his great age...well that big heart of his couldn't cope with all the rigours of being shaken up. Oh...it makes me so angry he had to go like that!"

"I'm sorry. I liked him even though I didn't know him well. He made me feel welcome in his world."

"He would. He was always hospitable but...but now we have to get on with our preparations. There will be time for remembrance later."

"I still don't really know what happened," Sam said. "Why was Mr Atkins using dynamite anyway?"

Charlie looked startled. "Of course, I was forgetting, you still don't know do you?" Charlie went to the door, opened it a little to check

whether anyone was coming. He had expected Cathy to have returned by now with a nurse, but although there was plenty of bustle in the corridor, there was no sign of her. He returned to Sam's bedside, spoke quietly, "It seems Atkins was after silver ore in the ground under the hills but didn't want anyone to know what he was up to so he brought in a group of his own men, bumbling idiots, the lot of them. Not a mining engineer or geologist among them, never mind an explosive expert. He wanted to use dynamite, but it turns out they weren't at all happy about it.

Jimander had found out what they were up to and tried to deter them with a little elven assistance. He thought if they supplied the men with enough silver and made them believe there was no more, they'd leave with what they had."

"How could the elves make them believe that? I wouldn't have thought they would want that gang to see them."

"Ah, yes. You see humans are susceptible to elven suggestion. It's a talent that has served the elves well over hundreds of years; their powers are countless, and they have made good use of them when the occasion called for it. When elves whisper into human dreams, the human wakes the next morning believing what they've heard. It's a very handy technique. It would have done again this time, but unfortunately, nobody reckoned on Atkins coming back just at the wrong time. He refused to believe it when his men told him the supply of silver was exhausted and forced them to go back. He must have thought they were lying to him, because this time, he insisted on going with them. From what I understand, he lost grip on reality down there and, when his men deserted him, he used the dynamite," Charlie stopped again, listening for noises outside. Satisfied, he went on.

"Apparently, he went down one of the tunnels they hadn't explored and, when they wanted to leave, he threatened them with a gun. One of them managed to stun him giving them time to get away, it was then he used the dynamite bringing the roof down on his own head or so we hear. His daughter, Meredith, not being very keen on her father or the company he keeps or, I should say, kept, had followed him and the others, to see what they were up to. Once they'd all disappeared down the tunnels, she got suspicious and called the police. They waited outside the cave and picked them up one by one as they emerged. One of them, quite a bit younger than the others, so I understand, came out

on his own before the others and told the police everything. The other four got out covered in dust from the roof-fall, but apart from that they were alright, until they were arrested that is! The police are still figuring how many charges they can bring against them. Of course Meredith was there when Jonah appeared and heard him kicking up a fuss about you still being in there.

"How did they get me out? I remember the roof caving in and thought I was dead for sure."

"Before the rescue teams could get in you had some 'very special' help. The police thought you must have crawled along the tunnel before you blacked out although they were surprised, in your condition, how far you managed to get. In fact the tunnel outside the cavern you were in, collapsed seconds after Jonah got through and was blocked completely. There was no way out that way. The elves knew you were there and needed help and it was Piggy, Claptrap, Halmar and Jerrill who found a way through, dug away the debris trapping you and between them carried you out, taking you back to the place where the tunnels separated, the place where you led Jonah away from the elves." He gestured towards the window indicating that Sam should look. Three small faces peered in waving cheerfully. Claptrap, Piggybait and Halmar were grinning back at him.

"Will you thank them for me, Charlie?" Charlie nodded.

Looking beyond the elves, Sam saw snow falling in large soft flakes. Sam beamed. "It's snowing. I've never seen a white Christmas before."

"Yep, they've made it snow for you again," Charlie grinned, "they thought you'd like it."

Sam thought about what Charlie had just said. "You mean, in the woods…when it snowed, it was the elves did that?"

"Well it helped you see better in the dark didn't it?" Sam opened his mouth to speak, but Charlie pre-empted him. "They won't come in. This isn't the place for them, but you'll see them again when you're well."

"Won't the police wonder why I was in the caves?" Sam was expecting awkward questions.

"They'll want to talk to you, of course," Charlie told him, "but I already thought of that. I told the police one of our dogs got out and you'd gone looking for him, then seeing the men going into the tunnel

you thought you'd better check what they were up to. Jonah's backed that story up already. He told them he heard you calling Benny's name while he was following you."

"But Cathy knows Benny didn't get out."

Charlie winked at him, "Don't worry about Cathy. She was asleep at the time."

The door opened and Cathy came in with two nurses.

"Good to see you awake at last, Sam. How are you feeling?" the older nurse asked.

"As though I've been smacked in the head by a mallet."

"That's only to be expected, considering. I'm Rosie Saunders and I'll be looking after you for the day shift. This is our student nurse, Rachel Askam."

"I know you!" Rachel smiled. "You're in my sister Susan's class aren't you?" Sam nodded painfully. "I must tell her I'm helping to look after you. It seems you're a bit of a celebrity at the school."

"Enough of the chit chat, Nurse Askam! We have a patient to deal with," Rosie put Rachel firmly in her place. Rachel pulled a face at Sam behind the older nurse's back. Sam stifled a chuckle.

"Now then, Sam," Rosie said, putting a digital thermometer just inside his ear to check his temperature, "It's good you're awake now. We'll have a better idea of any brain damage done now." Cathy winced. "We've notified the duty doctor to let her know you're conscious and she'll be in to see you in the next hour or so." She clipped something onto the end of his finger and checked his pulse. "So far so good," she said eventually. "Now, don't you stay too long," she told Cathy and Charlie. "We don't want our young patient to get overtired, do we," she finished, pointedly.

"What are my injuries?" Sam asked.

"We don't need to go into that now," she said briskly, "the doctor can discuss that with you when she arrives."

"I really think you should tell him," Charlie crooned softly.

Nurse Saunders shook her head, her expression blank. "Your injuries," she began in a monotone voice that neither Cathy nor Rachel seemed to notice, "are that you have concussion, you've broken your left arm and wrist and there's some nasty bruising to your left side. That headache's likely to last a few days and, after that, you should start feeling better. You will have to take things easy for a while as

concussion can be a funny thing. The doctor's prescribed you some painkillers. Do you need any now?"

"Yes please, and…am I allowed anything to eat? I'm starving."

Nurse Saunders vacant stare vanished and she smiled fully, "I'll see what I can do." She left, shooing Rachel out with her.

"It's Christmas Eve and you'll be wanting your Christmas presents tomorrow, but I don't suppose you're well enough for one now are you?" Charlie asked.

"Playing Santa again are we?" Sam asked, grinning.

"Hmm...I see you're feeling up to being a comedian anyway. Just wait here a minute. What am I saying? Where else are you going in your state?"

Sam waited impatiently for what seemed like a very long time then the door opened again. His mother came into the room pushing someone in a wheelchair. Sam could not believe his eyes. His dad was home! He tried to get up but pain shot through his side and he collapsed back onto the bed, groaning with the effort.

"No Sam, you just stay where you are!" his mother cried, "Don't try and get up," she said, hugging him carefully. "How are you feeling? What a terrible thing to happen? What were you doing there anyway?" Jane clearly did not know what to do first, laugh or cry, so she did both, at the same time.

"Now m'dear, don't take on," Charlie said, putting his huge arm around her small shoulders. "Sam's OK. He'll heal well and Steve's getting better too so you don't need to fuss. They can enjoy convalescing together at our place."

With his blond hair and blue-grey eyes, Steve Johnson was an older version of Sam. He wheeled his chair to Sam's bed and hugged him tightly, too tightly. Sam winced as his father squeezed his bruised ribs, but he did not complain. He was too pleased to have him home.

"It's so good to see you, son."

"And it's great to have you home Dad. Do you have to go back to South Africa? Are we moving over there?"

"No, no. We're staying, staying here in the UK."

"Yes!" Sam shouted as several pains shot through his arm and ribs but this time he didn't care.

Steve looked round at Jane and smiled, "OK, you win, I owe you a fiver." He turned back to Sam. "I've got to sort out a job, but we'll

worry about it after Christmas. We're staying here until New Year and Portia's fine with Ken and Emma for now, so we've got plenty of time."

Nurse Saunders came in with two tablets in a small plastic cup. She poured a glass of water for Sam and handed him the tablets.

The door opened again and Jenny stood waiting to be invited in. Sam felt his cheeks grow warm as she smiled fondly at him.

"Can I come in as well?" she grinned. "How's the hero? Getting better, I hope."

"You know you really shouldn't have too much excitement," Nurse Rosie Saunders was obviously not impressed and muttered something about too many visitors as she left the room.

"Well, Cathy my dear, time's getting on. Sam's got enough visitors and it's probably time we took our leave. See you later Jane, Steve. Jane, will you be alright giving young Jenny a lift back later or should we wait?"

Jane agreed to drive Jenny home when they left which obviously pleased Sam.

As they were about to go through the door, Sam heard Charlie ask Cathy, "Fancy a wee sherry my dear?"

"That would be very nice, Charlie." She pinched his cheek gently. At the open door she looked back at Sam and without Charlie seeing she winked and tapped the side of her nose.

Sam's jaw dropped. She knows, he thought, she knows who he is. She's known all along.

Sam winked back.

Acknowledgements

Over the years I have been grateful for the help and support of a number of people but in particular I have to give special mention to:

Helen Hollick is close friend and highly acclaimed historical author who has for a number of years been a support, an adviser and a damn good read. I would thoroughly recommend her books to anyone who enjoys the genre. Her Pendragon's Banner series, Harold the King and the Sea Witch series of piratical adventures are thoroughly researched and are excellent reads – I'm eagerly looking forward to the next in the series.

Cathy Helms of Avalon Graphics is a consummate graphic designer who has produced some wonderful covers, book trailers and artwork for other writers and I am delighted to now have her working with me. I am grateful for the wonderful cover Cathy has designed for this book and, I am glad to say, she's already started on the cover for 'Queen of Diamonds'. I hope this collaboration will continue well into the future.

I am very fortunate in having met some wonderful young people during the course of the writing competitions New Writers UK have run over the years. One of these talented young people is Megan Holmes, who has kindly drawn the map of Winterne Village which is to be seen at the beginning of this book. Megan is a gifted young writer who now also shows a considerable skill at artwork. She is also has an incredible aptitude for Maths and an ambition to achieve a career within Medicine. If she continues to excel in her medical and scientific studies, her future is assured but, just in case she doesn't, she can always turn her hand to literature and art.

Daniel Cooke, formerly of AuthorHouse UK, and now the Managing Director of New Generation Publishing has been real friend and ally who helped guide me through the minefield of publishing since 2005. I have always been able to rely on him and I trust his judgement implicitly.

My daughter, Rachel Malone (AuthorPress Editing), who is a qualified and experienced copy editor, has done a tremendous job working on this updated first book and I am grateful to her for all the time and effort she has spent on my behalf.

I also have to thank my husband, David, for his proof reading skills. He has an amazing eye for spotting the smallest typos and, having said

that, I hope you, the reader, don't spot any he or I might have missed! I also want to thank him for all the housework he has taken off my hands allowing me to write these books.

Jeremy Lewis and Dawn Bond, Nottinghamshire journalists, have given tremendous support over the years both to me personally and to New Writers UK. They have my heartfelt gratitude.

Lastly, Daniel Medley, Director of Wookey Hole Caves and his team for making us so welcome, giving support and encouragement in the writing of these books and holding book signings for me. Daniel, I hope to see you again later this year!

About the Author

Jae was born in Isleworth, West London then lived in Essex and Suffolk before spending the rest of her childhood in Sherborne, Dorset, close to the Somerset border. During those happy years, a visit to Wookey Hole caves and an inspiring History teacher at her school, Gerald Pitman, sparked her interest in the facts and myths that surrounded the Mendip Hills. Another teacher, Anne Osmond, was equally inspiring with her love of literature and encouraged Jae in her first attempts at writing.

In her early teens Jae moved back to London and, at 12 years old began writing her first book – a story set in Ancient Egypt and based on the life of Queen Hatshepsut – it was never finished!

As the years went on and career, marriage and children became her priorities, Jae forgot her writing but never her love of reading and almost always had at least one good book on the go; in particular, historical or fantasy novels.

Years later she moved back to the West Country to the village of Butleigh in Somerset, just four miles from Glastonbury, seven from Wells and fell in love with the area all over again, but this was to be a short stay.

Later, Jae met and married her second husband, David, and lived in Dumfries for six years. Then in 1996, the family moved back to England settling in Nottingham where they have lived ever since. Jae's children, Rachel and Greg, are now grown up and she has two grandchildren, Erin and Finn.

Having originally written 'Silver Linings' in 2005 and self-published in 2006, Jae met two other self-published authors and together they attended book festivals and other literary events and met a number of other self-published authors, all trying to find their way through the world of bookstores, journalists, publishers and agents.

In 2006 she founded not-for-profit New Writers UK and organised their first book festival in November that year. Participating were just eight very local authors and two designers and website creators. Having invited the Lord Mayor of Nottingham the Chairman of Nottinghamshire County Council, the Mayor of Gedling and a number of local journalists, New Writers UK was on its way.

NWUK now has well over one hundred members throughout the UK and overseas, runs an annual Creative Writing Competition for Children and Young People of Nottinghamshire and last year created a 'Silver Scribes' short story competition for people aged fifty-five. Both competitions are entirely free to enter.

Since writing her books and the formation of New Writers UK, Jae (under her given name of Julie Malone), is a regular on local radio, writes articles for newspapers and magazines in the Nottinghamshire area and for the New Writers UK quarterly newsletter.

For more information on New Writers UK please visit www.newwritersuk.co.uk.

'Silver Linings' is the first book of the Winterne Series. The second and third volumes are 'Queen of Diamonds' and 'Fool's Gold', all of which were originally written under the pen-name, Karen Wright, and have received very positive reviews. The fourth book 'Avaroc Returns' is well underway.

For further information about Jae please email her at jaemalone.author@gmail.com or contact her through Facebook

Queen of Diamonds

Chapter One

In August 1645, Mary Fuller was hanged as a witch in Bury St Edmunds, Suffolk, accused and convicted by the Witchfinder General, Matthew Hopkins. In 2014, her name was Armistice Endor Jenks, she was very much alive and worried about her previous ravens, Mélusine and Taliesin, who had not been seen for three days; a worrying and unusual occurrence.

"Look, look at them Merlin," she said to her more relaxed black and white Border Collie, who stretched drowsily on the kitchen hearth rug, "scores of crows, all heading back to their nests which is right and proper but, would you believe it, they're still nowhere in sight." Merlin lifted his head, acknowledging the mention of his name and wagged his tail but apart from that made no effort to comfort her.

"Oh! You're a great help," she smiled down at the unworried dog. "At least one of us is relaxed."

It was the Sunday before Easter and the bells rang across the village from the small church summoning the congregation to the evening service. Mrs Jenks was not one of them. She had never attended church services and had no intention of doing so just because it was Palm Sunday. She held her own beliefs and had far too much to do in her role as a healer to animals and those who preferred to use her services.

Steam rose from a saucepan on the black pot-bellied stove in the far corner of the window wall, releasing a strong herbal aroma into the kitchen as it bubbled and simmered in the pan. Mrs Jenks left the window to check on the contents of the pan; she stirred it with a large wooden spoon. Merlin sniffed and sneezed, twice.

Satisfied, she headed back to the window and pulled the curtain to one side. Her dark blue eyes squinted against the vivid golden rays of the sinking sun and she blinked hopefully as two small dots appeared, high above the trees, heading in the direction of Winterne. She smiled. Her treasured ravens were unharmed and almost home. She exhaled,

felt her shoulders relax. Relief.

She marvelled at the golden gleam of sunset shimmering on their blue-black plumage while they flew so closely together, their wingtips almost touched. "Brigid be thanked," she sighed, as the magnificent birds descended, skimmed over the treetops in a wide arc to land gracefully on the roof of the garden shed where they hopped onto the window ledge.

As was his habit, the male, Taliesin, immediately hopped inside, leaving his mate alone. Ignoring his calls, she hesitated; the breeze ruffled her feathers as her coal black eyes met those of the woman at the kitchen window. Again he called. This time she chose to join him hesitating just long enough for one last look into the crimson sunset.

Many local villagers called Mrs Jenks a witch and it was easy to understand why. Although she had never owned a tall black hat and her broomstick was used only for sweeping the floor, she was an expert in the use of herbs, had an uncanny affinity with animals and possessed a legendary talent for fortune telling using tarot cards. She also preferred to live alone close to the forest and was rarely seen in the village which only fuelled the speculation and allowed the more imaginative amongst them to create rumours and misconceptions about her.

Armistice Endor Jenks was born on Armistice Day 1918 and was well over ninety years old. She was tall, straight backed, unwrinkled and moved with an agility envied by people half her age. No-one would ever have called her beautiful. She was striking, with a strong handsome face and eyes so dark blue they were almost black, under arching grey eyebrows. She had a long straight nose, a firm jaw-line and a wide mouth often set in a determined line as she concentrated on herbal cures, but could switch to a smile in a heartbeat. She often wore her collar-length, iron-grey hair pinned up or tied back off her face to keep it out of her eyes while she worked.

Those who didn't know her thought she was arrogant but they were entirely wrong. Her few close friends knew her heart was as soft as goose-down and were privileged by her friendship.

When she did make one of her rare appearances in the village, people either stared or hurried off in the opposite direction, never quite sure how to react. But Mrs Jenks cared not a jot what anyone thought of her, indeed she thoroughly enjoyed her macabre reputation as it kept

away the local children, of whom she was not particularly fond. In her opinion, children were noisy, bad mannered, far too boisterous and only became tolerable when they reached her shoulder height, and she was very tall.

In fact it was customary to hear a harassed mother use the ultimate deterrent of 'Mrs Jenks will get you' when scolding their disobedient children, just as their mothers had done; no footballs were ever accidentally kicked into Mrs Jenks' garden.

Had the villagers known just how close to the truth they were, they would have been astounded and probably even more afraid, because Mrs Jenks was indeed a witch, although she had never cast a spell, jinxed or hexed anyone maliciously in any of her many incarnations, all of which she remembered very well. Particularly vivid were those in which she been starved and beaten, tortured with pins being jabbed into her skin or tied to a dunking stool and drowned; her memories of both times she was hanged were particularly distinct.

One person she hoped never to meet again, in any of her lives, was Matthew Hopkins the Witchfinder General, who had taken great delight in having over three hundred women killed during the trials he instigated in 1645. She shuddered at the memory of his condemnation of her for witchcraft and the satisfaction he seemed to derive from sentencing her to death. It was during her next incarnation she discovered the tables had turned on Matthew Hopkins when he too subjected to the 'swimming test' and executed for witchcraft in 1647. What goes around, comes around, she would say.

Thankfully, those grisly days were long gone and now she enjoyed her life with her cat, her dog, the ravens and her friends Charlie Nowell and the elves. But in truth, her magical abilities had diminished to such a degree over the centuries all that remained were her powers of healing.

As dusk fell, the light dimmed until the long narrow room was illuminated only by the wood fire in the grate, in front of which Merlin was resting, comfortable on the thick hearth rug and made dozy by the warmth. With fires in both the grate and the stove, the room was almost unbearably hot, but Mrs Jenks did not seem to feel it.

On the heavy round table in the middle of the room a cat sneezed.

"Bless you!" Mrs Jenks laughed. "Feverfew a bit strong is it? Never mind, it'll be done soon." The cat, an elegant grey animal with

enormous jade coloured eyes, had been grooming himself, licking his paw and rubbing it across his face. He looked up at the sound of her voice and purred. She moved closer and stroked his head, his purr grew louder and he arched his neck, rubbing his forehead against her hand.

"It's time to light the lamp, Bandit. Look how quickly darkness is falling." Going to the fireplace she stepped over the dog, took an oil lamp down from the mantelpiece and carefully lifted off the glass cover, then holding a long wax taper to the open fire until it ignited, she lit the wick, replaced the glass cover and placed the lamp on the table, away from the cat. A warm glow spread around the long, narrow white painted, room which served as both kitchen and living room.

The ceiling was quite low and crossed with dark wooden beams which, together with the dark furniture, made the room feel smaller than it actually was. This and the heat gave the room a near claustrophobic quality which neither of the animals or Mrs Jenks seemed to notice. Bandit was far too interested in a hairy-legged, black spider as it scuttled about anchoring a huge silvery web between a sheaf of dried flowers on a ceiling beam and the tapestry pole.

Bandit continued licking a paw as he observed, through lowered eyelids, licking a paw casually and biding his time. He would pounce when he was good and ready.

If she had one failing, Mrs Jenks was a hoarder; she rarely threw anything away. Shelves either side of the window and on the two large bookcases were crammed with books on botany or astrology, and every spare nook not jam-packed with plants and herb boxes, had photographs or rolled up horoscope charts squeezed in behind jars and plates. Astrological diagrams and palmistry charts were pinned haphazardly in spaces between the bookcases.

Pride of place above the fireplace was given to a fading tapestry depicting a scene from Greek mythology took pride of place. White-robed goddesses danced with fauns amongst the trees in a scene of tranquil joyfulness while Zeus watched from above protectively. Mrs Jenks was extremely proud of this tapestry having worked on it herself many years before.

Although the room was messy, Mrs Jenks knew exactly where to find everything she needed, with the exception of her tarot cards which regularly went missing, only to turn up somewhere other than where she absolutely knew she had not left them.

At the far end of the room two doors stood side by side, one was slightly ajar revealing a dark wooden staircase. The other led to a small, neat parlour Mrs Jenks used for the occasional visitor requiring a private tarot reading.

Her treasured birds now home Mrs Jenks was visibly more contented. Passing the stove, she gave the mixture in the saucepan a quick stir then, as she closed the curtains, something drew her gaze to the darkening sky. A chill breeze blew in through the open window and she shivered, pulling her paisley patterned shawl closer round her neck.

"It's colder than I thought," she said as the cat jumped onto the window ledge. "That wind's coming from the East. The North Wind blows cold but nothing good ever gets blown in with the East Wind. I have a feeling something's not…right. Trouble's coming," she said, almost to herself.

The breeze blew more strongly making the curtains billow out and she hurried to close the windows. Tugging at the handle of the first window she closed it easily but, as she tried to close the second, a strong gust of wind almost blew the handle out of her hand and she battled to keep hold of it until the wind eased allowing her to pull the window tightly shut.

Stretching, Bandit jumped down from the ledge and disappeared under the red chenille tablecloth. Merlin, disturbed by her struggle with the window, stood up, yawned loudly and padded over to where she stood. She stroked his head. "It's OK Merlin, you don't have to worry…I'm perfectly alright." Apparently reassured, Merlin returned to the hearth rug, flopped down, rolled onto his side and was soon snoring softly again.

Mrs Jenks returned to the saucepan, lifted the lid and stirred the gently simmering potion with a wooden spoon. The fragrant mixture had reduced nicely. She spooned out a little of the liquid and tried it for taste. Satisfied, she put the lid back on the saucepan. "Another half hour and it will be done to perfection," she told the smiling cat who leapt onto a chair and up onto the book and paper strewn table. He stretched his legs, arched his back and sprang over to the sink worktop, almost knocking over a couple of green coloured glass bottles containing a dark liquid. They wobbled threatening to crash to the floor, but Mrs Jenks caught them before they fell.

"Oh do be careful, you silly cat! I'm not in the mood for any mischief tonight!"

The cat made a plaintive mewing sound and nudged her hand with his nose as if asking forgiveness, which he received. She stroked him absent-mindedly and he purred pleasurably. Finally, back at the window Mrs Jenks snapped the curtains closed shutting out whatever was worrying her and the cat leapt lightly onto her shoulders and lay across her neck like a scarf, his claws retracted to avoid hurting her.

"Do you feel it, my boy?" The cat rubbed his face against her cheek. "What about you, Merlin?" The dog sat up, tipped his head to one side, his tongue lolled out of the side of his mouth while his tail thumped loudly against the chair leg. "No, it's no good asking you is it, you silly thing?" she smiled at him fondly. "I'll ask the cards."

Merlin lay back on his rug, his tail still wagging happily.

The cat still draped across her shoulders, Mrs Jenks went to a large dresser near the back of the room. A small bundle wrapped in purple silk caught her eye.

"I can't use them Bandit, they're for Isabel and I haven't blessed them yet. Now where are mine?"

The cat mewed.

Mrs Jenks chewed her lip. "You're sure you don't know where they are?" As she leaned forward to open a drawer, Bandit sprang onto the ledge above and paced up and down, miaowing constantly. Mrs Jenks rifled through the drawer, making more of a mess than there was before, but the cards were not there. She slammed the drawer shut and opened the next one, repeating the process at all four drawers. "Where are they? I used them recently."

Bandit paced the shelf agitatedly, purring constantly.

"It's no good you purring at me, Bandit. It's not helping!" She searched the untidy table, frantically pushing books and packets of herbs out of the way, accidentally knocking a couple of books onto the floor near Merlin. He raised his head and sniffed but, unconcerned, lowered his head and went back to sleep. Bandit dropped onto the floor and headed for a cupboard at the far end of the room. Sitting down at the door he miaowed forcefully.

"No, I didn't put them in there."

But the cat's mewing became more insistent; he scratched at the door.

"Alright, alright, I'll look, but I'm sure you're wrong."

On a shelf at the back of the cupboard, lying face down on a block of oak, were the missing tarot cards spread out in a long line. Small piles of salt in each corner of the block protected the cards from malign influence. "Brigid be thanked! They're here!"

Bandit mewed loudly, rubbing against her legs. "Sorry Bandit, you be thanked as well."

With a loud purr and a satisfied smile, Bandit leapt back onto the table and waited for her. Holding the pack of seventy-eight cards lovingly, she returned to the table and mixed the pack. Selected nine cards at random, she set them face down in a square formation, three rows of three, returning the remainder of the pack to the wooden block.

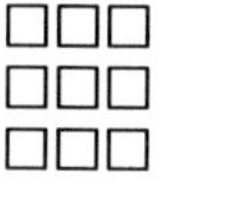

"Nine for the reading, and the tenth, when I close the cards," Mrs Jenks muttered quietly.

First, she selected the central card. "The Priestess, Bandit. That's me, I'm the enquirer, but you know that anyway. A good start."

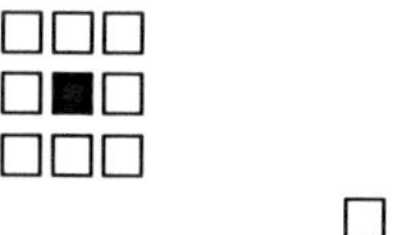

Her next choice was the first card on the top row. "The Empress! She's probably someone's wife or mother? I wonder who she is."

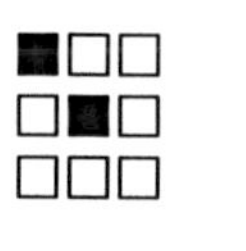

The third card turned over was on the right of the bottom row, giving a diagonal line, from top left to bottom right, of upturned cards.

“The Emperor. Hmm. There’s a connection to the woman, but how?”

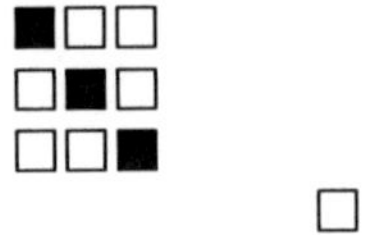

She next turned over the card at the far right of the top row. “The Chariot reversed, Bandit. Quarrels, possibly a defeat, it’s above the card representing the man. Hmmm. Let’s see what happens next.”

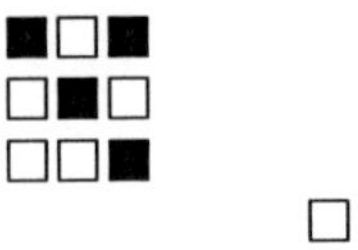

Her next card was the first on the bottom row. “It’s The Magician. Hmmm. This indicates a favourable change of position for the woman.”

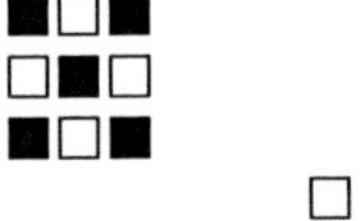

The upturned cards now formed an ‘X’. “Now then, the compass points.” The next card was in the middle of the top row, at the North position.

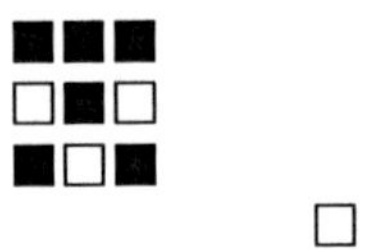

The cat inched closer, concentration creasing his whiskery eyebrows.

“The Moon and it’s reversed as well. I don’t like it, Bandit. This shows trickery, deception, maybe hidden enemies. This woman, whoever she is, had better be careful who she trusts.” Turning the

seventh card, at the South position, she gasped, her hand trembled.

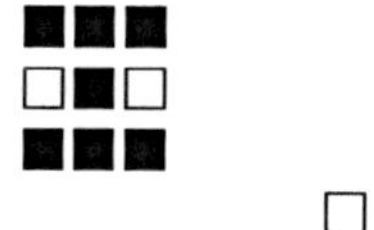

"Oh no! Death reversed! Possible serious loss and painful change and, from its position it's linked to the man again. If it had been the right way up it might have meant new beginnings, but it's a sinister card when reversed."

The cat nudged her hand with his nose. She turned towards him, his eyes locked on hers, he stared intently at her. "Yes, yes, I know you're right. We've come this far and must go on, but this really is quite ominous."

She turned the eighth card, at the West position. "No! This is just too much! The Tower! Disgrace and ruin!" Mrs Jenks clapped her left hand to her mouth, worry lines creased her forehead as she stared down at the cards. Merlin twitched and whined in his sleep, blissfully unaware of the drama going on at the table.

"This portends evil, Bandit. It's linked to the man, but there are two men on this card which foretells sudden and unforeseen calamity. But who are they and which one is it meant for?"

She scanned the cards spread out before her, her expression grave. On the top and bottom rows, all the cards were upturned, only one card in the middle row remained face down, the ninth card, in the 'East' position. The cat edged closer still. Mrs Jenks hesitated; her hand hovering in mid-air.

"I don't want to see this one, Bandit. It's odd too that they're all main cards, the Major Arcana. The cards are usually more mixed."

Bandit looked at the eight cards, and his eyes widened. She picked up the ninth card but, before she could turn it over, Bandit sprang forward, clamped his teeth tightly on it, snatched it from her hand and

dropped it over the side of the table onto the floor.

"Why did you do that?" She looked horrified. "You know you can't ignore a drawn card."

Bandit crept to the edge of the table. The card had landed face up, in the reverse position. Spitting furiously, hackles bushed out like bristles on a broom, he flew to the top of the nearest cupboard. Mrs Jenks bent to pick up the card and placed it with the others, her hand trembling. "The Devil and it's reversed! True evil!"

□

A smell of burning reached her nose. "Gwen's potion!" Rushing to the stove, Mrs Jenks found a smelly blackened mess of burnt herbs at the bottom of the dried up saucepan. "Damnation! I forgot all about it."

She was about to run the pan under the cold water tap when she looked again at the charred residue. With a sudden clarity she saw shapes in the cinders. "A black flag and a hawk. More bad omens!"

The cat sloped away into the shadows at the top of the cupboard.

Lightning Source UK Ltd.
Milton Keynes UK
UKOW02f2328290316

271122UK00002B/19/P